Nicole opened her mouth to argue with him and his mouth surrounded hers

A soft coo of satisfaction issued from her throat as he took her lips gently but possessively. Their lips parted and the kiss deepened and intensified, their tongues stroking and tasting, making love in an innocently erotic way. Their arms found their way around each other and the kiss went on and on until Lucien finally began to pull away from her, gently, reluctantly, with soft little nibbles and licks. She sighed softly and refused to open her eyes to face him until he put his finger under her chin and kissed her eyelids. She allowed them to flutter open and closed them again when she saw the hot light in his eyes.

"Look at me, sweetness. Didn't you like that?" His deep voice was even deeper and sexier, and the sound of it made Nicole dizzy with a longing to be even closer to him.

MELANIE SCHUSTER

started reading when she was four and believes that's why she's a writer today. She was always fascinated with books and loved telling stories. From the time she was very small, she wanted to be a writer. She fell in love with romance novels when she began reading the ones her mother would bring home. She would go to any store that sold paperbacks and load up! Whenever she had a spare moment, she was reading. Melanie loves romance fiction because it's always so hopeful. Despite the harsh realities of life, romance stories always bring to mind the wonderful, exciting adventure of falling in love and meeting your soul mate. She believes in love and romance with all her heart. She finds fulfillment in writing stories about compelling couples who find true, lasting love in the face of all the obstacles out there. Melanie hopes all of her readers find true love. If they've already been lucky enough to find love, she hopes they never forget what it felt like to fall in love.

trust
IN
Me

Melanie Schuster

KIMANI™
ROMANCE

Dedicated to my readers because I do it all for you.

In memory of a gracious lady, Katherine D. Jones

KIMANI PRESS™

ISBN-13: 978-0-373-86095-1
ISBN-10:   0-373-86095-1

Recycling programs
for this product may
not exist in your area.

TRUST IN ME

Copyright © 2008 by Melanie Schuster

This is a work of fiction. Names, characters, places and incidents are
either the product of the author's imagination or are used fictitiously,
and any resemblance to actual persons, living or dead, business establishments,
events or locales is entirely coincidental.

www.kimanipress.com

Printed in U.S.A.

Dear Reader,

Thanks for taking another journey with me. I hope you enjoyed revisiting the Louisiana Deveraux family.
Lucien Deveraux, the acknowledged playboy of the family, did something no one thought he would ever do—he fell in love. The minute he laid eyes on Nicole Argonne, he knew she was special. Once he got to know her he knew he had met the woman who was going to become his wife. All he had to do was convince her, which was probably the most difficult thing he'd ever had to do.

Nicole was more than a little gun-shy when it came to romance, especially with someone as handsome as Lucien. The big challenge for her was to learn to trust again. She had to trust Lucien and believe that he was a man of his word, but she also had to learn to trust her own instincts. One of my favorite inspirational sayings is "Jump and a net will appear." Sometimes you have to act on what's in your heart and take a walk on faith. In this case, the net was the love of a lifetime, if Nicole could forget about a past hurt and seriously consider what she could have with Lucien.

Trust is so important in relationships; it doesn't matter if it's a business, familial or romantic liaison, trust is the key to success. If you can't have complete confidence in the person you're involved with, your future can be pretty bleak. Lucien was determined to prove to Nicole that he was the man she could rely on for anything. But Nicole's role was even more challenging because she had to be strong enough to open her heart and receive the love he was giving her.

I hope you enjoyed *Trust in Me.* And I hope that you start looking with your heart as well as your head when you're considering life-altering decisions. Sometimes the answers you seek are right in front of you if you believe in yourself.

Melanie Schuster

ACKNOWLEDGMENTS

Even though I write the books, I don't do it alone.
I have a lot of special angels helping me. Thank you
to all my faithful readers who have been with me since
my first book was published in 2002. Thanks to
Betty, Gwen, Jeanette, Leslie, Janice Sims and
Janice Cochran for keeping me lifted up in prayer and
giving me encouragement. And a very special
thank-you to my wonderful physical therapists
for getting me moving again!

Chapter 1

There was nothing but love and happiness surrounding the big pavilion that separated the main house of Clay and Benita Deveraux from the guesthouse. The occasion was a joyous one: a double wedding had just taken place. The happy couples were Julian Macarthur Deveraux, Sr., and his bride, Ruth Bennett. His oldest son, Julian Jr., had remarried his wife, Maya, in what was actually a mere formality, as they had never been legally divorced. The ceremonies took place in Atlanta because Hurricane Katrina had laid claim to the beautiful city of New Orleans, the birthplace and home of the two grooms.

It had been a simple ceremony, but festive. The pavilion was full of beautiful flowers, fantastic refreshments and immediate family. The Deveraux family was a big one, and there were smiling faces everywhere. The Atlanta Deverauxes boasted five children, all of whom were married, with multiple children, and the Louisiana Deverauxes also had five children, four sons and a recently married daughter. "Immediate family" for the Deverauxes was a flexible term because there were in-laws, cousins, children of all ages and several lively pets who joined the outdoor reception with gusto.

Lucien Deveraux, Julian Jr.'s brother and, with his twin brother, Philippe, the last of the line, had eyes for only one person at the reception.

He'd met her before, when her brother Titus had married his only sister, Paris. Nicole Argonne. She was the youngest of Titus's sisters and had been one of the bridesmaids at the wedding. He'd thought she was gorgeous, with her dark chocolate skin, her long black hair and her huge, expressive almond-shaped eyes. After getting to know her throughout all the pre-wedding festivities and walking with her down the aisle, he'd planned to ask her out. But she'd brought a date to the wedding, so he'd missed his chance. She seemed to be alone on this trip, something he decided to remedy at once.

Lucien was about to make his move when she took the microphone from his young cousin Trey's hand and began to sing. Trey had the brilliant idea of charging people to sing at the reception with all the proceeds going to Hurricane Katrina survivors. Trey, although barely in his teens, was a born entrepreneur. The boy had executive producer written all over him. Both couples had refused wedding gifts of any kind, asking only for donations for the survivors of Hurricane Katrina. And Trey, knowing how much people enjoyed singing, whether they could do it or not, had hit upon this novel idea for the reception. It was karaoke to the ninth power with a live band accompanying the singers, and everyone was having a ball. Lucien took a seat near the makeshift stage and settled down to enjoy Nicole's voice.

She was wearing a soft pink dress in some kind of filmy

material that showed off all her best assets: her long, curvy legs with their slender ankles and dainty feet, her ample bust, small waist and big, rounded hips. She was just the kind of woman he craved, a soft, cushy, full-figured woman who looked like she would taste like chocolate and feel like a soft warm cloud wrapped around him. When she began singing Chaka Khan's "Through the Fire," Lucien was profoundly glad he was sitting down, because certain parts of his body were straining to catch every note of her beautiful voice.

"Luc, man, quit drooling. You're embarrassing us," Philippe said with a lazy grin. Lucien hadn't even heard his twin come to join him. He didn't even bother to front; he simply ignored him until the last notes had faded into the scented air.

"Dang, Luc, you look like you've been lobotomized. Somebody's gonna think that woman has you hypnotized," Philippe said.

"She does," Lucien answered, never taking his eyes from her face. "I'm going to marry that woman."

Philippe made a choking sound. "Are you crazy? Marry her? You don't even know her! And what makes you think you're ready to get married? You're the biggest hound in Louisiana and all of a sudden you're ready to settle down?"

He braced himself for an outburst of anger from Lucien. The Deveraux brothers were notorious hotheads. They were perfectly charming gentlemen with excellent manners and deportment when they were in public, but when they were alone they would do battle like samurai warlords. They could and did argue about everything from sports to law to music and they enjoyed every raucous moment of it.

Lucien looked at his twin for the first time. "Take a look around you. Look at Pop and Julian," he said.

His father and his oldest brother were both on the dance floor, staring down at their wives with such adoration it was as palpable as a warm wind caressing the faces of the persons witnessing their love. Lucien wasn't finished, though.

"Now look at Clay and Martin and Malcolm and Marcus. Check out Angelique and Donnie. Look at Paris, too, while you're at it."

Philippe obeyed, looking at all their Atlanta cousins. Each one was either dancing with his wife or holding her. In Clay's case, he was sitting next to his beloved Benita and stroking her rounded tummy; she was pregnant with their sixth child. Angelique, the only sister of the Atlanta Deveraux brothers, was being cosseted by her big handsome husband the way he always babied her when she was pregnant, like she was now. Marcus was holding his daughter Anastasia on his lap and he was kissing his wife, Vera, like there was no one else around. Martin was whispering something in his wife, Ceylon's, ear that was making her blush and giggle. And their sister, Paris, was sitting on her husband, Titus's, lap while he looked at her like she was the only thing of any importance in his world.

"Okay, I get it. All our cousins have found beautiful wives. Pop has found himself the perfect woman, and Julian has even managed to get back with Maya. So what's that got to do with you?"

Lucien narrowed his eyes at his brother. "Don't be dense, man. After what we went through with Katrina, how can you ask such a stupid question? Life is too short for playing around anymore. I can't just take my life for granted the way I used to. I need to follow the example of the men in the family and get my priorities straight. Look at all that bliss, man. I want some of that, too. It's time out for chasing around with a different woman every night. I want what they have, and I'm going to get it with her," he said, staring at Nicole as she left the stage. "That's my woman right there, and before the year is out, I mean to have her," he said confidently as he rose from his seat and headed in her direction. "And if you have any sense at all, you'll be looking for a woman of your own. This time next year I'm gonna be looking like Clay and Martin and Pop, and you're gonna be looking horny and mad like you always do," he added with a grin.

In minutes he'd reached Nicole's side and looked down at her with the smile that had been breaking hearts all over the South since he was in middle school. "Nicole, I hope you remember me—I'd love to dance with you while we get re-acquainted. And if you dance half as well as you sing, it would be my extreme pleasure." He laughed.

She looked at him, smiled, hesitated about thirty seconds before putting her hand through his extended arm and floating out to the dance floor.

Lucien was in heaven. Nicole was beautiful; she smelled like flowers and she felt warm and sexy next to him. His lines had always worked before, but this time, when it really mattered, he had managed to tempt the right woman into his arms. At that moment, life couldn't have been any better.

Chapter 2

Nicole didn't quite know what had come over her when Lucien asked her to dance. Her first instinct was to say "No, thank you" and rejoin her brother and sister-in-law at their table, but she found herself wrapped in Lucien's arms as the music became soft and romantic. She tried not to look up at him, but it seemed silly not to. She took a deep breath and was glad she had, because when she looked up, the expression on Lucien's face almost made her forget how to exhale.

His eyes were half-closed, and he was smiling at her with a tender, intimate look that turned her insides to jelly. She was trying desperately to think of something flippant to say, something to let him know that he wasn't making any kind of impression on her, not at all.

Just because he was tall, charming and handsome enough to be modeling, she wasn't going to let him get to her. *Why does he have to look so yummy?* She couldn't even hope that he was beautiful but stupid. because she knew he was one of the leading attorneys in Louisiana. He had a very lucrative practice with his brothers and they all had outstanding reputations. Lucien practiced corporate law, while his brothers specialized in tax law, entertainment and environmental law. *He doesn't even have the decency to be dumb as a rock,* she fretted, hoping her dismay wasn't apparent to him. It didn't seem to be, because he suddenly moved his arms so both of them were around her waist and pulled her closer to his long, muscular body. He smelled wonderful and he was a superb dancer, two things that were high on her list of preferred attributes in the opposite sex. She was jolted out of her musings when he suddenly kissed her on the forehead.

She found her voice and was about to let him have it for overstepping his boundaries, when he apologized. "I'm sorry, Nicole. I shouldn't have done that but that complexion of yours was just irresistible. You're too soft and sweet for your own good," he murmured. "By the way, if I didn't tell you before, your voice is amazing. You should be singing professionally."

Nicole was a very talented interior designer. She'd worked very hard to get her bachelors and masters degrees and to establish herself as one of the leading designers in the South. "I like my job," she told him. "I'm an excellent designer and I have a very large client base who wouldn't appreciate me becoming a torch singer. They rely on me completely. The owners of the firm won't like it, either." The small design firm was The Lennox Group and it was owned by Davie and Andrea Lennox, a happily married couple.

"Do you do residential or commercial design?'

"I do both. I just finished a new resort near Atlanta. My next couple projects are vacation homes for two of my best clients."

"Then you can just sing for me," Lucien said.

She laughed at his audacity and he smiled. "You smell wonderful," he told her. "That's a very sexy scent you're wearing." She couldn't think of anything smart to say so she just enjoyed the rest of the dance.

Thankfully the music changed to something hot and lively, and Nicole was about to leave the dance floor, when Lucien took her hand. "I think we'd better go sit down before I do something I really have no business doing in public," he said with a smile so sincere and warm Nicole felt heat all over her body. Before she could say a word they were on their way to the table where her brother Titus was feeding his new wife, Paris. He was giving her small bites of their shared plate of hors d'oeuvres. At least this gave her something on which to comment, now that she was pretty sure she could talk without stammering.

"Umm, Titus, the last time I looked, my sister-in-law was capable of eating on her own. I don't really think it's necessary for you to feed her," Nicole said tartly.

She sat down across from the couple, and she had to smile. Titus, the last of the hard-hearted loners in the world, had fallen head over heels in love with Paris, and now he was acting like he'd invented the emotion. Paris was looking at him the same way, like he was the entire world to her, which he was. They finally tore their eyes away from each other long enough to look at Nicole and Lucien with sparkling eyes and big, secretive smiles. Finally Titus came clean with the whole story.

"Yes, I'm quite sure my wife is capable of eating on her own. It just so happens that I'm not feeding her," he drawled.

Nicole raised an eyebrow and looked at Lucien. "My eyesight is still twenty-twenty, and I saw you putting food in her mouth. Lucien saw it, too, didn't you?" She looked at Lucien for confirmation. He was still holding her hand.

"I was looking at *you,* to be perfectly honest, but it did seem like the two of them were involved in some strange newlywed ritual," he admitted.

Nicole was caught up in the tender thrill that ran up her body, so caught up that she almost missed what Titus said next. "Well, sis, it seems like we brought a little something back from the honeymoon with us. I was feeding your niece or nephew to be, if you really want to know," he said proudly.

"Oh. Well, that's a different story," she said absentmindedly, and then the full import of what he'd just revealed hit her.

"You brought what? You were what? My *what?*" she sputtered. "Are we having a baby? I'm gonna be an auntie?" Tears sprang to her eyes, and she had to jump up and hug Paris, then Titus, and then Paris again. And she hugged Lucien, too. "A baby, Lucien, isn't it wonderful?" And before she realized what she was doing, she kissed him, a kiss he was only too glad to return.

It was a brief kiss born out of pure excitement, but the reason for the kiss didn't lessen its impact on the grateful recipient. Lucien felt a swift heat enflame his manhood when her soft, tender lips touched his. He didn't say anything; he simply smiled at her.

Her joy in her brother's announcement was obvious; her face was lit up with genuine love and happiness. She was so captivating that he continued to look at her as though he'd seen her for the very first time that day.

He liked everything about her, from her thick, shining black hair to her slender feet. Her eyes were amazing. They were big and clear, with long eyelashes and a slight almond shape that made them mysterious and sexy. Her smooth chocolate-brown skin looked soft and kissable, and she had high, sculpted cheekbones that he wanted to press his mouth against right there at the table, but he knew better. In the meantime, he just enjoyed the view.

He gradually became aware that Nicole was speaking. "So why did you wait so long to tell me?" she was asking with a little pout. "You know I like to know things before anyone else. I like to be the first stop on the grapevine. It's my job to pass things on properly," she reminded Titus.

Titus was busy nuzzling Paris's neck and almost didn't hear her question, but he managed to pull away from his wife long enough to answer. "That's precisely why we didn't tell you anything. We wanted to tell the parents first. We wanted them to be the first to know. So we took a little trip to Charleston and Savannah and we told Mac and Ruth when they got here."

"I wanted to tell the whole world," Paris said dreamily as Titus went back to kissing her neck. "But we wanted to do it the traditional way, so parents come first," she said with a soft little sigh of happiness.

Titus actually had two sets of parents. His adoptive parents were Nicole's parents, too, and they lived in Charleston. He had just met his birth parents earlier that year and they lived in Savannah. Even though Nicole recognized the respectful aspect of their way of announcing their impending parenthood, she was still a little put out, or she pretended she was.

"I still don't see why you couldn't have given me a little heads-up. A little word on the side so I'd know before Nona and Natalie, that's all. They always know everything before I do. It's not my fault I'm the youngest sister."

"Nicole, sweetie, get over it, please. And if it'll make you happy and get you to shut up, you do know before Nona and Natalie. We just told Mom and Pop. We're saving the big announcement for later today," Titus said with an amused grin. "So whip out that cell phone and get to gloating. You know that's what you want to do."

Nicole immediately took her hand away from Lucien's and retrieved her cell phone from her tiny bag with a look of utter glee on her face. She called her sisters, her best girlfriends, her bosses and was probably about to call her hairstylist when Lucien finally took the tiny phone from her hand. He looked into her surprised eyes as he closed it and put it into the pocket of his suit coat. Her eyes widened and she was about to smart off when Lucien gave her another devastating smile.

"I'm feeling neglected. I'm sitting here with the most beautiful woman at the wedding and she'd rather talk on the phone than talk to me. What do you suppose we do about that?" He took her hand as he was speaking, and she did something she rarely did when she was being flirted with so blatantly: she smiled so he could see her dimples.

"Well, I wouldn't want to be the cause of any hurt feelings. What do you suggest I do to remedy the situation?"

Lucien put his free hand over his heart. "Just keep smiling at me like that and I think we're halfway there."

Nicole lowered her eyes and then stared at him. "Just a smile?" she said in a low, sexy voice.

"I said halfway there," he reminded her as he leaned closer to her. "There's also dancing, drinking champagne, dancing, eating together, dancing and letting me take you home so I can kiss you good-night."

Nicole's dimples deepened and she looked even more alluring. Lucien was looking so sincere and delicious she simply couldn't find the inner fortitude to resist his charm.

They danced together over and over to every song, they toasted the happy couples and they shared the sumptuous

meal. There was a wide array of Creole and Southern special-
ties, everything from barbecued ribs to jambalaya, and everything was unbelievably tasty. Lucien even coaxed Nicole into
trying to eat crawfish the proper way, by breaking off the
heads and sucking the juice out before consuming the succulent meat. She made a face as she watched him do it a couple
of times and flatly refused to imitate him.

"Nope. That just looks gross. I can't do it," she said firmly.

He wiped his mouth with a linen napkin and gave her a
smile of encouragement. "Just try one and I won't ask you
again," he coaxed. "I think you'll find them quite to your
taste," he promised. "If you don't like them, I won't ask you
again. I'll never try to get you to do something you don't want
to do," he said persuasively. "I just don't want you to miss out
on something wonderful."

Nicole looked around and saw all of the Deverauxes
digging into the nasty-looking little critters with gusto, even
the youngest children. Even her brother Titus, a notoriously
picky eater, was sucking them down with great appetite.
"Okay," she mumbled. "But if I don't like them, you're going
to owe me big-time, Lucien." She daintily imitated the method
he used to eat the shellfish, and a look of pleased surprise
came over her face. "Ooohh, these are *good*," she said rapturously. "Where have these delicious things been all my
life?"

"Aww, sugar, they've been waitin' for you in Louisiana,
same as me. It just took us a while to get to you, that's all."
He watched the delight with which she consumed the deli-
cacy, and he could feel his attraction to her growing. The way
her luscious mouth drew the juices out of the shellfish was
more than enticing: it was mesmerizing. Normally, he would
have said something slyly suggestive to get the mating dance

started, but tonight he held back. He couldn't keep his eyes off Nicole, even for a moment. She was without question one of the sexiest, most desirable women he'd ever encountered and he meant everything he'd said to his twin, Philippe. For reasons he couldn't completely explain, he knew without question that the laughing, adorable woman at his side was destined to be his. At the moment it didn't occur to him that Nicole might have something to say about his plans.

After the meal, the dancing, the entertainment and toasting were over, the cake was cut and it was time for the happy couples to depart for their honeymoons, after, of course, the traditional tossing of the bouquets and garters. Nicole did what she always did when this part of the festivities arrived: she left.

On her way out, she kissed her brother and sister-in-law, thanked Lucien for being a wonderful dance partner and made her way across the pavilion at the speed of light. She was so intent on getting away she collided with a slender woman with very short, very chic hair. As they were laughing and begging each other's pardon for their clumsiness, an unwelcome but beautiful bounty of flowers landed at their feet. They looked at each other dumbly before bursting into uncontrollable laughter. Nicole picked up the bouquet and smiled at Chastain Thibodaux.

"This must be for you, because I have no intention of getting married," Nicole said emphatically as she tried to push the flowers into the other woman's hands.

"Oh, no, honey, Maya must have been aiming for you. because I took a vow of celibacy," Chastain protested.

Nicole's eyes widened. Chastain Thibodaux was sharing a guest suite with Nicole. She was Paris Deveraux's lifelong best friend, and Nicole had met her during the wedding preparations for Paris and Titus's wedding since both of them had been bridesmaids, but this was the first time Nicole had ever heard of her taking religious vows.

"I didn't know about that," Nicole said apologetically.

"That's 'cause Chastain ain't goin' nowhere but the nuthouse if she doesn't quit tellin' big whopping lies like that," Lucien said with a big smile as he caught up with Nicole.

"Luc, you need to mind your own business for a change. I have no intention of getting married now or ever, so Nicole gets this thing all to herself," she said as she accepted his kiss on the cheek and shoved the flowers firmly into Nicole's unwilling hands.

Lucien's eyes lit up with merriment. "Well, seeing as how I got the garter, I think our timing is just right. And speaking of timing, Philippe is headed this way," he added as he saw his twin making his way through the crowd.

Chastain's pretty face hardened into a frown. "Then that's my cue to leave. Good night, y'all."

She vanished into the guesthouse, leaving Nicole staring after her. "Hmm. She seemed pretty emphatic about not running into your brother. Any ideas as to why?" She gave Lucien a sideways glance with one arched eyebrow slightly raised.

"Aww, she's probably just tired. She had to fly in from New York to be here," he said carelessly. He took the flowers from her hand and put the lilac bridal garter around her wrist. Before she could say a word, he'd kissed her on the forehead and slipped his arm around her waist. "Now, which one is your suite?" he mused as they walked toward and entered the Deveraux guesthouse.

With their family growing so rapidly, the elder Deverauxes had purchased the house next door to them some years before and converted it to a guesthouse. There were several individual suites, all of which were filled with relatives. Some were from New Orleans, taking refuge from the destruction of Katrina, and others were like Nicole and Chastain, visiting for the wedding. Nicole looked up and down the hall with a slightly confused look on her face. "You know, I'm not sure," she said slowly. "I was moving so fast to get ready, I forgot which one. It's on the second floor, though."

Lucien pulled her even closer. "We'll find it, no problem. We may have to bang on a few doors, but it's all good. In the meantime, I'm staying right here, so we may as well go in and get comfortable until we figure out where you belong," he said smoothly.

In seconds Nicole was swept into the tastefully decorated living room of the suite where Lucien and his brothers were staying. Lucien escorted her to the long sofa and invited her to sit down. "I'm going to put these in the refrigerator for you so they'll stay fresh." He waved the bouquet in her direction as he went into the kitchen.

Nicole made a face as he left the room. *You can grind that thing up in the disposal if you want to,* she thought. Her train of thought was interrupted by Lucien's voice from the other room. "Would you like something to drink?"

"Yes, I'd love a glass of milk," she answered.

His head popped into the living room so fast she had to smile. "Milk? Like from a cow, or is that the name of some new cocktail?"

"The moo-cow variety," she said, laughing. "I happen to like it."

Lucien disappeared into the kitchen again. "There's bottled

water, fruit juice, beer and some other stuff, but no milk," he said, rubbing the back of his ear with his index finger.

"Water would be nice if it's no trouble," Nicole said sweetly.

"For you, nothing is too much trouble," he replied. He went to get a bottle of Evian water and a goblet.

"Oh. In that case go to a farm and milk me a cow," she said in the same sweet tone.

Lucien sat down on the sofa next to her and burst into laughter until he saw the serious look on Nicole's face.

"Why are you laughing? You said nothing was too much trouble, and I want some milk. So go get me some."

Lucien poured her a glass of icy-cold water and handed it to her. "I see you got jokes," he told her. "I like a woman with a good sense of humor."

Playfully, Nicole crossed her arms across her enticingly rounded bosom and widened her eyes slightly. "You think I'm joking? Do I look like I'm playing with you?"

Lucien stared at her intently. Her eyes were amazing, flashing black fire and intense intelligence. A lesser man would have been intimidated, but Lucien was aroused by the sight. "You look like you want to be kissed." He put the water on the table in front of the sofa and moved as close to her as possible. Nicole reacted at once, relaxing into the soft pillows of the comfortable sofa.

"You must need glasses," she said. "Either that or you're the most conceited man in the state of Georgia."

Lucien was too busy looking at the curve of her lips, the lush fullness of her mouth and thinking about the delight that awaited him to pay her words any attention. "You promised me a kiss. When we were at the reception you promised me dancing, champagne and a good-night kiss," he reminded her. "This kiss is inevitable, Nicole. Sooner or later you're going to be in my arms, so we might as well enjoy this first one. You only have one first kiss, so let's make this one memorable," he murmured.

Nicole opened her mouth to argue with him, and his mouth surrounded hers. A soft coo of satisfaction issued from her throat as he took her lips gently but possessively. Their lips parted and the kiss deepened and intensified, their tongues stroking and tasting, making love in an innocently erotic way. Their arms found their way around each other and the kiss went on and on until Lucien finally began to pull away from her, gently, reluctantly, with soft little nibbles and licks. She sighed softly and refused to open her eyes to face him until he put his finger under her chin and kissed her eyelids. She allowed them to flutter open and closed them again when she saw the hot light in his eyes.

"Look at me, sweetness. Didn't you like that?" His deep voice was even deeper and sexier, and the sound of it made Nicole dizzy with a longing to be even closer to him.

He kissed her again, this time in the corner of her mouth, flicking his hot tongue in and out. He kissed her chin and was angling his head to cover her neck with more sensual licks. "Nicole, you didn't answer me. Do you like me kissing you?"

Nicole took a deep breath and tried to sound nonchalant. "It's okay," she murmured.

"Damn, you're a bad liar. You like this as much as I do. And I love it. Your lips are so luscious I could kiss them all night," he said as he found the tender spot at the base of her throat that made her shiver all over.

"Then shut up and kiss me, you—" Her words were drowned out by another onslaught of passion from his lips, the most talented ones that had ever touched hers. She felt like she was drowning in the sensations he was creating. One hand was making its way into the thick, soft hair at the nape of her neck, and she could feel his other hand caressing her breast. She was supposed to stop him, to pull away and put an end to this encounter but somehow she couldn't. She wanted more of him, more of his touch and his taste. She was sliding down the pillows into an even more seductive position on the sofa, and she couldn't have cared less; all she wanted was more of what she was getting from him. She arched her back and opened herself into the kiss even more.

What would have happened next was a moot point since the door to the suite opened and in walked Lucien's brothers Philippe and Wade.

A little later Wade returned to the suite just in time to break up what was about to become a full-fledged fist fight between Lucien and Philippe. He shook his head as he stepped between his younger brothers, holding them apart with his long arms. "Are you two trying to wake up everybody in the county? Why don't you two grow up? Or at least shut the hell up so people won't think you're crazy?"

"Because he owes me and Nicole an apology, that's why. It's bad enough you came bustin' in here without knocking, but to stand there and watch and snicker say 'Are we interrupting something?' was just crude. You embarrassed her! I'm not takin' that from you. You don't come up in here and make my woman ashamed of something that was totally private and extremely personal. You owe her an apology and you're gonna give it to her or I'm a give you another black eye to match the one you already got."

True enough, Philippe was holding his hand to his left eye, but there was also a slight trickle of blood on Lucien's lip. Wade gave up trying to be neutral and sophisticated and laughed at both of them. "Damn, what is wrong with you Negroes? Okay, so we didn't knock before we came in, it's not a capital offense, man. But why didn't you call us and tell us to stay away or lock the door? We weren't trying to embarrass Nicole, she's a beautiful lady and she's real sweet, too. I don't think she was that embarrassed. I walked her to her room and she was real cool," he said in a conciliatory voice. All that did was set Lucien off again.

"That's another thing, jackass. Don't nobody walk my woman nowhere but me, you got that, slick? The only reason we were in here was because she couldn't remember which room she was in and we were just taking a minute to figure out which room she was in. If anybody was supposed to take her anywhere it was me and here you come, all 'I know where you are, I'll be happy to escort you.' What the hell are you, a damned Eagle Scout? You need to mind your own damned business, that's what you need to do."

Wade looked at Philippe with total confusion on his face. "What the hell is he talkin' about? All I did was take the lady to her room and he's acting like I committed a crime? When did Nicole get to be his woman? Where was I when all this happened?"

Philippe shrugged as he went to get ice for his eye, leaving Lucien mumbling to himself as he went to the bathroom to inspect his now-swollen lip. "Aww, man, he's gone crazy, that's all. He told me he's gonna marry the woman and as far as I know this is only the second time he's laid eyes on her. He's done lost his little rabbit mind if you ask me," he grumbled.

Wade laughed out loud at that point. "How hard did you hit him, bro? Hound Dog Deveraux is talking about getting married? Was he drunk or just plain horny?"

Lucien joined the two men in the small kitchen, shirtless and still fuming about his swollen lip and the fact that his brothers had busted in on him like he was sixteen with his first girlfriend. Without a word of warning he'd pinned Wade up against the wall by his throat. "Say it again. Say it three times and see if you don't have two black eyes when you apologize to my future wife in the morning. Say it, I dare you."

Philippe cursed under his breath, threw the makeshift icepack of paper towels and crushed ice into the sink and pulled him off his older brother. "Damn, Luc, if this is what falling in loves does to you I promise God I don't ever want it to happen to me. Calm down, man, Wade was just trying to be funny. You know he has no basic sense of humor," he said as he made a gesture with his head to encourage Wade to go along with it.

"Yeah, Luc, I was, ah, just kidding. We'll apologize to Nicole first thing in the morning. Sorry, bro."

Lucien abruptly let him go, glared at both men and availed his swollen lip of the discarded icepack in the sink. He left the room muttering fiercely, leaving his brothers staring at his broad-shouldered back. They crossed their arms and tilted their heads at identical angles as they watched him leave.

Wade was the first to speak. "I think that joker is serious. He meant every word of that," he said with wonderment.

Philippe touched his tender spot where his eye was swelling. "I think you're right."

They looked at each other and said in one voice, "We better make a real good apology tomorrow."

Chapter 3

When Wade and Philippe had burst into the suite unannounced, teasing and laughing, Nicole wanted to sink into the plush carpet and vanish like lint being sucked up by a vacuum cleaner. Luckily, Wade, who appeared to be the most refined of the Deveraux brothers, finally came to her rescue by first pretending that he didn't notice the fact that she and Lucien were entwined in each other like they were delivering a new form of CPR. He even offered her a way out, asking if she wanted him to walk her to her suite. "This place is a little confusing," he'd said quietly. "But Chastain mentioned that you two are roommates, and she's right upstairs. I can show you if you like."

Nicole had gotten to her unsteady feet with as much aplomb as she could muster and accepted his offer. "Wade, that's very kind of you. Let's go."

She was pleased that Wade didn't ask any questions that

required an answer, but he did make pleasant conversation, none of which she could recall. They reached the second floor and Wade stopped in front of a door with an orchid-colored panel on the front. "Each one of the doors has a different color," he explained as he knocked on the panel. "You probably didn't notice it. Most people don't. I told Benita she should number the doors, but she says it would feel too much like a hotel," Wade said with a smile.

Nicole returned his smile. "I know what she means. But it would make it easier to remember where you are," she added as she observed, for the first time, that each suite door *was* painted a different pastel. Just then, Chastain opened the door to the suite and Nicole's entire being was flooded with relief. She thanked Wade again for escorting her and entered the suite, barely saying good-night to him. The door closed and she leaned against it. Her eyes closed tight and then rolled up in her head as she said, "Take me now, Lord. Just take me and get it over with."

Chastain was watching her with both sympathy and amusement. She had already changed out of her dress and was wearing a short silky robe patterned with soft flowers. "You poor thing. You've been 'Deverauxed,' haven't you?"

Nicole peeled herself away from the door slowly. "I've been what?"

Chastain reached over and took both Nicole's hands in her own. "You've been Deverauxed, honey. That's what we call it at home. You bear all the unmistakable signs of a woman who's been subjected to one of those overgrown passion poles known as the Deveraux boys. Come on in and get comfortable and tell girlfriend all about it," she invited.

Nicole actually brightened up at the other woman's words. In the absence of her sisters, Chastain would do just fine, and for some reason Nicole felt the need to unburden herself.

"Let me get out of this dress, take a quick shower and I'll meet you in the living room."

Soon, the two women were seated on opposite ends of the couch, the latest from Mary J. Blige was playing on the stereo and they were each enjoying their favorite drinks. In Chastain's case it was pineapple juice, and Nicole was savoring a big glass of milk at last. And it was chocolate milk, too, which made it even better.

"Benita makes it a habit to know what all her guests like, and she makes sure that every suite is supplied with whatever their little hearts desire. She is without question one of the best hostesses in the world. If I could, I'd spend every weekend here just to get pampered," she admitted.

"You're right about that," Nicole agreed. "I love visiting here. Bennie has a beautiful family," she said as she stared pointedly at her glass, trying to avoid eye contact with Chastain.

Chastain was ready to have some fun, however, and she gently started picking at Nicole. "She does have a lovely family," she agreed. "But are you talking about her big, handsome husband and those pretty kids of theirs, or her fine brothers from Detroit, or those fine brothers-in-law, all of whom happen to be married to very lucky women?" she mused, tapping her lower lip with her forefinger. She waited a full beat before getting in the real zinger. "Or could you mean those overly tall, overly charming, too-handsome cousins-in-law from Louisiana? Are they the ones you're really talking about?"

Nicole made a face as she sipped more milk. "I was just beginning to like you, too. I'm not even sure that cousin-in-law is an actual relationship," she said sternly.

"You know I'm just teasing you, Nic. But you forget, Paris and I have been partners in crime since we were little girls, and I've had years in which to observe her brothers. I know the effect they have on women. I saw Lucien glued to your side all evening, and when you came in here looking like you'd been run over by the love train, it wasn't too hard to figure out that you've been Deverauxed. That's what we call it back home when some poor innocent woman gets caught up with one of them."

Nicole looked relieved for a moment. "Oh, so you've dated one of them before?"

Chastain choked on a swallow of juice. She sputtered and wiped her mouth inelegantly with the back of her hand. "Ewww! That would be like dating my cousin or something. I've known them all forever. They're like family. I just know the signs when I see them. Dreamy eyes, soft sighs, hair all tangled, breasts heaving…."

Nicole threatened to pour what was left of her milk on Chastain's head. "If you don't want to drown, you'd better hush. I didn't look all that crazy," she said haughtily. *At least I hope I didn't. But she came real close to describing just how I felt,* she thought grumpily. She looked at the other woman and decided to confide in her. In the absence of her big sisters, a new friend would do just fine.

"I have no idea what came over me," she confessed. "He asked me to dance and I started to say no, but then I thought, well, that's ridiculous, this is a party. So we danced. He kissed me on the forehead, which normally would have gotten him a broken nose, but it was sweet, you know? Then we went back to the table and I find out that Paris and Titus are having a baby and I get all excited and happy and I'm hugging and kissing everybody in sight, which happened to include Lucien," she said, twisting a lock of her long hair around her forefinger.

"Then we just danced and danced and we ate together and he taught me how to eat crawfish and we made a lot of toasts and everything. Then you stuck me with that stupid bouquet," she said, narrowing her eyes and pointing her index finger at Chastain. "Remind me to put you in a headlock for that tomorrow because you know you were the one who caught that thing, you just pushed it off on me.

Chastain laughed loudly and shook her head. "Girl, you need to quit! You know you caught that thing fair and square. I think Maya was aiming at you if you want to know the truth."

"Well, she wasted a perfectly good toss because I've been there, done that and got the T-shirt. There is no marriage in my future and especially no more pretty men. Oh, hell to the naw, or however they say it. No, no, no."

"I didn't know you'd been married. I'm sorry I was teasing you," Chastain said contritely.

Nicole rolled her eyes expressively. "I said I'd been there and done that. I didn't say I'd been married. I almost got married once to a big idiot who was almost as good-looking as Lucien. That mess is what made me swear off marriage and good-looking men in that order." She paused for a second. "Maybe it's the other way around, no handsome men and then no marriage, I can't remember which. Anyway, after that debacle I promised myself, my God and two other responsible people that I was done with that kind of man permanently."

Chastain looked absolutely stricken. "Nicole, I'm so sorry. I didn't want to bring up any bad memories for you. I was just trying to have a little fun. At your expense," she mumbled and looked even more sorry. "I really apologize, truly I do."

Nicole waved her hand to brush away Chastain's chagrin. "Honey, please. Do you want me to put you in a headlock now? Because I can, my brother taught me how to fight dirty. My mother tried to make a lady out of me, but I got some skills. If you quit apologizing, I'll tell you the whole story and I promise you I am not scarred for life or anything close to it. My ex-fiancé, now he had to leave town," she said with an evil grin.

Chastain got up from the sofa and headed for the kitchen. "Wait a minute, hold up, this sounds like a tale that's going to require more sustenance. Do you want some popcorn?"

"Yep, and something else to drink. This is a long story."

"Give me five minutes and we'll be good to go," Chastain promised.

Five years earlier—

Nicole was remarkably calm, considering the fact that her wedding was taking place in a mere two weeks. All the weeks of dating that had led to a steady relationship with her man, Leland Fricke, were just a happy collage of memories. She had met Leland in graduate school, and the attraction was immediate. Besides being in law school, he was tall, dark, handsome and brilliant, as well as being charming and very loving. They had met on a blind date arranged by one of her sorority sisters, and the couple had clicked immediately. Leland was just the kind of man she always imagined marrying, someone with good manners, high ambition and a strong sense of family. He planned to practice law, and she was going to continue her studies in art until she became a professor of fine arts. They were going to live in Winston-Salem, North Carolina, and they'd planned on two, possibly three children.

Leland was self-assured and articulate and he knew how to treat a lady. That was one of the things Nicole liked about him the most: the fact that he was so much a gentleman and yet so passionately ardent in his pursuit of her. They enjoyed the same things: fine dining, dancing, concerts and travel-ing—when they could work those activities into their busy schedules. As she often told Nona and Natalie, her older sisters, it was the perfect partnership.

"He understands my goals and respects them. We're so good together. I still can't believe we met on a blind date. Yvette really knew what she was doing when she introduced us. Usually I just blow those things off, but something told me that I might have a good time with him, and I did. It was the best date I've ever had and everything just fell into place," she told them.

They were all sitting in Nona's living room, putting together the gift bags for the bridesmaids' luncheon. The decor she had selected for the wedding was pink and green, her sorority colors. Everything had been planned down to the last detail, including ivy in the bouquets. Besides having a special meaning to her sorority, ivy meant fidelity in a relationship; although that was the last thing Nicole was concerned about. She looked at her sisters with a dreamy expression in her eyes. "Being in love is so wonderful," she said with a sigh. "I can't tell you how secure and happy I feel knowing that in two short weeks I'm going to marry my soul mate."

Her sisters couldn't quite meet her look of ethereal joy. They were looking at each other with deliberately neutral expressions on their faces. Nicole caught the look and stared at each sister in turn. "I know that look," she said flatly. "Something's going on that I need to know, and you're scared to tell me. What is it?"

Both sisters exchanged another look, this one resigned yet full of despair. After a long pause, Nona finally spoke up. "Nic, sweetie, we didn't want to say anything, but there's been a lot of talk around town about Leland and this other woman. Now you know we're not going to come to you with some idle gossip, so we didn't say anything to you."

Natalie then chimed in. "And you also know that we

wouldn't let you get married to some cheating, conniving, lying baboon, either. So we did a little investigating," she said.

Nicole's voice was much lower than normal, a sure sign of distress. "And you didn't find anything, right? All that snooping around was just a big waste of time, wasn't it?"

Her fingers were laced together and her gaze was fixed on them. She slowly turned her clasped hands so that she could see her engagement ring, the ring that was supposed to be joined by the matching wedding band as she joined her life to the man who said he'd love her forever. "You're not answering me," she said in the same low, dull voice. "This is the part where you tell me that you found out it was all a pack of lies and my fiancé is perfectly innocent. This is when you tell me that you found out that people in Charleston have nothing better to do but stand around and hate on people who are really in love. So what are you waiting for?"

Nona and Natalie pried her hands apart and each took one in her own grasp and held it tightly. Once again, Nona started speaking first. "Nic, I wish with all my heart I could tell you that. But I was hearing a little of this here and a little of that there, and I tried to ignore it. But when I overheard my coworker talking about her sister's new man, I couldn't ignore it anymore. Her cubicle is right next to mine, and she was talking on the phone and I could hear every word. She was saying that her sister was involved with some new man and that the man was supposed to be getting married but he was calling it off because he didn't really love the woman." She had to pause to tighten her grip on Nicole's hand because she had begun to struggle to get away. "Now, I will say that the reason my coworker was even discussing it is because she says her sister is a big ol' hoochie who slings it at any and every man she can. And she said she knew good and well that he wasn't about to call off the wedding because she knew the woman he was engaged to, that she worked with her sister, that being me."

Natalie had to get a firmer hold on Nicole's other hand. "So we followed him one night, and, sure enough, he met this woman in the parking lot of the mall and they went to his town house. And when we were sure the coast was clear, we went around to the patio and looked in the window."

By now both women were holding on to Nicole with all their might because she had risen to her feet and was trying her best to pull away from them. "Quit hanging on me like I'm going go tick-tick-boom," she said irritably. "I'm just going to get a glass of milk. Nona, do you have anything for a headache?"

"Oh, of course I do, sweetie. It's right in the cupboard next to the refrigerator on the first shelf. Do you want me to get it for you?" Her voice was soft and full of concern.

"No, I can get it. I need to process this information," Nicole answered as she left the room.

"She took that awfully well," Natalie said as her troubled eyes looked at the doorway to the kitchen.

Just then the back door slammed and they could hear Nicole's engine start as she gunned the motor and backed out of the driveway like she was the lead car in the Indy 500. "I think she took it *too* damned well. Let's follow that girl before she does something that could land her in jail," Natalie said. In mere seconds they were in Nona's car, tearing down the street as they followed Nicole to Leland's town house.

Chapter 4

Chastain's light brown eyes gleamed with interest and her hand was buried in a bowl of popcorn. "What happened? Was it the truth, was he really having an affair?" she asked breathlessly.

Nicole curled the corner of her shapely mouth. "No, he wasn't 'having an affair.' That always sounds so genteel, so refined. So does 'I couldn't help myself, I was weak, please forgive me.' What he was doing was humping the brains out of this girl who was barely out of high school. I had let myself in with my key and followed the noise to the bedroom and they were going at it like baboons in mating season," she said dryly. "Nasty buzzard," she added. "Thought he was going to be carrying on all over Charleston and not have me find out about it. Me, who has the two nosiest sisters in this hemisphere and a brother who's one of the best investigators in the country. How long did he think he was going to be able to cheat on me? I mean, is there a bolt in my neck? Does it look like my head screws off at night and I just set it on the nightstand or something?" She made a sound of utter disgust at the memory.

"So what did he do when he realized you were there?" Chastain nearly knocked over the popcorn as she reached for her glass again. Nicole handed it to her and took the bowl.

"Calm down, it's coming. My, you do get excited, don't you?" she teased. "I didn't let him know I was there. While I was driving over there like a bat out of hell, I got my little digital camera out of my purse and had it in my hand, just in case. I took pictures. Lots of pictures, snap, snap, snap. They were so into it they didn't even realize I was there. Luckily I got through just about the time my sisters rolled up, so they didn't come busting in there with baseball bats or something. We don't play, honey. Remind me to tell you about the beatdown we gave a skank who was messing over my brother," she said as she daintily ate some popcorn.

"Well, why didn't you beat him down?" Chastain demanded. "Girl, I'd a choked him so hard they would've had to sedate me to get my fingers off his neck. They would have been, 'Well, Your Honor, it had to be temporary insanity 'cause it took us damn near an hour to pry her hands off the corpse,'" Chastain said with just the slightest roll of her neck.

"I didn't want to let him off that easy. I had a plan, honey. My sisters couldn't believe how calm I was, but they had no real idea of how hurt and mad I was. I wanted to get him good, and I did. I made prints of the best picture, the one where you could see him but not the girl's face, and I got on my little computer and made nice little cards that I sent to everyone who'd been invited to the wedding. I put a nice note in there explaining that the engagement was off and they could draw their own conclusions as to why. I returned all the wedding gifts, but since I couldn't get the money back for the catering,

I turned the reception into a big party for the women's shelter, the rescue mission and the children's home. It was actually fun, too, because I got covered in the news and there was a write-up in a couple of magazines.

"And the best part is there was a poor woman whose house burned down and she lost her entire wedding party's outfits. Everything went up in smoke, so I gave her mine. All my bridesmaids donated theirs, and they got the flowers, the church, everything. It was by far the most cathartic thing I've ever done in my life. I was still brokenhearted, but somehow, seeing Leland Fricke having to leave town in disgrace went a long way toward easing the heartache."

"He left town?"

"Damned skippy. He had planned on being this big-time lawyer, and the last I heard he was a public defender some-place in Arkansas. While I was busy dismantling the wedding, my brother got busy digging up every speck of dirt he could find on Leland's family. His father had this law firm, and they had some…unorthodox methods of handling certain cases which my brother assured him would come to light if he ever used my name in any way, shape or form, including interviews, rebuttals, retaliation or revenge. His own daddy wouldn't let him practice with him, he was so disgusted with the fool. Plus, the poor little girl who had the misfortune to get caught with him ended up pregnant and he's now married to her with some kids," she said with a satisfied smirk.

"And the chump probably gave her your engagement ring, too," Chastain said.

"Oh, he didn't get that back," Nicole said quickly. "I don't return things, especially jewelry. I sold that sucker and took my mama and my sisters on a Caribbean cruise, and we had a ball. And best of all, I didn't have to go through life answering to 'Nicki Fricke.' See, there's a reason for everything, and I was saved from that horrible name."

Chastain was laughing out loud by now, and she held up her hand to give Nicole a high five. "I knew I was going to like you. We have too much in common not to get along. We're both artists, we don't take no mess and we know how to get revenge. But just tell me that this hasn't made you bitter and cold toward all men. He doesn't sound like he was worth giving up on dating and love and all that good stuff."

Nicole's expression changed. She looked quite serious as she admitted that she still dated and often. "But I did stop dating the gorgeous ones. With the exception of my brother, they're all worthless," she said firmly.

"Oh, don't say that! Look at the Deveraux men. They're all *foine,* and each one of them is happily and devotedly married. Look at Judge Deveraux and Julian—they would no more cheat on their wives than they would flap their arms and fly to the moon. Just because a man is handsome doesn't mean he's a jerk. Are you telling me you never met a homely man who was a dog?"

Nicole was pretending great interest in the remaining kernels in the communal bowl, and then she put it on the table and wiped her hands on a napkin. "Let's use those Deveraux cousins as an example. Did you not use the term 'Deverauxed' when I came in here looking crazy? And did you not say that was a common term in Louisiana for any hapless female who found herself entranced by one of them? They don't sound like keepers to me. I just don't get involved with men who look like Lucien Deveraux. Men like that are incapable of being faithful, as far as I'm concerned."

Chastain hurriedly defended her friends. "Oh, no, he's not like that. I mean they used to call him Hound Dog because he dates a lot. And I mean a *lot,* honey. That man has more women than you can count. If he could convert his conquests into cash money he'd have more than Bill Gates, Oprah and Warren Buffett," she said with a laugh that died in her throat as she observed the look of horror on Nicole's face. "What did I say?" she asked plaintively.

"Hound Dog? *Hound Dog?* Are you telling me that I was making a fool out of myself with a man commonly known as *Hound Dog?*" Nicole's face was flushed, and she was obviously even more flustered than when she had first arrived at the suite. "See, this is why I stay away from men like that. This is the very reason I keep away from the so-called fine men, the handsome ones that run through women like I run through panty hose. They have no morals, no principles and their only ambition is to bed as many women as possible in as short a period of time."

By now Nicole had risen from the sofa and was pacing back and forth with her arms tightly crossed in front of her. "Why is it when I decide to do something crazy I pick the worst possible candidate in the free world to do it with?" She paused a moment in her pacing. "With whom to do it? I can't even remember proper grammar anymore. I swear there's a curse on me when it comes to men. There were at least forty decent single men at the wedding, and I end up with Hound Dog." She looked at the ceiling dramatically and said, "Okay, that's it, I quit. I'm through with men for life. Tall ones, short ones, fine ones, bald ones, I'm done. Finished," she said as she took her seat on the couch again with an expression of total disgust on her face.

Chastain was holding her hands to her cheeks, which were by now bright red. "Nicole, I'm sorry, I'm giving you the wrong impression of Lucien. He's not a bad guy, really he isn't. He's just very popular. All those men are. Paris and I used to watch all these girls make fools out of themselves over them and we used to make a lot of jokes about it, but they really are nice guys. All of them," she said earnestly. "They go to church on Sunday, they work with different charities, they're smart and successful attorneys, they're brilliant, really. And I've never known any one of them to mistreat a woman in any way. They've all had women chasing them since they were in elementary school. They can't help it because they look good. They're fine on the outside and sweet on the inside, they really are. You can't be mad at them for being handsome, can you? That would be like somebody hatin' on us because we look good," she said with a weak little laugh.

To her relief, Nicole took the remark in the spirit in which it was meant. "Well, yes, we do look good," she said thoughtfully. "I think it's fair to say we're some fine examples of womanhood, and we're very sweet, too. I think we're sweet, don't you?"

"Absolutely," Chastain said enthusiastically. "And so are the Deveraux brothers. Just give them a chance, girl, you'll see how wonderful they are. Especially Lucien."

Nicole's expression told her new friend that she'd gone just a wee bit too far. "This would be 'Hound Dog' Deveraux? I don't think so. I was with you right up until the dog came back into the conversation." She pursed her lips and shook her head firmly.

"Look, Nicole, I've known Lucien forever and I've never, ever seen him look at a woman like he was looking at you tonight," Chastain said softly.

"That's because he was probably looking at so many women at the same time he was looking all cross-eyed and crazy! You probably never saw him look at one woman at a time before, and that's why he looked strange to you. I'm sure it had nothing to do with me."

"Ooh, girl, you're more hardheaded than I am, and my daddy used to say you could break bricks on my head! If you don't believe me, wait until you see him tomorrow and see if he doesn't react the same way," Chastain challenged her.

Nicole gave her a wry smile. "Well, in order to do that, he's gonna have to come to Charleston, because I'm leaving here first thing in the morning."

"You're not even going stay for breakfast? Everybody's going to be saying goodbye to everyone, and it's like an after-party, really. You're just going to run away instead of facing the man?"

"I sure am leaving, with a quickness. I heard everything you were saying, but I made myself a vow. I promised myself that the only men I would be involved with from now on are the dependable kind. I only date men who are calm, honest, down-to-earth and housebroken. I don't think a Hound Dog fits in any of those categories," Nicole told her. Chastain looked so stricken Nicole had to go give her a hug.

"Don't look like that, sweetie. I know they're your friends. They're Paris's brothers and I'm sure they're every bit as sweet as she is, but I'm not trying to get into a new relationship with anybody. But I promise to stay in touch. I have your address in New York, your e-mail, your cell, your home phone—girl, you couldn't lose me if you tried," Nicole laughed.

"Just remember I'm not going to be using that New York address much longer. I'm moving back to New Orleans for good. I have elderly relatives who need help. Hell, the whole city needs help. It's my heart, that city. It's where I grew up, where all my roots are. I have to come home and fight for its survival," Chastain said. Her expression was serious and resolute and Nicole could see that she meant every word.

"Well, Charleston isn't that far away. If you need me, holla and I'll be there."

Chastain's face lit up. "Promise?"

"You bet, and I never break a promise. Especially the ones I make to myself. Now I need to go to bed because I'm going to be skulking out of here at the first glimmer of dawn, which is just a few hours away."

Chapter 5

The next day was rather hellish for Lucien. When Wade and Philippe came back to their shared suite to report that the mission of apology was not accomplished, Lucien was about to erupt. His brothers held up their hands and called for calm.

"Look, Luc, we went up there and knocked on the door and Chastain said she'd left two hours ago. Said she had an important meeting on Monday and she needed to get ready for it. You can't hold us responsible for that," Wade said.

Lucien's response was immediate and angry. "Like hell I can't. If you hadn't embarrassed her in the first place, she wouldn't have flown out of here at the crack of dawn. Business meeting my foot—can't you see she was just making up an excuse to get as far away from here as possible?" He was dressed casually in jeans and a pale blue oxford shirt and was still barefoot.

Philippe shook his head in disgust. "Look, we'll send her

an e-card, flowers, whatever. We'll apologize for busting in here and embarrassing her. We'll even apologize for having you in the family, but you really need to chill. You can stay up here and pout the rest of the day, but I'm going to get breakfast. See ya." Without another word, he left the room.

Wade gave his brother a long look. "Luc, I can understand what you see in Nicole. She's a beautiful lady, smart and sexy, too. But you've only met her a few times. What's the big deal?"

Lucien raked his long fingers through his wavy hair while Wade was talking. He spotted one of his expensive loafers by the sofa and went to retrieve it. He sat down heavily and stared at the shoe as though he was trying to remember what it was. Finally he answered Wade in a more subdued voice than his brother was used to hearing.

"Wade, I know it might sound crazy, but I know this is the woman meant for me. And like I told Philippe, when a man knows, he knows. There's something about her that is so easy to be around. I knew it the more we hung out over Paris's wedding weekend. But then she was with some Poindexter for the reception and I wasn't going to try to put some cheap moves on her. I knew I'd see her again, and sure enough, she was here. Like it was planned or something," he said as he searched for his other shoe. He gave up the hunt momentarily and fell back against the cushions of the sofa.

"Maybe I'm just like Pop and Julian," he said reflectively. "They took one look and knew that Ruth and Maya were the ones for them. That's what happened with Mom, too. Pop told me once they went out on one date and he knew this was the woman he was going to marry. It might not make sense to you, Mr. Levelheaded, or to Philippe or anybody else, but I know what I know. Nicole Argonne is going to be my wife."

Wade opened his mouth to point out the many flaws in his

brother's impassioned statements, but thought better of it. He wasn't in the mood to try to argue with Lucien. Furthermore, Lucien didn't look as though he was in any mood to have a calm, logical conversation. He'd never seen his brother so bent out of shape about a woman, and it wasn't a pretty sight.

His empty stomach reminded him of the wonderful brunch that he was missing, and he decided to make a break for it. "Luc, I think you need to get some food in your system. I'm going down to eat, so come on down when you're ready." He turned to leave the suite and noticed the errant loafer by the console table near the entrance. He tossed it to Lucien. "Here. Put this on and come eat. You'll feel better."

He had reached the door when Lucien had to get the last word as always. "I'll feel better on my wedding night, that's when I'm gonna feel better. Don't eat all the food before I get down there," he warned Wade.

It still took Lucien about fifteen minutes to join the family for brunch. In one sense, it cheered him up to see all of his loved ones, especially since everyone was so happy and there was so much love flowing around. He was hugely gratified when his niece Corey ran over to greet him. Corey was Julian and Maya's five-year-old child, a fact that Julian had just discovered earlier in the year. She was a true Deveraux from head to toe, from her long black hair and creamy complexion to her deep dimples and her forthright way of communicating.

"Good morning, Uncle Luc," she said, holding up her arms for a hug and a kiss. "I already had my breakfast, but I'm going to eat some with you, okay?"

"Nothing would give me more pleasure, sweetheart. I'll fix us a plate and we can share it, if that suits you," he answered.

"Yes, it does," she agreed.

Soon they were seated at one of the tables on the pavilion with a huge plate of pecan pancakes, scrambled eggs, grits, fresh fruit, biscuits and sausage gravy, apple-cured bacon and salmon patties. He also got a glass of milk for Corey and a cup of coffee for himself. Corey made herself comfortable in his lap and carried on a conversation with all the aplomb of an adult.

"Did you have fun at the wedding, Uncle Luc? I did. I like being in weddings. I was a flower girl before," she said before taking a bite of watermelon from the end of his fork. "When Aunt Paris married Uncle Titus, I was a flower girl then, too. I like it."

"You make a wonderful flower girl, sweetie. You looked very pretty. And yes, I did have a great time yesterday." He took a bite of the pancakes, which literally melted in his mouth, followed by a sip of the rich black coffee. Corey's mind was still on weddings, which was evidenced by her next words.

"I'll be your flower girl, too, Uncle Luc. When are you getting married?"

The old Lucien would have dropped Corey and run for the hills at a question like that, but he relaxed into a huge smile. He didn't answer her right away, which was fine since she was still sampling the colorful ripe fruit and bites of pancake. He looked around, watching his Atlanta cousins and all their children. There was Martin, his arm around his wife, Ceylon, who was holding their newest baby, a little girl named Jordan. Martin's twin brother, Malcolm, was bouncing the latest addition to his family on his knee, a sturdy toddler named Gideon. After having three girls, Malcolm was pretty pleased to have a son who looked just like him.

His cousin Marcus was doing what he usually did at family gatherings—he was trying to keep up with his young son, Chase. He often commented that they had picked the perfect name for him because all they ever did was chase him from one daring exploit to another. He was gregarious, fearless and totally charming and his grandmother Lillian often said he was just like his father when he was a little boy. Marcus's wife, Vera, was taking pictures of the two of them and their older child, Anastasia.

Lucien looked around at all the familiar faces of his loving family and smiled down at Corey as she helped herself to the last bit of bacon on his plate. Before popping the crispy morsel in her mouth, she repeated her question. "When are you getting married, Uncle Luc?"

He kissed the top of her head and smiled as he gave her a tight hug. "Soon, sweetie. Real soon."

Chapter 6

After sharing brunch with Corey, Lucien figured it was time for him to get started on his master plan to capture Nicole's heart. He sought out Paris and found her relaxing in a lounge chair while Titus was getting her something to settle her stomach. She was lying back, looking completely comfortable and happy, with her eyes closed and a smile on her face. Lucien almost hated to disturb her, but she had information he needed.

"Coco, wake up, sweetie," he said, using her childhood nickname, the name he always used when he was feeling particularly affectionate or when he wanted a favor. "I need to talk to you about Nicole."

Paris's eyes flew open and she stared at him with open inquiry. Her career in television suited her perfectly because she had an insatiable curiosity. Paris was also a matchmaker with no shame in her game. She loved nothing better than getting a couple together, a couple that she considered to be perfect for one another. The fact that her brother was asking about her new sister-in-law should have filled Paris with glee, but for some reason his words had the opposite effect. Paris rose up on one elbow and fixed him with a serious look.

"Stay away from Nicole. You have enough women trailing behind you. You don't need to try to add another conquest to your harem. Nicole is a good woman. She's smart and ambitious and talented, as well as being beautiful and sweet. She needs a man who's going to be interested in her for real, not somebody who just wants another one-night stand. You just leave her alone, Luc. You are not what Nicole needs in her life right now," she said firmly.

Lucien was stung to his heart. He dropped down onto a wicker ottoman that was next to Paris's lounge chair. "Coco, how can you say that? In my entire life have I ever treated a woman badly? I might date a lot, but I don't lead anyone on or lie to them or try to make them think they're getting into something permanent. As a matter of fact, I only get involved with women who feel the same way I do just so nobody's feelings get hurt. I only deal with grown women who can handle that kind of relationship. So what's the problem?"

Paris made a face at him and then proceeded to tell him precisely what she felt was the problem. "That's exactly what I'm talking about, Luc. Nicole isn't one of your usual good-time party girls. She's a woman of real substance and heart, and she's not gonna go for your ol' player nonsense."

Lucien turned pale, a sure sign that he was beyond angry: he was stunned. "Paris, you sound like you think I'm pond scum or something. You're acting like I'm not good enough for her." He had to work hard to keep his voice down, because like all of his brothers, he could bellow when enraged and Paris had pushed a button in him he didn't realize had been installed. He couldn't have admitted it, but his sister had actually hurt his feelings.

She knew her words had hurt him, and she patted his arm in a gesture of apology. "Luc, I wasn't trying to say that you aren't good enough for Nicole, but I'm also not saying that you're ready for her. Unless you plan to get real serious, I suggest you just keep on looking for a new hottie. Besides being a wonderful person, she's my sister-in-law and my friend. She deserves someone who's interested in something long-term, something real. She's not the type of lady to have a little fun with and then move on," Paris said gently but firmly.

"Is that what you're worried about? I should have explained my intentions, Coco. I'm not trying to push up on her for the sake of getting a little sumthin-sumthin. I have something totally different in mind," he assured her. "That's the woman I plan to marry."

Paris sat up straight and whipped off her sunglasses to look her brother straight in his eyes. "Do what?" she said faintly.

"I didn't stutter, baby. You heard me. Nicole is going to be mine. That's why I'm trying to find out more about her. You've gotten to be real close to her, so I thought—" His words were cut off by a sharp gesture from Paris.

"Oh, no you don't. My name is Bennett, and I ain't in it," she said hastily. "I'm out of the matchmaking business."

"C'mon now, sis, you know you live for that. You're always trying to hook somebody up. That's your favorite hobby, Paris. You're known for it. And you're not gonna help me get with Nicole?"

Paris had the grace to blush a little. It was true; she was a world-class yenta and loved nothing better than to get two people together when she saw the potential for love. But she had never considered trying to get her brothers involved with anyone, not after what her oldest brother, Julian, had gone through with Maya. She'd always felt guilty because their first marriage had ended up so badly and she had introduced them. Besides, Lucien juggled women like he was a headliner in the UniverSoul Circus. This was the first time he'd ever mentioned settling down, and if he was serious he was going to have to prove it to her before she believed him. She told him so, too.

"If you want Nicole, you're going to have to go for it on your own. I'm not getting involved in this in any way. I love you to death, you know I do. But I know you too well to take you seriously. I'm taking a leave of absence from matchmaking. And you'd just better make sure you're really sincere before you start down this path, because there'll be hell to pay if you try to mess her over." Her expression changed as she saw her tall, handsome husband returning with some ginger ale and saltines to ease her morning sickness.

Lucien rubbed the corner of his mouth with his thumb. "I'm not scared of your husband, if that's what you mean. Is he gonna jump me if he thinks I mistreat his sister or something?"

Paris shrugged. "I certainly wouldn't count that out. He's as protective as you guys are when it comes to his sisters, and y'all kept me from having a date until I was in college. Remember how you used to run off every man who looked at me?" She gave him a stern glance and they both laughed because it was true. The Deveraux men were known far and wide for blocking any play that came at their only sister. Lucien had to hold up his hands to acknowledge that Paris was right on point.

Paris leaned back in the chaise longue again before making her summation. "What I meant was you better watch out for Nicole. She knows how to take care of herself and she's perfectly capable of making you wish you'd never laid eyes on her. I'm trying to tell you, Luc, Nic isn't like those women you date in bulk."

Lucien gave her a lazy grin. "In that case, we won't have a problem, because I plan to make her the happiest woman on earth. When I get done she'll be blessing the day I was born." He stood, kissed her on the forehead and strolled away, singing under his breath.

Titus had reached her side by then and made sure she was comfortable as he handed her the goods. "Lucien seems real happy all of a sudden. What happened to light up his world?"

Paris took a long sip of ginger ale before answering. "My brother says he's found the woman of his dreams and he's getting married," she said. "Lucien says he's through with his player ways and he's ready to settle down."

Titus gave her the smile that never failed to make her heart flutter. He rubbed her tummy and reminded her that until he met her marriage was the last thing on his mind. "All it takes is the right woman to make a man get his priorities straight. He may have found her, sweetheart."

Yeah, and she's gonna give him a run for his money, too. I hope he means business, 'cause she'll break him down if he doesn't, Paris thought.

Even though he hadn't been able to get any further information from Paris, Lucien was nothing if not resourceful. He obtained Nicole's home telephone number from directory assistance in Charleston and called her. Since this was the first time he called, he expected a little awkwardness on her part. She'd been practically ambushed by his boisterous brothers, after all, and she was still due an apology for that. And she'd left before he could let her know how interested he was, how much he wanted her. He was sure he could bridge that gap quickly and suavely and then get on with the process of winning her heart. He called her on Sunday evening. He was alone in the suite when he made the call. Leaning into the pillows at the head of his bed, he stretched out comfortably, listening to her phone ring. He smiled when she answered.

"Hello?"

Lucien almost forgot to reply; he was too taken with the melodic tone that stroked his ear. Just hearing her speak made him relax all over in a way that was totally new to him.

"Hello?" This time Nicole sounded impatient, as well she should, since he hadn't said a word.

"Nicole, this is Lucien," he said, using his best voice. "How are you?"

"Lucien who? Do you have a last name?" she asked crisply.

Lucien's smile widened. "Oh, you got jokes."

Nicole's tone didn't change. "No, I've got Luciens. I know three men named Lucien, so I need a little clarification. Which one are you?"

He got out of his comfortable position and brought his legs over the side of the bed. "Nicole, this is Lucien Deveraux, Paris's brother. You haven't forgotten me already, have you?" he asked, feeling less like a man of the world and more like a gawky teenager.

"Oh, *that* Lucien. No, of course I haven't forgotten you. I have an excellent memory. How are you?"

Only slightly relieved by her admission that she remembered him, Lucien plunged ahead. "Listen, Nicole, I wanted to apologize for my brothers. They really didn't mean to embarrass you. If they'd had any idea that we were in the room, they would have knocked. I'm really sorry if you were uncomfortable in any way," he said with the natural confidence that was so irresistibly sexy.

"Uncomfortable about what, Lucien? Why do you think your brothers owe me an apology?"

Lucien was taken aback slightly by Nicole's cool disinterest, but he was determined to stay the course. He was supposed to call her, apologize, remind her of the wonderful time they'd had and arrange a date in the very near future. Nicole apparently hadn't read the manual, because she wasn't on the same page. This wasn't the reaction he'd expected, not at all.

"I'm talking about the fact that they came stomping in there when we were getting to know each other. I know how upset you were about that whole thing, which is why you left early," he said, his confident tone slipping into something like an adolescent plea.

"Lucien, we were just kissing. It wasn't that big a deal," she said airily. "I had to drive back to Charleston because I have a presentation tomorrow morning. A rather complex one, actually. As a matter of fact, I'm working on it now, so I'm going to have to cut this short. It was nice hearing from you," she said sweetly, "but I really need to get back to work. Take care and thanks for calling."

Before Lucien could say another word, she ended the call. He stared at his cell phone with utter puzzlement. What the hell had just happened? He had to smile because Nicole had put him in his place like no woman ever had. On the one hand, the results weren't as stellar as he'd hoped, but on the other hand, it gave him a better idea of what he'd be dealing with. Paris was right about one thing: Titus's little sister was no pushover.

In Charleston, Nona and Natalie also had questions. They were at Nicole's condo getting the details of the double wedding, which they had missed due to prior commitments.

When Nicole claimed to know three Luciens, their eyes met and both of them looked suspicious. As soon as the call was over, they pounced.

"You don't know any Lucien except Paris's fine brother. Was that him on the phone?" Nona asked.

Natalie was helping Nicole unpack, but she stopped with her hands full of makeup to help interrogate her sister. "And if it was him, why were you playing games with him? Why were you trying to pretend that you didn't know who he was? And what were you doing kissing him, anyway?"

"Honey, if she was kissing him, it's because he's *foine*. That's a good-looking family, girl. If I'd been there, I'd probably have been doing some kissing of my own," Nona said saucily.

"They're all younger than you," Nicole said smugly. Nona was the eldest sister and Nicole rarely got an opportunity to needle her because she was so self-contained and composed. Her little dig didn't work, though.

Nona raised an eyebrow and said, "So what? Honey, a man that good-looking could be *twenty* years younger and I wouldn't care. As long as he's potty-trained and can drink from a cup, we'd be good to go. Now don't change the subject. What were you up to in Atlanta this weekend, you little harlot?"

When Nicole hesitated, Natalie put down the cosmetics, with the exception of a bottle of Philosophy lotion. It was Pure Grace, one of Nicole's favorite scents, and Natalie threatened to pour it down the sink if she didn't confess.

"I didn't do anything," Nicole said as she tried to snatch the bottle from Natalie. Natalie tossed it to Nona, who ran out of the bedroom with it clutched to her chest.

Nicole screamed and ran after her. "If you dump that out, you're gonna pay me for it," she warned. "Okay, let's go in the kitchen, and I'll tell you. But I need something to eat. I'm hungry."

Soon they were sitting around the kitchen table and Nicole was enjoying the plate of food her sisters had brought her. Nona had to miss the wedding because she had hosted a baby shower for one of her coworkers. But she had a bounty of leftover delicacies that Nicole was savoring.

"I know you brought me some dessert," Nicole said with a dimpled smile. "Where is it?"

Natalie held up a white baker's box. She had a way with sweets that was amazing. "You know what's in here? *Cake*," she said with a wicked grin. "And not just any cake. It's my homemade Italian cream cake, which, if I'm not mistaken, is your very favorite dessert. There is also a red velvet cupcake and some petits fours. And there's milk to go with it, too. Not that nasty stuff in the carton—the kind in the glass bottles from the deli that you like so much."

Nicole made a little sound of anticipation and held out her hands, only to have Natalie snatch the box away. "You don't get a crumb unless you tell us what you got up to this weekend. If you try to lie, we'll know and you'll never get this box. So go on and give it up, sister."

"Okay, okay, okay. Pour me some milk and I'll tell you the short version of how I made an absolute fool out of myself and got caught doing it."

Natalie and Nona raptly listened to her explain how she'd met Lucien again at the double wedding and how he'd given her the full-on where-have-you-been-all-my-life treatment until they had been so unexpectedly interrupted by his brothers. "He was attentive, sexy, charming, all of that," Nicole said glumly. "I couldn't remember which suite I was assigned to in the guesthouse and he offered to escort me, but not before we stopped at his suite. Then he kissed me. Then his brothers came busting in like it was a police raid or something. I wanted to go through the floor, but his brother Wade rescued me. He knew which suite Chastain and I were in and he escorted me out of there before it got ugly. And that's all." She took a long swallow of milk and finished the last crumb of the cake. The other things would be saved for later. She looked up to find Nona and Natalie laughing so hard that tears were rolling down Nona's face.

"See, this is why I don't tell you heifers anything. You're supposed to be giving me sympathy and all you can do is laugh like hyenas. Ugly, mean hyenas," Nicole said with a pout.

"I'm sorry, sweetie, I'm just picturing you and Mr. Gorgeous all caught up and then getting busted. I would have paid to see that," Nona said as she tried to contain her laughter.

Natalie nodded in agreement. "So was it worth it? Is he a good kisser?"

Surprising even herself, Nicole answered in the affirmative. "'Good' doesn't even begin to cover it. He's so tall and sexy and smart it doesn't make any sense. He's a great conversationalist and he has wonderful manners, just like all the men in that family. He's a great dancer and he smells good. You know that little place at the base of a man's throat that your nose touches when you're slow dancing?" she asked in a dreamy voice. "His skin smells so delicious, just like summer and clean linen and rain. And his lips are lethal. I've never kissed anyone who could kiss like Lucien. I swear I heard a voice going, 'What's my name? What's my name?' Because I couldn't remember my name! If somebody had asked me who I was, I would've said Pippi Longstocking, because that man kissed me right out of my mind."

Her sisters applauded happily, and Nona pumped a fist

over her head. "Go, Nicki! It's about time one of us got some action. So why were you playing mind games with him? It's obvious he likes you. Just go with it," she advised.

Nicole pursed her lips and looked at her cheery sisters with disgust. "Have we just met? You know I don't do pretty playa-playa men and you know why. I'm staying far, far away from him from now on. Unlike a lot of women, I learn from my mistakes. No, no, no, Mr. Lucien Deveraux is off-limits for me."

Natalie reached for the box of pastries and took out the red velvet cupcake. "You don't deserve this. I thought you had good common sense, but I was wrong," she said grumpily as she removed the paper wrapping and took a dainty bite of the cake. "Just because that idiot ex-fiancé of yours was a fool, does it mean that all men are equally stupid?"

Nicole braced herself for another round of the argument that had been going on for years among the sisters. "No, of course it doesn't. And it's not like I don't date. You know I date. I have a very rich and varied social life, thank you very much. I go to concerts, to plays, I go out to dinner, and I go boating and everything else there is to do. I date plenty and you know it," she said defensively.

"Yes, but all you date is Urkels," Nona pointed out. "Don't try and deny it—ever since that Leland fool, you've avoided all good-looking men. You only date mild-mannered nerdy men who're terrified of you. You ignore all the handsome, successful, intelligent men who want to go out with you and go straight for the little Endicotts who are so intimidated that they do whatever you want them to do. You're turning into quite the little princess, I might add. You're getting real warped in your perceptions and treatments of men."

"I think that's an insult, but before we go there I have to ask, what is an 'Endicott'? I know what an Urkel is, someone like that kid on that old TV show, but what, pray tell, is an 'Endicott'?" Nicole asked.

"It's from a song by Kid Creole and the Coconuts. Way before your time, honey. I found all of Daddy's old albums and cassettes and I put a lot of them on CD. This song is hilarious." She began singing the lyrics, which were about a very neat, tidy little man named Endicott who had no faults and was being used as an icon for male behavior.

"I remember that song!" Natalie joined in with Nona, and they even got up and did a little dance to Nicole's intense annoyance.

"Y'all need some hobbies. You're just a little bit too caught up into this thing," Nicole said dryly.

When their performance was over, the sisters sat down at the table again. Natalie looked at Nicole with love and said, "Sweetie, we're just trying to get you to see that you're becoming narrow-minded and you could miss out on someone really wonderful. You didn't make a mistake with Leland. *He's* the one who made the mistake. It was his loss, not yours. And quiet as it's kept, I didn't think he was all that handsome. His eyes were a little bit too close together for my taste. Besides, look at Daddy and Titus. Two of the most gorgeous men walking the earth, and both of them are as sweet as pie. You can't dump on poor Lucien just because he's handsome. That would make you just as shallow as that ex of yours," she said wisely.

Nicole was running her fingertip along the edge of the tiles on the table, trying to pretend that what her sisters were saying didn't make perfect sense, which it did. "Yeah, well, it's not just that. His nickname is Hound Dog because he has so many women," she said with a little sniff. "Now do you see what I'm talking about?"

Nona shook her head. "Not really. I've heard worse nicknames in my life. Hey, they used to call Franklin 'Mandingo' when we were in college, and I still married him," she said with a wistful smile. "And he was a wonderful husband. I couldn't have asked for better, God rest his soul."

Nicole was momentarily ashamed of herself. It was hard to believe that her vibrant, beautiful sister was also a widow. Sometimes Nicole could kick herself for blurting something out without thinking about how callous it might sound to someone who'd lost the love of their life tragically, like Nona had. But Nona was resilient and always serene, especially when she could get in the last word.

"Besides, Nic, honey, any woman can turn a hound dog into a puppy dog if she knows how to handle him. Aren't you up to the challenge?" she teased.

For once, Nicole didn't have a snappy comeback.

Chapter 7

In an ironic way, Lucien welcomed the chaos of the next month. Even though his Garden District home escaped damage from Katrina, he, like everyone else, had to remain evacuated from the city. Now he was back within the city limits with his brothers, all of them working feverishly to help the survivors. There was nothing too menial, too dirty or too horrifying for them to tackle. The Deveraux men worked side by side with the scores of others who were all working toward the same goal: to house the survivors and help rebuild the city.

Seeing what was left of what had once been a magnolia-scented jewel was beyond depressing. The realization that it would take years before the place known as the Big Easy was returned to its former glory was daunting. But there was hope. Lucien found that if he concentrated on one task at a time, it was easier to get through the days. To think too deeply about the hundreds of displaced families, the hundreds of people who had lost their lives, the total destruction of parts of New Orleans as well as other areas on the Gulf Coast was to court madness. But Lucien never lost sight of the fact that he and his family were among the lucky ones. They had their homes, they had each other and they had the opportunity to help the survivors. It was like a tiny beacon of hope radiating through a sea of chaos.

The nights were hard because he couldn't control his thoughts as easily. Lucien didn't sleep well, the way he had before the storm. He woke up often and dreamed often, mostly disturbing dreams of what he'd seen during the day. But sometimes he'd dream about Nicole. That was the only time he'd get any peaceful sleep. Sometimes they'd be talking and laughing; sometimes they would be dancing. And sometimes the dreams were tantalizingly erotic.

He would recall with complete clarity the taste of her lips, the feel of her soft curves. He could smell her delectable scent, and even though the dreams were so real they were a form of sweet torture, they were his secret delight. It was the only time he could stop thinking about everything that had happened since the storm. When he would dream about Nicole, he'd wake up rested and smiling because in every dream, every single one, he'd been wearing a thick gold wedding band on his left hand.

Finally the need to hear her voice got to be too much for him, and he had to call. He didn't question the urge that made him call; he just followed his craving. He was naked, having just taken a shower, and was covered to the waist with the top sheet of the bed. He was listening to a Mark Murphy CD as he waited for her to answer.

"Hello?"

This time, he didn't hesitate. "Nicole, this is Lucien

Deveraux, Paris's brother," he said quickly. "I hope I'm not calling too late."

She sounded amused rather than put out. "Hi, Lucien. How are you?"

"Exhausted," he said at once. "It's still kinda rough around here."

A soft sigh sounded from her end. "I'm sure it is. How are you dealing with it?"

Even though he was happy to hear the concern in her voice, suddenly he was just too spent to talk about what the days had been like since his return to the Crescent City, as New Orleans was also known. He swallowed hard. "Nicole, it's like…being in hell. Not for me," he explained hastily. "My father and my brothers, we were all really lucky in terms of our houses staying intact and all that, but… So many people have died. So many were missing, and there's so much destruction."

He talked for a few minutes and then stopped in the middle of a sentence. "I can't talk about it anymore, Nicole. I just can't. Can you do something for me? Can you just talk to me for a while?"

"Of course I can. What would you like to talk about?" she said in a soft, sweet voice.

"Anything you want. What have you been doing since I saw you?"

And just like that, she started chatting away about this and that, little inconsequential things that sent a wave of relaxation over him. She could have been reading *Vogue* magazine to him and it wouldn't have made a bit of difference. It was her voice, the calm, soothing sound of her voice that made him feel like a new man. Unfortunately, he got a little bit more relaxed than he realized. The soft murmur of Nicole's seductive voice combined with the background music and the welcome sense of well-being that surrounded him put him to sleep. He drifted off with a smile on his face and never heard her say, "Good night, Lucien." He simply slept better than he had for weeks.

Nicole was smiling when she hung up the phone. Under normal circumstances if a man had the nerve to fall asleep on her while she was talking to him, her reaction would have been very different. She would have been verbally abusive if not physically violent. She wasn't above delivering a good hard pinch or a sharp smack on the hand when a situation called for it. And the men she dated would allow it, too. But she couldn't find it in her heart to be angry or insulted. Lucien was bone-tired, she could tell. And she thought what he was doing was admirable.

She had a lot of friends who'd lost family and friends to Katrina's rage and she knew that dealing with the aftermath, even a few years later, had to be daunting at best. It was perfectly understandable that the poor man had fallen asleep on the phone. What she didn't completely understand was why she was being so reasonable about it. *I should be upset,* she thought. *Am I getting soft in the head?*

She was sitting at the dressing table in her bedroom, studying her reflection in the big round mirror. Her bedroom reflected her personality. It was decorated in soft pastel shades of pink, peach and coral, but the hard angular lines of the Art Deco–era furniture she'd bought and painstakingly restored made it look sophisticated and chic instead of overly feminine.

Her elbow was propped on the table and her chin was resting in her hand. Her sisters' words were echoing in her ears after hearing Lucien's voice. Was she narrow-minded and unable to take chances? Was she dating only mousy little men

who were scared of her? She crossed both arms on the
dressing table and stared at her smooth complexion intently.
She was thinking about the men with whom she went out.

*Let's see, there's Milton, the CPA. Medium height, medium
brown, medium brains, quiet and always punctual,* she
thought, making a little face. *Then there's Herman,* she
mused. *He's quiet, polite, almost tall, a little thin, always a
little early, also an accountant.* She studied her fingernails
carefully as she thought about yet another of her usual dates,
Charles. *He's a little taller than Herman, a little more talka-
tive and somewhat more spontaneous.* Her eyes widened as
it suddenly dawned on her that *he* was also an accountant.

"Oh, Heavenly Father, I'm dating a posse of bean
counters," she said aloud. "Nona was right! I've gone to the
Urkel store and picked out a whole selection of...*nerds.*" She
got up abruptly and knocked the chair in which she'd been
sitting over in her haste. She hurriedly set it upright on her
way to the bathroom. There was no cure like a bubble bath
and that's just what she was going to do.

A nice, hot scented bath in tons of bubbles would make her
feel worlds better. She set the water to running, adding a
generous amount of Pure Grace body wash and watched the
bubbles rise until the water was deep enough for her to bathe.
She took off her pink terry-cloth bath wrap and stepped into
the tub. Soon she was lolling in the scented water, enjoying
the steamy warmth and the clean, fresh scent of the bubbles.
She adjusted the bath pillow behind her head and began to
analyze her angst.

Nona was right about her, and so was Natalie. Nicole had
let her experience with Leland sour her on men. Nicole
frowned slightly as she looked over at the small glass-fronted
cabinet within which one of her favorite possessions resided.

It was a figurine of a plump, glamorous woman taking a bubble bath. Her head was wrapped in a towel and her leg was extended out of the tub. She had a very pretty, serene face, and Nicole had bought it the moment she'd seen it. She'd been with her mother and giggled when she caught a glimpse of the bathing lady. "Mama, look! It's me! I have to have that," she'd said.

Her mother had been charmed by it, too, although she pointed out that Nicole's thighs were nowhere near as big as the statue's. "But that's what makes it so cute," Nicole explained. "The proportions are exaggerated so her foot looks really dainty and adorable. I love her, and I'm taking her home."

Now she looked at the plump diva for confirmation of her thoughts. "I actually let that idiot Leland have power over me. I'm letting him control me. Because he was cute, I've been assuming that all good-looking men are worthless, and that makes no sense. I'm a smart, sophisticated adult who's able to make intelligent decisions, and I haven't been doing that, have I?" Waiting a moment as though the bubble goddess was going to answer, she nodded.

"You're right, it wasn't my fault. He did treat me badly, and I was so traumatized that I made an emotional reaction into a lifestyle. I let my anger and pain box me into a corner, and I stayed there. The men I've been dating are very nice, but they aren't really my type," she admitted. "And I don't think I've been particularly nice to any of them. I boss them around, and they let me do it because…because…" She paused and looked at the figurine again for answers.

"Well, yes, I am rather delicious, just like you," Nicole said, batting her eyes with false modesty. "But beauty like ours comes with responsibilities. I can't be taking advantage of nice little men just because they let me. I should be ashamed of myself. And I need to stop it, too. I wouldn't want anyone judging me, but I've sure been handing out some rough sentences to some innocent men. How could I be so neurotic?"

Just then, her cell phone rang, and she leaned out of the tub to pluck it off the cabinet next to the figurine. "Hello?"

She smiled happily when she heard Chastain's voice on the other end. "No, I'm not busy. Of course I can talk. I'm taking a bubble bath and talking to the Bath Diva."

Chastain asked, "What's a Bath Diva? I don't think I've ever heard of one."

Nicole explained and laughed along with her friend when Chastain started laughing. "Yes, I'm sitting in the tub talking to a statue. I do it all the time. She likes me and she always agrees with me, unlike some people who don't seem to recognize that I'm brilliant. So how are you doing?"

"Hanging by a thread, honey. I'm not going to lie. It's really been rough now that I'm back in New Orleans, Nicole. I knew it would be bad when I came here, but I had no idea how awful the conditions would be. We're all taking it one day at a time, doing the best we can to accomplish something. I'm working with some really good people," Chastain said gamely, "but it's really rough, Nicole."

Nicole could hear Chastain struggling not to cry, and her heart was touched. "I know it's hard, and I know you're tired, but you're doing something to change things. And don't forget, you were a big part of the reason we did that big fundraiser through my sorority. We'll be there on Thursday," she reminded Chastain.

This time, Chastain did give in to tears. She sniffled a little, saying, "I'm sorry to be yowling in your ear, but it's starting to get to me."

"Don't apologize," Nicole said firmly. "I know it's been

rough, and that's why we're coming. Just look for a pink-and-green caravan on Thursday. And try to get some rest, too. You can only do so much every day, and if your body becomes run-down, you won't be able to accomplish anything. Try to take a day off, if you can." She was going to New Orleans with her sorority to help with the aftermath of Katrina. She was also going to stay in New Orleans for a month, working with Chastain to restore artwork damaged by the flooding.

"I'll do that after you get here," Chastain promised. "We'll look for you on Thursday. Finish your bath, and you get some rest because you're going to need every ounce of strength you've got," she said sadly.

Nicole ended the call and put the cell phone back. She shivered a little and used her toe to let some more hot water into the tub. Neither she nor Chastain had mentioned the obvious, a certain devilish Deveraux, but it was all good. And she was going to have an opportunity to do some really good work, something else that satisfied her deeply.

"It's all going to be good," she murmured. "Better than good."

Philippe was watching Chastain, who was looking up every five minutes or so. They were standing side by side in the store that was owned by Chastain's family. It was located near Bourbon Street in the French Quarter. It was a typical souvenir shop, but it had a distinct atmosphere. It was a tall, skinny brick building with a big glass front window and hardwood floors. Inside was an eclectic mix of artwork, posters, framed prints, photographs and sculptures by local artists. There was also locally made jewelry, incense, body oils, massage oils, Mardi Gras beads, spices, masks and T-shirts.

The name of the store was Gris-Gris, a term for a charm or talisman that was supposed to bring good luck or ward off evil spirits. The roots of the phrase were hazy. Some scholars said it derived from a West African word, *Juju,* which meant essentially the same thing. Some thought it was from a French word, *Jou-jou.* In any case, it was a word that immediately made the hearer think of New Orleans, which, of course, was the intention. At one time Chastain's Uncle Toto concentrated on selling candles, faux voodoo paraphernalia and the like, but over the years, Chastain had exercised her artistic influence to make the store more artsy than ominous, which had actually improved sales.

Now the store was functioning as a meeting place for people like the Deverauxes who were keeping the city cleaned up and running again. Chastain made sure there was always bottled water, tea, food and coffee, the latter heavily laced with chicory the way many in N'awlins preferred their brew. Philippe was sipping a cup while he watched Chastain fidget. She was dusting things that didn't need to be dusted, since she had already spent several days cleaning the place from top to bottom, even though it hadn't been damaged in the storm. She wouldn't admit it to anyone, but she couldn't sleep for worrying about her family, her friends and if the city she'd loved all her life would ever be the same. Now she was standing behind the main counter pretending to read a newspaper, but she was really staring out the window. She'd look up every five minutes just as though she'd been programmed to do it.

"Your neck is spinnin' around like a broken toy," Philippe said irritably. "Why do you keep looking out that window? You waiting for Prince Charming or something?" While he was getting on Chastain's case, the door opened and in walked Lucien just in time to hear his twin's words.

"Somebody looking for a prince? Here I am, *cher,* at your

service," Lucien said as he walked over to greet Chastain with a big kiss on the cheek.

Chastain returned the gesture of affection and looked him over with a big smile. "You always manage to look good, even in that getup. How come when you guys wear jeans and a T-shirt, you look like a Ralph Lauren ad and your twin looks like he's on work release?"

Both men were wearing well-worn jeans and equally ancient T-shirts, but Chastain was right; Lucien looked like he'd just left a country club, while Philippe resembled someone from a police lineup. Lucien's hair was beautifully cut and his mustache was meticulously groomed, while Philippe's hair was growing longer and wilder every day. He also hadn't shaved since the double wedding, and he looked very different from his brother, something Lucien was happy to point out.

"I've been expecting this ever since he went into environmental law. It was only a matter of time before he started looking like one of the critters he's trying to protect," he said as he flicked a bit of lint off his shoulder.

Chastain disagreed. "He looks more like Smokey the Bear, if you ask me."

Philippe was about to retort when the front door opened again and a cheery voice was heard.

"We're here at last. Please tell me there's a bathroom in here, because there are about twenty women out there who really need some facilities," said Nicole.

Chastain burst around the corner of the counter to embrace her. "You made it!"

It was indeed Nicole, wearing a sorority T-shirt and cute knee-length khaki shorts that showed off her gorgeous legs. Her hair was in a ponytail, and she didn't look like she'd just driven in from South Carolina: she looked as fresh as a dewy rose. Chastain hugged her twice, saying, "Nicole, you have no idea how glad I am to see you!" She couldn't resist taking a peek at Lucien, whose surprise was evident. *I think somebody else is glad to see you, too,* she thought.

Chapter 8

Lucien's pleasant surprise turned swiftly to anger as Philippe practically jumped over the counter to join the two women. When Philippe put his arms around Nicole and gave her a big hug, he could feel a slight throbbing in his temple that usually heralded a huge argument. He could have easily gone off on his brother for encroaching on the woman he felt was his exclusive province but something stopped him from making a scene. Two things, really; one, he knew instinctively that Nicole wouldn't appreciate it in the least, and two, she smiled at him.

When Philippe finally released her from what seemed to Lucien was an overly familiar embrace, Nicole turned and flashed the beautiful smile that he'd been dreaming about for weeks.

"Hello, Lucien. How are you?" Before he could answer, she added, "Where's my hug? I get a nice hug from Chastain and Philippe, and you're just going to ignore me? What's that about?"

"I was just waiting my turn, *cher.* I was surprised to see you. Shocked is a better word. Why didn't you tell me you were coming here? You never mentioned a word," he said reproachfully.

Her eyes twinkled merrily. "I kept it a secret because I wanted to see the look on your face when I walked in. I like to keep life exciting," she said with a mysterious smile. "It's good to keep you on your toes. My sorority wanted to help out with the recovery efforts and so I took a leave of absence from my job. I'm going to be helping Chastain with some art restorations while I'm here," she explained. "So where's my hug?"

Lucien gave her a sexy smile. "I was waiting for my heart to slow down, *cher.* It's good to see you again, Nicole." He was gratified by the warmth in her voice. He took both her hands in his and smiled down at her before putting a kiss on the back of each hand.

Nicole protested. "I said a hug. Are you trying to lick my hands? You need instructions or something?"

Lucien just laughed and pulled her into his arms. He held her closely, so close that he could smell her light fragrance and feel the warmth of her body. This was what he'd been wanting, what he'd needed from her alone. He angled his head so he could whisper in her ear. "When I lick you, you'll know it, Nicole. And you'll enjoy it as much as I will."

Nicole's eyes narrowed, and she twisted out of his arms so fast it was like she hadn't even been there. The door opened, and Gris-Gris was suddenly crowded with Nicole's sorority sisters, who really were in need of the ladies' room. The level of conversation rose to a near-din, and Lucien lost Nicole in the crowd of women. But judging by the look she'd given him, it was probably best that he gave her a little space.

Lucien wasn't dense; he knew he'd probably gone a little

bit too far with that licking thing. Paris's words were coming back to haunt him. She'd warned him not to use any of his old player tricks; she'd told him in no uncertain terms that Nicole wasn't going to go for anything in his sizable arsenal of amorous moves. He took a deep breath and walked over to lean on the counter so he could watch her animated expression as she introduced her friends to Chastain and Philippe. She was such a welcome and pretty sight that he couldn't take his eyes off her. *Okay, you went a little overboard. But you can make up for it,* he told himself. *Just need to take it slow and easy.*

He relaxed against the counter and feasted his eyes on her. She looked even more desirable than he remembered, and he had a good eye for detail. The essentials were the same, but there were tiny things he hadn't noticed before. Her skin looked softer than he recalled, her hair was shinier and her dimples were even more fascinating. He could see more of her legs this time; the shorts she was wearing showed them off much better. She had some world-class legs; they were big and curvy and smooth, and he knew these were the legs he wanted entwined with his every night for the rest of his life.

Philippe came up behind him and poked him roughly in the back. "If you don't get that stupid look off your face, I'm going to have your birth certificate revoked. You can't be my brother if you're going to stand here drooling with a blank look on your face. Cut it out, dummy," he said in a low voice that only Lucien could hear.

"I'm not drooling, I'm just admiring the view," Lucien said in an equally low voice. "I didn't know she was coming, and I was caught off guard, that's all."

Just then, Nicole looked at him, and the look was anything but warm. Philippe gave an exaggerated shiver and mumbled, "Damn, it's gettin' cold in here. You better get your guard up, bro, because that woman ain't nobody to play with." As much as he wanted to disagree, Lucien could see for himself that his twin was on point.

In a short while, the women were assembled at the stately home of Mac and Ruth Deveraux. Ruth had prepared a huge buffet for the ladies, and they were gladly taking part in it. Lucien had invited himself along, since it was his father's house, after all, and he had a lot of questions. Evidently everyone in New Orleans knew that Nicole was going to be in town and no one had bothered to inform him beforehand. He didn't even know why all those women were there. Was this some kind of sorority conference or something? He cornered Ruth in the big kitchen and started asking questions.

"Why are all those women here, and why didn't anyone tell me they were coming?" he demanded.

Ruth was refilling a tray of crudités and hummus and didn't answer him at first. He stood behind her and put his hands on her shoulders, repeating his question. "Why didn't you tell me they were coming?"

"Luc, sweetie, I'm sure I mentioned it. Their chapter did a lot of fund-raising for the hurricane survivors, and they're here because they've brought truckloads of building supplies, clothing, food and cash donations. They'll be leaving soon, because they're going to Houston next. They started this caravan in Charleston, and they've driven down the Gulf Coast, leaving supplies in the neediest areas. Nicole is staying here with us since she's family. I'm sure I mentioned it to you and your brothers," she said.

"Yeah, maybe. You probably did and it just didn't register," Lucien said moodily. He released her shoulders and made a move on the tray of fresh vegetables.

"Hands off. There's plenty in the refrigerator. Make yourself useful and take this into the dining room, please."

Lucien still wasn't satisfied. "Yeah, but nobody bothered to mention that Nicole was coming. I would have remembered *that,*" he said emphatically as he walked out. "I would have remembered for sure."

Ruth finally turned around to look her son-by-marriage, as she referred to Mac's children, in the eyes. "Oh, really? Am I to assume by your tone that you have an interest in Nicole?"

Lucien gave Ruth a calm, level gaze. "I'm more than interested. I'm going to marry her," he said confidently.

"I see," Ruth replied drolly. "So why is this the first time I'm hearing about this? You haven't mentioned it to your father because I'm sure he would have told me, unless you've sworn him to secrecy or something."

Lucien had gone to the refrigerator to start rummaging around. Sudden hunger had seized him and redirected his energy for the moment. He took out a bowl of shrimp salad and turned around to find Ruth's green eyes wide with curiosity.

"You can't drop a bomb like that and then stuff your face. I want details, young man. Sit down at the counter and explain yourself. Let me put this on a plate for you, I plan to have some left for your father this evening and I know how much you can eat," she reminded him. "Wash your hands and I'll fix this up for you."

He did as she instructed and after he dried his hands he straddled one of the tall chairs at the work island in the middle of the kitchen and watched Ruth as she made a nice plate for him with salad, vegetables and a big dish of her fabulous fruit salad. He started talking as he observed her quick, efficient movements.

"I guess I didn't tell y'all about this because I just realized at the weddings that she was the one. I'd met her before at

Paris's wedding, of course, but she had a date so I couldn't really do anything. I thought she was gorgeous, but I had to mind my manners, you know. But when she came to your wedding, I knew she was the woman I'd been looking for all my life," he said, eyeing his food appreciatively.

Ruth waited until he'd said grace and picked up his fork. "But why haven't you said anything about this before, sweetie? Didn't you think your father might be interested in knowing he was getting another daughter-in-law?" she asked with gentle amusement.

Lucien nodded as he swallowed his first bite. "This is really good, Mom. You can throw down in the kitchen," he said gratefully. "You and Pop went off for your honeymoon and when you got back we were all so involved in the clean-up it just never came up. It wasn't like it was a secret or anything," he said thoughtfully. "I talked to Paris about it, and Wade and Philippe knew about it, too. Paris told me to stay away from her and Wade and Philippe think I'm nuts. But I'm not," he said calmly. "I just know what I want and what I want I go after. Nicole is going to be my wife. Any more rolls?"

Ruth got him another of her homemade rolls and offered him more herb butter, which he refused. "So if I'm following this correctly, you met Nicole on one other occasion and decided after you saw her at the wedding that she was destined to be your bride, is that right?"

Lucien answered her firmly and confidently. "That's about right. When I saw her the first time I knew I wanted to get to know her, but when I saw her again I knew why I felt that way. It was because she was going to be mine. Can I have some more of this? This is really good." The Deverauxes' cat, Bojangles, appeared to agree with Lucien because he showed up in the kitchen demanding his fair share.

"Flattery will get you some more chicken salad, but your father is getting the rest of the shrimp. And Bojangles, you're getting that high-priced cat food. You're not supposed to eat rich people food."

Lucien had just slipped the cat a sliver of chicken from his plate and looked guilty, which Ruth couldn't see because her back was to him. Getting the container out of the refrigerator, she put a generous helping of chicken salad with artichoke hearts, pesto and lemon fettuccine on his plate. "So you believe in love at first sight, Lucien? Because that's what this sounds like."

Lucien shook his head. "Technically it's love at second sight, Mom. And it's not really like that. Love at first sight sounds like infatuation, like something that happens to you when you're young and impressionable. This is *knowing* at first sight. I looked at her and I knew. I touched her and I knew. I kissed her and, man, that was it. I never felt anything like that in my life and I know I'll never have it with another woman. She's it. She's the one," he said simply, but with deep conviction.

Ruth was watching him with great interest. "You're completely serious, aren't you, sweetie?"

"Absolutely. I'm just like Pop and Julian. My cousins all fought like Bengal tigers because none of them wanted to get married, well, except Marcus. But the Louisiana Deveraux men don't play that. We don't mess around. We know our destiny when we see her and we go get her, simple as that."

"And does Nicole know how you feel about her? Does she return those feelings?" Ruth was leaning on the work island with her arm up. Her chin rested in the palm of her hand and she was smiling at him with warmth and love.

Lucien's confidence didn't waver as he answered her. He put down his glass of sweet tea and answered no on both counts. "But she'll know soon. It has to be soon before I put my foot in my mouth like I did today. I said something really stupid to her and she got offended. She gave me this look that put the fear of God into me," he said with a laugh. "I'm going to have to slow my roll or she'll think I'm the village idiot or something."

Ruth patted his hand reassuringly. "There's no chance of that, Luc." She went to the oven and took out a pan of rolls that she put into a napkin-lined basket. Before going into the dining room she reminded him to bring the vegetable tray. "And don't worry, you'll have plenty of time to get to know her. She's going to be staying with us for a month. Bring that other pitcher of tea, too, would you?"

Lucien stared at Ruth as she went through the French doors to the dining room. Then he smiled widely. If this wasn't a sign he didn't know what was. He was right about everything; he and Nicole were meant to be. Why else would she be dropped into his arms like a gift from above? Any tiny bit of doubt he'd been entertaining disappeared as he picked up the tray and the pitcher and headed for the dining room to help Ruth. Everything was going to work out just fine.

Nicole watched Lucien like a wary lioness for the rest of the afternoon. All during lunch, when he kept making appearances to help serve, to refresh the women's drinks and even to clear off the table, she watched him. She was hotter than a jalapeño pepper. He had his nerve making an ol' cornball pass at her like that. She was perfectly justified in feeling angry about that nonsense. But she was way beyond angry, she was boiling, hopping mad, and not at Lucien but at herself. She was furious because she knew better than to get smitten by another good-looking womanizer. She knew firsthand that handsome men were generally not to be trusted, that they acted like gentlemen to cover up their basic player behavior. She'd already been down that road once.

When Lucien had taken her hands in his and kissed the back of them, Nicole should have been able to step back and smack him across the mouth. Instead, the feelings that rushed through her at his touch were amazing, surprising her with passion. His touch was gentle, tender and assured. So warm and tender that the intensity of her reaction actually frightened her a little. Like most attractive women, Nicole was used to men making passes at her. She knew how to protect herself against that kind of boring behavior. But what she wasn't used to was the secret thrill she felt at Lucien's touch. It wasn't supposed to happen like that. She was supposed to be cool, calm and disinterested in Lucien. She had already decided that if he put another move on her, she wasn't going to get all soft and mushy. While she was chastising herself, she felt warmth on the back of her neck and knew without turning around that it was Lucien. She got a grim satisfaction out of thinking *Your eyes might shine and your teeth might grit, but none of this brown sugar is you gon' get.*

She was about to start giggling, and then she looked up to see Lucien's broad shoulders that tapered down into his slender waist. Her eyes traveled down to his muscular butt and his long, slightly bowed legs. A quick burst of heat in her middle filled her with dismay.

Even a woman of very strong resolve and principle had a hard time resisting the irresistible.

After the luncheon, the ladies went to distribute some of their bounty. Nicole was slightly aggravated that Lucien was still tagging along, but she decided it would be childish to resent his presence since he was being helpful. They had rented three trucks and two vans, and getting the supplies unloaded was no joke. Neither were the contents of the vehicles. One of Nicole's sorors was from Pass Christian, Mississippi, a small town which had been almost completely destroyed in the storm. Her parents had survived, but everything they owned was gone. Her tragedy, among so many others, was what had spurred their chapter to start a fund-raiser to end all fund-raisers.

The women of Nicole's sorority had solicited corporate donations, held crab boils and fish frys, a huge yard sale and a bachelor and bachelorette auction. They had urged the congregations of their various churches to take up special collections and each member of the group had also donated between five hundred and one thousand dollars apiece. The results of their hard work were visible in the supplies they brought with them. Brand-new clothing and shoes were neatly packaged in plastic with the sizes plainly labeled on the outside. There were basic first-aid supplies, personal hygiene items, food staples and bottled water.

She was watching Lucien's T-shirt clinging to his body as he perspired from his exertion. A sudden poke in the arm jarred her back from her reverie. It was Chastain, wearing an innocuous expression that didn't fool Nicole for a minute.

"Have I told you how glad I am you came? Bringing all the goods and helping to restore that artwork and rebuild a legendary arts collective is really going to help the artistic community," she said in a voice as innocent as her expression.

"Cut it out," Nicole said, giving her a stern look. "You're trying some of Paris's old tricks, aren't you? That's why you really wanted me to come here." She glared at Lucien's fine frame and had to repress a slight tremble as she watched the sweat trickle down Lucien's brow while he hoisted another box. She let out a stifled little sigh before starting in on Chastain again. "It didn't have anything to do with any ol' artwork. You're up to something else entirely, aren't you?"

"No! I'm not trying anything underhanded or sneaky, I swear I'm not! I really need you. *N'awlins* needs you, Nicole. You have no idea what a service you'll be rendering to us in our hour of need," she said fervently.

Nicole rolled her eyes, but she smiled at Chastain. She knew her friend was up to something, but she also knew she'd be doing some really good work while she was here. That didn't mean she wouldn't give Chastain a hard time.

"I took a leave of absence from my job to be here. I had to turn over a really big contract to someone else at the design firm just so I could come here for a month," she said in a martyred tone. "And I didn't do it so that gigolo could put some cheap moves on me. I don't want to have to put out a restraining order on him."

Merriment filled Chastain's eyes. "Did he say something to you at Gris-Gris? I kinda noticed that you looked at him a little strange," she said coyly.

Nicole was about to answer when the object of her disdain appeared by her side. Lucien was wiping his face and hands with wet wipes that held a soft citrus scent. Even that mundane little detail didn't make him less eye-pleasing. She still got the same little chill that radiated down her traitorous spine every time he was this close to her. She tried her best to look coolly disinterested as he asked her a question.

"Nicole, may I have a moment of your time?"

He didn't exactly wait for a response; he was talking as he

took her elbow and guided her a few feet away from Chastain so that they were alone on the sidewalk, facing each other.

She crossed her arms and glanced at him with a carefully neutral face. "What do you want?"

"Nicole, I want to apologize for what I said to you at Gris-Gris. I was completely out of line. My only excuse is that I was so happy to see you," he said. Sincerity emanated from him and washed over her like a summer breeze. "I was so shocked to look up and see you, and you felt so good in my arms, I lost my mind. I promise you it won't happen again. I have no intention of ever disrespecting you in any way," he told her. "I'll be talking to you soon, if that's okay," he added.

Once again, Nicole's knees turned to rubber and that same tingling feeling came over her. Lucien was slipping under her ultrasensitive radar. All she knew was that she had to watch her every step or she could end up in some serious trouble. She watched him walk away. The back view was almost as good as the front—she had to admit it. Suddenly he turned around and smiled at her, a really sweet, sexy smile. At that moment she was truly glad she was standing still because otherwise she would have fallen down flat on her face. She knew it for a fact.

That evening, Nicole got settled in at Mac and Ruth's house. When Chastain told them that Nicole was coming to the city to deliver goods and to help her with some restoration projects, they insisted that she stay with them. Ruth had also reminded Chastain that she was more than welcome to come, too.

"I worry about you down in the Quarter, honey. We have plenty of room here and there's no reason for you to be staying on top of Gris-Gris," Ruth had told her.

Chastain was indeed living on top of the store in a furnished apartment that had been the home of one of her uncles, who was currently in Baton Rouge until things were more back to normal. He was elderly and Chastain felt it would be best for him to take some time to visit with relatives for a while. She had thanked Ruth for the invitation, but told her that her uncle had begged her to stay there to protect his belongings and the store, and she never broke her word, ever. "Mrs. Deveraux, I'm fine, I really am. There're more people coming back to the Quarter every day and I've known most of them since I was an arm baby. I've got all the bouncers and bounders and bartenders keeping an eye out for me, so I'm cool," she had told her.

She wasn't opposed to eating well, however, and had several dinners with Ruth and Mac, usually joined by Lucien, Philippe and Wade, singly or en masse. Tonight, because Nicole was there, she was expecting Lucien to join them, but he was conspicuous by his absence. Wade and Philippe were there with good appetites and their usual boisterous charm, and no one seemed to miss Lucien except Nicole. Chastain caught her darting a glance at the front door several times as though she expected him to appear. She filed that information away for a later discussion and complimented the food instead.

"Judge, you put your foot in this *maque choux,*" she said appreciatively. "No one makes it like you do. Yours is the best in N'awlins."

"It may be the second best from now on. My lovely bride made this batch," Mac said with pride.

Chastain covered her mouth in embarrassment. "Me and my big mouth! I'm sorry, Mrs. Deveraux. I'm just used to eating the judge's food and it's so good I thought he'd made this, too," she said hurriedly.

"Why don't you put your other foot in your mouth while you're at it?" Philippe said dryly.

"Philippe, hush," Ruth chided him. "I'm very flattered that you like it, honey. And that is Julian's recipe. I've been getting him to teach me all kinds of Creole dishes because I love to cook and I love the local food. This is like fried corn but I'd never thought of putting the pepper and okra and other things in it. I used to make fried corn all summer in Chicago but this is so much better. It's elegant but down-home," she said. "Would you like some more? Or some more eggplant?"

Chastain readily accepted seconds on both. She took a quick glance at Nicole, who was staring at the front door again. Damning the inevitable consequences, she put on her sweetest expression. "Where's Lucien tonight? I thought he'd be here." She had to put her napkin to her mouth to stifle a shriek because Nicole, who was sitting next to her, had given her a sharp pinch under the table. The unexpected pain gave her a little jolt and she almost missed Mac's words.

"He's probably still at the Rescue Mission. He volunteers there a few nights a week," he said. "Anyone want dessert? We'd better get it dished up in a hurry because poor Nicole looks like she's about to fall asleep. It's been a long day for you, dear. Why don't you turn in and Ruth can bring you some crème brûlée on a tray."

Nicole thanked him for his offer, but said she would pass on dessert. "*Today,* that is. I don't eat a lot of sweets, but I have a feeling that yours will convert me, Mrs. Deveraux. You're an amazing cook and the meal was superb. Thank you so much," she said nicely. "I think I will go to bed, though. We left Charleston at four this morning and I'm starting to feel it. Chastain, can I borrow you for a minute to go over tomorrow's agenda?"

After saying good-night to everyone, she and Chastain headed for the room that Nicole would be staying in for her visit. As soon as Nicole closed the door Chastain ran behind the comfortable-looking club chair in the corner and pleaded for her life.

"Now, Nic, don't hit me! It might leave a mark and what would people think?" She laughed as Nicole snatched her purse off the bed, saying that her straight razor was in there somewhere.

"It's a nice sharp one, too, so it won't take too long. This is what happens when you meddle in grown folks' business," she said tartly. She tossed the bag aside and stretched out on the bed. "What went wrong with you at the dinner table? Why did you have to mention his name?"

Chastain emerged from her hiding place and sat in the chair. She leaned back and stretched out her long legs, crossing them at the ankle. "Well, how could I not? This is his parents' home, after all, and he usually has dinner here, at least he has lately. It was a perfectly proper remark. I think a better question is what are *you* up to?"

Nicole's face went blank. "I don't know what you're talking about."

Chastain rolled her eyes impatiently. "Look, you can spill it or I can badger you to death. You want to get in that nice comfortable bed and close your eyes and I want to find out what happened with you and Luc today. You want to do this the easy way or the annoying way?"

Nicole bared her teeth tiredly at Chastain. "I have two older sisters and you're, like, four times as inquisitive as they are. It hardly seems possible. Could we be related in some way that I'm not aware of, do you think? Dang, you're nosy!"

"Yes, it's why Paris and I are such good friends. We were known as the Snoop Sisters when we were growing up. No secret was safe with us, so if you want to go to bed, tell me everything. I can whine," she warned. "That's something you don't want to hear, trust me."

"Okay, you win, but I have something in store for you. One day when you least expect it, you're going to get got, so be ready for it. Here's the short version: when we were at Gris-Gris, Lucien said something to me that I didn't appreciate. He was supposed to give me a hug and he kissed my hands and I said something about why was he licking my hands and he said something corny about when he licked me I'd know it and I'd like it and so would he," Nicole said in a dry voice. "Then he took me aside this afternoon and apologized for being a jerk and said he shouldn't have said anything like that and he would never disrespect me. And that's the whole story. Now go home."

Chastain didn't budge from her seat. Her face was gleaming with interest and admiration. "Well, that's one to Lucien," she said. "He passed that test with flying colors, didn't he?"

"What test? I wasn't testing him, I was trying to ignore him." Nicole yawned widely.

"Look, everything is a test of some kind. When you meet a guy you have to kind of feel him out while you're getting to know him. Lucien passed a test today. He did something really stupid and he had enough sense to admit his mistake, apologize and leave the door open for further exploration. I'd say round one goes to Lucien."

Nicole opened her mouth to argue with Chastain and she abruptly closed it again with a calculating look. She looked like someone who was on the verge of solving a complicated formula in a physics class. Chastain had to call her name twice before she responded.

"Huh? Oh, sorry, I was just thinking about something.

Listen, I really am sleepy, so let's talk about this tomorrow, okay? What time do you want to meet?"

"I'm sorry, Nicole. I keep forgetting that you've had such a long day. How about we hook up at eleven? I'll pick you up here and show you around and we can get started."

Nicole nodded, but she looked like her mind was far away. "Okay. See you tomorrow at eleven."

Chapter 9

The next day dawned sunny and bright, and Lucien was in good spirits. He had taken a quick shower and was dressing in his now-usual attire of jeans and a T-shirt. The Bose stereo on his dresser was blasting Clifton Chenier, and the raucous zydeco music suited his good mood. He'd made a big mistake with Nicole, but he'd recovered nicely and felt that he'd cleared the way for some serious courtship. He felt so good he was dancing and singing along with the CD. He glanced around the room and slid to a stop in his sock-clad feet. He was looking at his furnishings in a whole new light.

The bed was king-size, to accommodate his height. It was beautifully burnished dark cherrywood with four posters. It, like the dresser, the armoire and nightstands, was an antique. The floors were gleaming hardwood and the walls were painted a creamy ivory with crown molding. A fan, also in cherry, whirled in the center of the ceiling and there were a few paintings of old New Orleans on the walls. They were the only decorative touches, except for a few family pictures on top of the dresser. He enjoyed his house, too, especially his bedroom, but it suddenly occurred to him that the room was too masculine. It looked too hard, too manly for a woman. That was because it was planned for him alone, with strictly his comfort in mind. But that was about to change.

He left his house and in ten minutes was parking his car in front of Mac and Ruth's house. He walked to the back and knocked once before entering. Ruth was in the kitchen fixing breakfast, and his father was making some of his special coffee. They both greeted him, and Mac went even further by asking him why he was there.

"What brings you out this morning? Not that I'm not glad to see you, but isn't this kind of early for you?" he asked.

Lucien was saved from having to answer the question by Nicole's entrance. He had a physical reaction to seeing her, as usual. He could actually feel warmth from the aura that surrounded her. It was like a combination of her light fragrance, her powerful personality and her essence. And she smiled at him, which both relieved and encouraged him. At least she wasn't looking as him the way she had the day before.

"Good morning, Nicole. I hope you slept well," he said.

"I did, thank you. And good morning to you, too," she replied.

"You look beautiful," he added thoughtfully as he took in her appearance from head to toe. She really did look cute, wearing light blue jeans and a sorority T-shirt with sneakers.

She smiled again, and he could feel the heat building up inside him. Who knows what he might have blurted out if Ruth hadn't invited everyone to sit down.

"Breakfast is ready," she said, placing a pitcher of orange juice on the table. "Nicole, I hope you like shrimp and grits."

Nicole looked sheepish for a moment before she answered. "I've never had them," she admitted.

"Really? Charleston is such a seafood-oriented city, I thought this would be a familiar dish. I think you'll like it, although you can just have plain grits if you like. There's some turkey bacon and sausage, too."

Lucien moved quickly to hold out a chair for Ruth and then Nicole, who was still looking a little self-conscious. "I've never had *grits*," she said softly.

Ruth, Lucien and Mac all stared at Nicole, and she started laughing.

"I know, I know, it's ridiculous that a black woman raised in the South has never eaten grits, but I've never had them. My mother used to make them all the time, but I just never tried them. I didn't like the way they looked, and my big brother Titus used to eat mine for me when my parents weren't looking. I don't think they know to this day that I never ate them."

Lucien reached over and took her hand. "Well, if you want to try them I can assure you they're delicious. But if you don't want to, no one is going to think anything. Have anything you want," he invited.

"I'm going to try them," she said. "It's time I discovered what everyone else already knows about," she said cheerfully.

Lucien was cheered by the fact that she didn't seem to resent him touching her. In fact, when Mac said grace, he continued to hold her hand, releasing it when everyone said, "Amen."

Ruth put a small helping of grits on her plate, along with a little of an appetizing-looking mixture of shrimp cooked with onions, bacon, peppers and aromatic spices. "Usually the mixture is put right on top of the grits, but I think you might like to try them plain first," Ruth said.

Nicole picked up her fork and took a bite of the hot, creamy grits. Her eyes widened, and she smiled. "This is good!" she exclaimed. "I don't know what I thought they tasted like, but this is delicious." She tried another bite, this time with shrimp, and her eyes closed in appreciation. "Oh, this is wonderful! And I've been missing out on this all my life," she said with a hint of sadness. "I can't believe it. I was passing on something that tasted this good just because I didn't know any better."

Everyone laughed at her regret and her honest enjoyment of the time-honored combination. Mac told her that she could go back to South Carolina with her head held high now.

"You may not know this, but grits are the official state food of South Carolina," he told her.

She nodded as she polished off the last of her helping. "I know they are, and I always felt a little guilty about not supporting my home state. Now I can fully participate in everything that makes me a good citizen of Charleston," she said happily. "May I please have some more?"

Everyone laughed again, except Lucien. He decided that tonight would be the first night of many more. He was going to take her out that night and begin the process of making her feel like she never wanted to leave New Orleans.

After breakfast, Nicole insisted on clearing the table and tidying the kitchen, and Lucien insisted on helping her. Ruth and Mac exchanged a look and graciously accepted their help. "We've both got a full agenda today, so we certainly appreciate it. But don't start making this a habit. You're not here to work for your room and board," Ruth said with a warm smile.

The couple left the room, leaving Nicole and Lucien alone. She felt completely at ease, something she wouldn't have expected the day before. But the fact that he had, as Chastain put it, passed a test was another epiphany for Nicole. She didn't feel any resentment or uneasiness today; she felt calm and relaxed. She turned to Lucien and gave him a smile.

"How about if you bring me the dishes and I load the dishwasher," she said. "Or do you think we should just wash them by hand?"

Lucien was already clearing the table, working quickly and efficiently. "Let's just put them in the dishwasher. We won't turn it on unless there's a full load, though. No point in wasting water for a half-filled machine," he replied.

Nicole looked at him appraisingly. "Good point."

Lucien elaborated. "My twin brother is Mr. Conservation. He's indoctrinated all of us into behaving in a way that does less harm, as he puts it. He lives, breathes, eats and sleeps environmental law. He's a total vegan, for example. Won't eat anything that has a face on it and won't wear any leather or fur, and that kind of thing," he said as he put leftovers into containers and stowed them in the refrigerator.

"Good for him," Nicole replied. "We need more socially conscious people in the world. Have you ever thought about going vegan?"

Lucien made a face. "Not me. I'm a total omnivore. If it's smaller than me and can't get away, I'll eat it. Speaking of eating, would you like to have dinner with me tonight?"

Nicole's eyes widened slightly. "You're very direct, aren't you?" she said with a tinge of amusement. "Why do you want to take me out to dinner?"

Lucien had cleared the table and was wiping it down with an antibacterial spray and a clean dishcloth. He stopped what he was doing and looked at her with a penetrating gaze that made her heart speed up just a little.

"Because you're good company. I want to get to know you better, and a nice meal is a good way to do that. And I think you're gorgeous, and I like the thought of looking at that pretty face across the table," he said with unmistakable sincerity.

Nicole returned his gaze with an equally steady stare. He was pretty gorgeous himself, even in a purple-and-gold fraternity T-shirt that had seen better days and a pair of jeans. The sunlight that streamed into the kitchen surrounded him and made him look even better. "That was a very nice invitation, Lucien. I think I'd really like having dinner with you."

She waited for a bit of cockiness to flash into his dark eyes, but all she saw was a pleased expression that looked totally genuine.

"I'll pick you up at seven, is that okay?" he asked.

"Who's picking who up when?" Chastain asked as she joined them.

Lucien looked less than happy to see her. "How did you get in here?"

"I picked the lock, a talent left over from my misspent youth," she quipped. "Your father let me in, of course. I'm here to pick up Nicole. And nobody answered my question. Who's picking somebody up and when?"

Nicole and Lucien spoke at the same time. "None of your business!"

Chastain raised her eyebrows but didn't take offense. "Someone seems to be on the same wavelength as someone else," she said archly.

Nicole ignored her question and pointed to a glass on the counter. "Make yourself useful and hand me that, please." She took the glass from Chastain and put it into the dishwasher, closing the door when she was done.

"Okay, all finished, we can go now," she said brightly. "Are you coming with us, Lucien? Chastain is taking me on a tour of the city before we start working on the restoration projects."

Lucien looked pleased, but he had to refuse. "Ordinarily I'd love to, but I need to get to work. The courthouse is still closed, but I have some work I need to catch up on. My clients still deserve my attention even though a lot of legal things ground to a halt and are just now starting to pick back up. But I'll see you this evening at seven. Dress casual, very casual, okay?"

"Okay," Nicole replied. Conversation stopped as they looked into each other's eyes. Nicole didn't move from her post by the dishwasher, and Chastain was looking wide-eyed from Lucien to Nicole and back again.

"I'll see you later," Lucien said quietly.

"I'm looking forward to it," Nicole said in an equally subdued voice. She used the back of her hand to brush her bangs away from her face, and the movement was both graceful and provocative, at least to one observer.

"To hell with it," Lucien muttered and crossed the kitchen in a couple of steps to cup Nicole's face in his hands. He put a lingering kiss on her mouth and pulled away slowly. "Tonight," he said, and then he turned to leave. "Later, Chastain," he added, and disappeared through the back door.

Nicole tried not to let Chastain see how strongly she'd reacted to the kiss, but subterfuge was unnecessary because Chastain was doing enough reacting for both of them. "Oh, snap! What's going on around here? When did you kick it up a notch? Why didn't you tell me?" she demanded.

Nicole didn't answer her; she just gave her a maddeningly serene smile. Chastain moaned in frustration.

"All I'm sayin' is I get to be a bridesmaid. I don't have to be maid of honor, 'cause I know you have sisters, but I get to be a bridesmaid," she said firmly.

"You're getting a little ahead of yourself, aren't you? It was just a little kiss. C'mon, let's go and get this day started. We don't have time to waste in idle chitchat," she said airily as she went to the back door.

"You're just wrong, Nicole. You are just *wrong!* How can you keep me in the dark like this?" Chastain was dangerously close to whining as she followed Nicole.

Ruth came into the kitchen with Mac, the two of them in search of more coffee. They'd overheard Chastain's demand to be a bridesmaid and Mac was curious. "Is someone getting married around here?" he asked with mild interest.

"Well, darling, if Lucien has his way, he'll be married to Nicole in the very near future," she said with a smile.

"Lucien? And Nicole?" Mac asked as he inspected the coffee situation and began to make a fresh pot. "Didn't they just meet? I mean, he hasn't known her that long."

"No, but he says she's the one," Ruth replied.

"Oh," Mac said, as if that word explained everything. "I guess he follows in my footsteps after all. We know what we want and we go get it. She's a lovely woman and she'll make a fine addition to the family. Hand me that French roast, will you, honey?"

Chastain's badgering questions might have kept up indefinitely, but the sight of the damage from the broken levees was a sobering one. Nicole was speechless. She'd seen the news footage and magazine coverage, but nothing could have prepared her emotionally for what she was seeing. Chastain narrated the scenes in a dry voice that did little to cover the pain she was obviously feeling. She stopped the car and pointed out the window.

"Over there, that was used as makeshift morgue," she said, indicating a huge tentlike structure. "They sifted through the remains to determine who died from the storm and who was washed out of the grave. We couldn't bury the dead here because we're under sea level. Everyone goes into above-ground graves or mausoleums, and the storm just destroyed a lot of them," she said dully. "They had to fly in a lot of forensic pathologists and coroners to help. It was way too much for us to handle on our own."

There wasn't anything Nicole could say to that. She reached over to grab Chastain's hand and give it a tight squeeze as they continued their tour. Chastain pointed out places from her childhood. "There used to be a candy store right there. My great-aunt Mahalia ran it. She's in Baton Rouge with Uncle Toto and the rest of the family. They're all getting old, and I thought they didn't need to have to try to deal with this…mess," she finished.

Nicole's heart turned over when she saw Chastain's eyes fill with tears. "I think you've shown me enough today. This has to be hard on you. Why don't we get something to drink and just chill for a minute?"

"You're right. I had to come home because I knew this was where I belonged. I couldn't stay in New York while all of this was going on and my family was in jeopardy. But I can't lie and say it hasn't affected me. I'm supposed to be so hard and tough and sophisticated, but honest to God, Nicole, this is hard. And I'm one of the lucky ones," she said, hastily wiping her tears with the back of her hand. She closed her eyes briefly and swallowed hard. "Come on, there're a couple of places where we can get something to drink. Let's go." She put her car, an elderly Crown Victoria that belonged to Uncle Toto, into Drive, and they headed back to the French Quarter.

There was a little café that was open with a limited menu, which suited them fine. Soon they were seated in a booth by the window, after the proprietor, a large burly man named

Dutch with long blond hair and a beard, greeted Chastain like his long-lost sister. "Sit on down, *cher.* I'll bring you some sweet tea in a minute."

"Do you know everyone in New Orleans? Everywhere we went today someone was calling you by name," Nicole observed.

"There aren't too many people in town right now," Chastain said with a fair imitation of her usual smile. "But I do know a lot of folks. I come from a large family, and most of them are in business. Nightclubs, jook joints, cafés, shops—you name it, we're in it. I guess that why it seems like I know a lot of people."

Nicole could hear the underlying sadness in Chastain's voice, and she wanted to be able to take away her pain. Knowing that she didn't have the power to do that, she tried to distract her. "Did I tell you that Lucien asked me out today?" Her ploy worked beautifully as Chastain's eyes lit up at once.

"So that's what I walked in on! I hoped it was something like that!"

Nicole could answer her honestly now. "He asked me this morning, and I saw no reason to say no," she said. "He's actually rather intriguing, in a way. I was thinking about what he did yesterday and how he was man enough to admit that it wasn't the brightest thing he'd ever done, and it made me look at him a little differently."

"See? I told you he'd passed the test. It doesn't matter if you were testing him or not, he proved himself worthy by that apology. And he actually passed another test this morning," Chastain said, smiling as Dutch brought them tall glasses of sweet tea filled with crushed ice and garnished with lemon slices.

Nicole's forehead puckered. "What are you talking about?"

"This morning when he kissed you right in front of me, that's what I'm talking about! He looked at you and you looked at him and he couldn't leave the house without kissing you goodbye. That's a test, Nic, whether you realize it or not. Most men aren't going to do that unless they're real serious about a woman, especially not a reformed player like Lucien. He's never done anything like that as long as I've known him. He'd sooner go to the gallows than show his hand in front of his family, and he and I are like brother and sister. It was another A-plus for him. He passed that test with some serious flying colors."

Nicole felt heat rising to her face, but she ignored it. "What do you mean, 'reformed player'? You told me he was the Big Easy Man-Slut of the Decade. How did he suddenly lose his title?" She took a long sip of tea while she waited for the answer to her question.

"You must have worked some magic on him, because the word around the campfire is that Lucien has cut all ties with his former flames. The well is dry from what I hear, and I hear *everything*. There've been a whole lot of women hoping to cry on his shoulder about everything that's gone down since Katrina, and his shoulder is not available. So that tells me that Lucien is serious about you. What I want to know is what are you going to do about it?"

Nicole tried looking out the window, examining her fingernails and surveying the nearly empty café, but she could feel Chastain's inquisitive eyes staring a hole in her. Giving in, she emitted a weak laugh. "I'm going to have dinner with him. That's all, just dinner. He told me to dress casually, so I'm assuming we're not going anywhere fancy. We're going to have a nice meal together and see what happens."

"But this is such an abrupt change of heart for you. You were so determined not to get involved with him, and now you're practically dating. You were ready to tear a hole in him yesterday, and today you're letting him kiss you in public with no protests. What's going on in your head? I can hear the little wheels turning, so give it up, sister." Chastain stopped talking only because they were brought fresh glasses of tea.

Nicole thought about her answer carefully, because even though she liked Chastain, there were some things she wasn't ready to share. "I had a talk with my sisters before I came here, and they convinced me that I was having a permanent reaction to a temporary bad situation. Leland did me a favor by screwing another woman. I could have married that jerk, and that would have been a disaster because orange is not my color."

"What's that got to do with anything?" Chastain asked.

"If he'd tried something like that after we got married, I'd a had to shoot him and I'd a wound up in one of those hideous orange jumpsuits they make you wear in jail. It was good luck in disguise that he couldn't keep little Leland in his pants. But instead of cutting my losses and getting on with my life, I really let that incident dictate my social life. So when I came here, it was with a clean slate. Lucien is a nice guy, very entertaining and intelligent, and there's no reason that I shouldn't go out with him. That's all there is to it," she said matter-of-factly.

"Is he a good kisser?"

Nicole choked on her tea at the question. Chastain reminded her of the unexpected kiss Lucien had given her that morning. His lips had been moist, warm and sweet, and the sensation that had ricocheted through her body had almost sent her to the bathroom for a cold shower. Chastain started giggling, which meant that she could read Nicole's lustful thoughts, so the jig was up.

"Yes, he's a good kisser. He's a wonderful kisser, as a matter of fact. He could give lessons in the art of kissing. Does that make you happy?"

Laughing at Nicole's deadpan delivery, Chastain shook her head. "It doesn't do anything for me, but it should make *you* happy. You're going to have a good time tonight. I have a feeling that Lucien is going to be trying to impress you, so there's no telling what he might do. Ooh, I can't wait to hear about it!"

"You'll be the first to know," Nicole said in a voice rich with sarcasm. To tell the truth, she was a little curious herself. Just what did Lucien have up his sleeve for that night?

Chapter 10

Nicole had just finished dressing when Ruth came to her room to tell her that Lucien was downstairs. Nicole took a quick look at the alarm clock on the bedside table and saw that it wasn't even seven. "He's early," she said with surprise. "Well, I'm done, I think. How do I look?"

She was wearing a pair of pink linen pants and a matching pink blouse. On her feet were sleek little black-and-pink flats. Her thick black hair was out of its ponytail and lay on her shoulders in soft waves. She was wearing silver hoop earrings and a minimum amount of makeup. She really didn't need any because she was quite pretty without it, but the mascara and rose lip gloss made her glow. Ruth assured her that she looked lovely.

"Honey, you could be wearing a sack and Lucien wouldn't care. See you downstairs," she said.

Lucien was talking with his father and he smiled when he

saw Nicole. He rose to greet her. "Hello, Nicole. You look wonderful. These are for you," he added, handing her a small bouquet of roses in various shades of pink.

Nicole took the bouquet and thanked him sweetly. "Lucien, these are so pretty. How did you know I love roses?"

"Lucky guess. I'm glad you like them. Are you ready?"

"Of course. I just need to put these in water," she said, only to have Ruth take the flowers from her hands.

"I'll take care of these," Ruth said. "You two go have a good time."

After saying good-night to Ruth and Mac, the couple left. Mac joined his wife in the kitchen, where she was opening the bouquet to trim the stems before putting the flowers into a round crystal vase. He watched her work for a moment, and then went behind her and slipped his arms around her waist, kissing her neck and breathing in her scent.

"I think you're right, honey. My son has the unmistakable look of a man in love. It's a look that all Deveraux men have worn when they find the woman of their dreams. I think Nicole had better brace herself because I don't know how long Lucien will be able to keep himself in check. I don't want him to scare the poor girl off," he murmured.

Ruth put down the flowers and turned around in her beloved husband's embrace. "I don't think we have to worry about that, Julian. I didn't run from you, did I?"

"No, you didn't. But we had age and maturity on our side, not like those impetuous youngsters," Mac replied.

"Oh, I think we had our share of impetuous moments. In fact, if you come upstairs with me right now, we can have another one," she said with a provocative smile.

"That sounds like a plan, honey. Let's go."

* * *

Lucien glanced over at Nicole, who appeared to be completely relaxed. She was looking at the old houses that lined the street with great interest. "I know I said this before, but you look really pretty, Nicole. And you smell great. What are you wearing?"

Nicole gave him a mischievous look. "Why do you want to know? Are you going to buy me some?"

"If you want me to, sure I will. Anything you'd like," he told her.

"Well, in that case, it's called Juicy Couture," she said promptly. "And my birthday is coming up, so I expect you to remember that."

Her teasing tone reassured Lucien because it let him know that she was at ease with him. In his experience that was a good sign. He wanted her to have a really good time with him tonight so there would be many more nights to follow. It was what had made him decide on the site of tonight's dinner. He turned down a side street and parked the car in front of a white house with black shutters and trim. It was a stately home with homey touches, like the pots of flowers that hung on both sides of the door as well as the ones that flanked the sidewalk leading up to the stairs. Nicole looked at the place with a bemused expression.

"That's an unusual restaurant. What's the name of it? I don't see a sign," she said.

"That's because it isn't a restaurant, it's a home," he explained.

"Your home?" Nicole's voice had just the merest hint of suspicion in it, something he rather expected.

"No, Nicole. This is my brother Julian's home. We're having dinner with Julian and Maya tonight."

As they walked up to the front door, Lucien was congratulating himself on his brilliant ploy. He was accomplishing several things at once by taking Nicole to dinner with his brother's family. One, they would get to spend time together, two, she would see him in a totally nonthreatening way and three, she'd see how happy Maya and Julian were and it might start giving her ideas. It was the perfect plan.

They were greeted at the door by Maya and Corey. Corey was thrilled to see her uncle as always, but she remembered Nicole, too.

"Hi, Nicki! I didn't know you were coming to our house!" Corey seemed very happy to see Nicole, holding up her arms for a hug and a kiss.

Maya was also glad to see Nicole. "Come on in, Nicole. When Lucien told us you were in town, we insisted he bring you over. It's so good to see you!"

The two women embraced and started chatting like old friends. They went into the living room to sit down and enjoy a nice long talk. Corey took it upon herself to entertain her uncle.

"My daddy is outside making meat. Do you want to go see him? Can I ride on your back?"

They went out to the patio, Lucien carrying Corey on his broad shoulders. He had to smile at the sight of Julian masterfully grilling chicken. All of the men in his family were dedicated cooks as well as being great eaters. They took food as seriously as they did the law. He greeted Julian with a smile. "Thanks again for having us over, man. I know how busy you and Maya are, so I really appreciate it."

Julian brushed aside his thanks. "It's not like it's an imposition, bro. We have to eat, too. We're trying to make sure we always have breakfast and dinner together as a family. Something you should think about, since you plan on—" He abruptly changed topics since Corey was hanging on his every word, as always. "How is Nicole enjoying her stay?"

"I plan to make sure she enjoys it," Lucien replied confidently. He was sitting on one of the wrought-iron chairs that surrounded a matching glass-topped table. Corey was leaning on the arm of his chair, her little fingers examining the thick gold bracelet he wore on his right wrist.

"Uncle Luc, I'm getting a surprise tonight," she informed him.

"You are? What is it?" he asked.

"I don't know yet, but I'll find out tonight," she said. "After dinner, I think. Are we going to have dinner now, Daddy?"

"We'll be ready in a few minutes, angel. Why don't you ask Mommy if she needs any help with anything?"

As Corey dashed off to find her mother, Julian directed his full attention to his brother. "I have to tell you, man, when you first said you were going to marry Nicole, I thought you'd lost your whole mind," he said. "And now here you are bringing her to dinner like you two belong together."

"Well, that's because we do belong together. I tried to tell you fools, but you wouldn't listen. So now you know," he said smugly.

Julian was putting skewered shrimp on the hot grill and didn't respond at first. When he'd finished his task, he pointed a long fork at his brother and warned him about sounding too cocky. "Don't get too full of yourself. You might have made a believer out of me, but I'm not the one you have to convince. Nicole doesn't strike me as being a pushover. Get that platter and bring it in for me, would you? I haven't even said hello to our guest yet. She's going to think I'm some kind of barbarian."

"She'd be right," Lucien said amiably and ducked when his brother threw a small set of tongs at him.

The dinner was just as nice as Lucien knew it would be. His sister-in-law was an amazing woman. Besides being a loving wife, doting mother and gifted physician, she was a great cook, and she liked nothing more than providing a good meal to anyone who dropped by, something he and his brothers knew all too well. They all took advantage of her meals as often as Julian would allow. Since they remarried, he was very protective of his wife's company. He wanted her all to himself, and no wonder: she was warmhearted, beautiful and brilliant.

She and Nicole were getting along like they'd known each other for years, just talking about any- and everything. The food was delicious. They started with the grilled shrimp and moved on to the chicken and a fantastic combination of vegetables that had also been cooked on the grill. Maya had sliced zucchini, yellow squash, eggplant, onions and red peppers and seasoned them well, then wrapped them in foil and put them on the grill to cook. There was also a green salad and homemade garlic bread. Nicole complimented her on everything, especially the vegetables.

"Maya, did you use butter on these? I have to learn how to do this because I love veggies and these are wonderful!"

"Thanks, Nicole. I used olive oil, or EVOO as my girl Rachael Ray would say. I'm addicted to it, and it gives everything such a great flavor. I'm also addicted to her show. Julian TiVos it for me."

The two women were so deep in conversation that they didn't really notice when the men got up and cleared the table to prepare for dessert. Corey was starting to get fidgety, which was unusual for her. She was a child who could keep still for the most part, but she was too revved up about her surprise. She'd mentioned it at least three times during dinner.

Lucien was in the kitchen with his brother when a loud squeal of pure joy was heard from the front of the house. Julian grinned and said that Corey's surprise had arrived. They went in the direction of the noise and found Corey sitting on the living room floor with a little white puppy climbing all over her, trying to lick her face.

"Oh, Uncle Philippe, she's so pretty, I love her! Look, Mommy, look, Daddy, see my surprise? Isn't she pretty? I love her," Corey exclaimed.

Philippe had gone to the car to get the puppy's supplies, which consisted of a crate, food and water dishes, a couple of chew toys and food. Lucien was amused by the sight of his niece's delight in her new pet. He and Nicole were sitting side by side on the sofa watching her play. Julian and Maya were on the love seat, and Philippe was lounging on the floor to make sure that the puppy didn't get too riled up. Lucien had his arm around Nicole's shoulder, and he liked the feel of her very much, as well as the subtle scent of her sweet fragrance. The evening had gone well, better that he could have hoped for. Nicole had a chance to spend time in his company with no pressure, no agenda other than having fun, and it had worked. She was relaxed and laughing and appeared to be having a great time. She was watching Corey and her puppy intently and asked Philippe where he'd gotten the little dog.

"I've been working with a group that's been trying to rescue animals, Nicole. A lot of pets got lost during the storm. People had to abandon them to go into temporary shelters or out of state, and they couldn't take care of them. Some were strays to begin with, but some were family pets. That's a Westie, a West Highland white terrier. I found her with her mother and two other pups in a wrecked car. I don't know how they managed to survive. Terriers are tough little dogs, but this was above and beyond the call. I took them to the vet, got their shots, got them checked out and cleaned up. I asked Julian and Maya if they thought Corey would like a puppy, and they assured me she would," he said quietly.

Nicole's voice was full of admiration as she told Philippe what a wonderful thing he was doing. "Philippe, that's so caring of you. I don't think I've ever met anyone as compassionate as you are."

Lucien was having a physical reaction to her words. His face felt hot, and he could feel his heart rate increasing as he experienced jealousy for the first time in his life. He'd never understood jealousy before but he'd never had a reason to be jealous. Now he did, or thought he did. She wasn't supposed to be praising his brother like that. He momentarily forgot his angst as Nicole got up from the sofa to sit down on the floor with Corey.

"Would you like to hold her? She's very nice, isn't she?" Corey held the wriggling puppy out to Nicole, who took her gladly.

"She's adorable! What are you going to name her?" she cooed as the puppy licked her chin.

"Popcorn! I'm going to call her Popcorn because she's white and fluffy like popcorn. Do you want to be Popcorn, puppy?"

Apparently she did, because she leaped out of Nicole's lap and ran to her new owner. Nicole made a sound of longing. "I want one of those," she said with a sigh.

"Well, I still have her sister. You can have her if you want," Philippe said.

Nicole's eyes lit up, but she looked guarded. "I would have to ask your parents first, because I can't very well bring a dog into their house without notice. Maybe I could drive her up to Charleston and my parents would keep her for me until I go back home," she said, smoothing her hair away from her face as she spoke.

"I'll keep her," Lucien said in a rough voice. All the adults turned to look at him as if he'd just announced that an alien mothership was landing. "What? You think I can't take care of a little bitty puppy? I'll be happy to keep her for you, Nicole. I'll get the crate and stuff and we can get her tomorrow," he said grandly.

"Lucien, that's so sweet of you. Are you sure you want to do that? Puppies can be a handful," she cautioned.

"She won't be a problem at all, Nicole. Trust me," he said.

Philippe had some doubt, too. "I don't know, bro, maybe you ought to let her stay with me until Nicole goes home. Terriers can be really stubborn. They're hard to train because they want their own way, especially Westies. They want what they want when they want it. You have to give something to get something with them," he warned.

Lucien had to exercise superhuman control to keep his voice level as he answered his twin. "I can handle it, Philippe. Don't worry about it."

Nicole didn't seem to sense his rising temper, however. She got to her feet gracefully and resumed her seat on the sofa, surprising him with a big kiss on the cheek. "Lucien, that's one of the most thoughtful things anyone's ever done for me," she said, her eyes glowing with excitement. "Are you sure you want to?"

Lucien felt all the anger ebb away, replaced by desire. "Anything for you, Nicole. Anything at all."

Chapter 11

The ride back to his parents' home was too quick. He didn't want the evening to end, and Nicole seemed to feel the same way. She was talking about her puppy, and she sounded as excited as Corey.

"I think I was meant to have a Westie," she said. "I started wearing Juicy Couture because I saw an ad in a magazine with these adorable little dogs, which were Westies. There was a sample strip in there so you could smell the perfume, and I liked it so I went and bought some that day. The bottle has a crest with two little dogs on it and everything," she said. "It was just meant to be. I still can't believe that you're going to babysit her for me."

It was dark in the car, but Lucien could hear Nicole was smiling. Even better, she reached for his arm and curved her hand around it. He smiled and told her again that it was nothing. "I told you, Nicole, I'd do anything for you."

"Anything?" she repeated.

"Anything to make you happy," he said.

They were in the driveway at Mac and Ruth's house now, and he had turned off the engine but left the key in the ignition so the CD player was still on. The soft sound of Kurt Elling's latest album filled the car, and he couldn't remember feeling more content to have a woman's company. The sound of her voice was an incredible turn-on for him; he wondered if she knew how much it affected him.

"So you'll do anything to please me, hmm?" Nicole sounded thoughtful.

"What would you like? Just ask and it's yours," he told her.

Her eyes sparkled like jewels in the moonlight, and she leaned toward him. "I would like this," she said so softly he almost didn't hear her. The next thing he knew, she kissed him. He was stunned for a few seconds while he adjusted to the feel of her luscious lips and the sensations her touch created in him. Then her hand came up to touch his face, and he was gone. He pulled her as close to him as possible and took over the kiss, opening his mouth so that he could taste every bit of her. Their tongues met, dancing over each other and yielding sweet explosions of bliss.

They were necking like teenagers parked on some secluded lover's lane, but they were adults in his father's driveway. Lucien wanted to put the car in Reverse and take her to his bed, but he didn't want to break the spell. He wanted to rip her clothes off and take her right there. He was being driven out of his mind by the feel of Nicole's hands on him, the taste of her lips, the scent of her, and her soft sounds of surrender. The passion rose in him to a dangerous level; he had to put a stop to this *now* or he wouldn't be able to control himself.

"Nicole," he whispered between kisses. Her only answer

was a soft murmur that he couldn't understand, but all it did was incite more of the fire that was about to consume him. He had to stop this now, and the only way he could was to pull away from her—but he couldn't. Her fingers were tangled in his hair and her lips and tongue were so sweet, so hot, that taking his mouth away from hers was impossible.

"Mmm, Lucien," she sighed.

He took a deep breath and began pulling away from her, forcing himself to ignore the soft sound of protest she made. They were finally apart, and he was as spent as though he'd just run a marathon. He leaned his head back on the seat and expelled a long breath. Then he started laughing.

"And what, may I ask, is so funny?" Nicole sounded breathless but indignant.

"Look at the windows! You should be ashamed of yourself," he teased her. The windows were so steamed up it was impossible to see out of them.

"Ooh, look what you did." Nicole giggled.

"What *I* did? I think *we* did that, sweetheart. I was the one who had to put a stop to it. In fact, I'm taking you in the house right now before you try to violate me in some other more devious way. You're a dangerous woman, Nicole." Before she could say a word, he was out of the car as quickly as his unfortunate erection would allow him to move. He limped around to her door and opened it, holding his hand out for her.

"I'm dangerous? I don't think so, Lucien. You were the one who kissed me back until I almost…" Her voice trailed off, and she tried to look innocent.

"Until what, baby? Tell me," he coaxed as they walked to the back door of the house.

"I'm not saying another word. Anything I say could incriminate me, isn't that what you lawyers are always saying?"

Lucien used his key to open the door, and they were in the kitchen. Bojangles had apparently been patrolling the house and came to see what they were doing. The cat took one look at them, disheveled and sweaty, and he arched his back and hissed his disapproval before dashing off.

They laughed at the cat and looked at each other. "We do look pretty bad," Nicole admitted.

There was a mirror on the wall by the back door, and they turned to inspect themselves. They were a hot mess, with tousled hair, rumpled clothes and kiss-swollen lips. Nicole covered her face, and her shoulders shook with laughter. Lucien put his arms around her and joined in the laughter.

"We don't look that bad, baby. Look at us," he told her. She turned to face the mirror and laid her head on his shoulder. He bent down so they could see their reflections better, and to his eyes they looked just right. They looked like a real couple, like they were supposed to be in each other's arms. He could feel Nicole's warmth as her body melded to his, and he didn't hesitate—he bent his mouth to hers once again. It didn't seem possible, but the kiss was even better because this time he could feel her soft curves against his body. He moved his pelvis against her, and it was a kind of erotic torture, but he could no more control his reaction to her than he could stop breathing.

"Lucien," Nicole sighed. "We have to stop this."

"Yes, we do," he agreed. "We really have to stop," he murmured just before he kissed her again. He could feel her hands braced against his chest, and when she pushed gently, he reluctantly stepped away so their bodies weren't touching anymore.

"I'll see you in the morning," he said as he rubbed his thumb behind her ear. "I'll get the crate and stuff and come over to get you so we can go pick up your baby. What are you going to name her?"

"I'll tell you tomorrow. I have a name in mind, but I have to make sure it's right for her," she said sleepily.

"You need to get some sleep," Lucien said before kissing her forehead.

Nicole gave a tiny little yawn. "So do you."

Lucien felt his inner thermostat going up again. *What I need is you in my bed, but what I'm gonna get is a cold shower.*

The next morning, Nicole woke up before the alarm went off. She was still wearing the same smile she'd gone to sleep with, and no wonder: she'd dreamed about Lucien all night. She couldn't recall any of the details other than more of the same blindingly passionate kisses they'd shared the night before. She most assuredly remembered those delights, and without a bit of shame, either. Last night had been a revelation for her and a very pleasurable one. She got up and went to the adjoining bathroom to brush her teeth thoroughly and take a nice hot shower. Normally she'd have been singing at the top of her lungs, but she wasn't at home.

Her mood just seemed to call for singing or some other expression of happiness. She'd had a wonderful evening, and she was getting a puppy: what could be better than that? And she'd had the opportunity to get to know Lucien better, and that was turning out to be a real pleasure. He was warm and attentive, funny and smart and sexy as hell. The unexpected gallantry he'd shown by bringing her flowers was a bonus, as was his generous offer to care for her new puppy. It was such a kind gesture and an unexpected one, too. Lucien was proving to be much more interesting than she'd ever thought he'd be. She turned off the water and got out of the shower. When she saw the big mirror all steamed up from the heat, she had to laugh. It looked just like the car windows last night.

As she toweled off, she began humming "Come Away With Me" from Norah Jones, one of her favorite songs. She dressed quickly and casually but took her time with her hair and makeup. She wanted to look her best when Lucien came to pick her up. By now, Bojangles was aware that she was awake, because he came into the bedroom and gave her a look that said he knew she was up to something. She talked to him like she would anyone else.

"Yes, I'm getting a puppy, but I'm not bringing her here. You'll still be lord of the manor," she assured him. "Now why don't you move so I can make the bed?"

He continued to sit on the bed until Nicole told him she was making breakfast, too. "That is, if you get out of my way. Do we have a deal?"

He jumped off at once, and she made the bed quickly and expertly. The two of them went downstairs to the kitchen, and Nicole looked in the refrigerator. She found some fresh raspberries and decided to make muffins. Looking in the cupboard, she also found a can of almond paste. "Ooh, Bojangles, these are going to be really good. Raspberry-almond muffins, omelets and turkey bacon. I think that sounds good, don't you?"

When Ruth came downstairs she was amazed to find Nicole setting the table for four and a delicious aroma filling the room. "What's all this? I told you about that room and board, you're a most welcome guest here, sweetie. You don't have to do things like this," she protested.

"It's my pleasure," Nicole said. "I hope you don't mind my going into your cupboards and stuff, I realize that's kind of pushy," she apologized. "But I woke up early this morning and I just had the urge to cook. I'll clean everything up afterward."

"You'll do no such thing. We're going to enjoy this lovely meal, and you're not going to lift a finger afterward. It was sweet of you to do this, Nicole." She looked at the table and asked if the fourth was Chastain.

Nicole surprised herself by blushing a little. "Actually, Lucien is picking me up this morning." She explained about their dinner with Maya and Julian and the puppy that Philippe was giving her. "So he's going to get her a crate and everything, and he's going to keep her for me until I go back to Charleston."

Ruth's eyes widened. "Lucien is keeping a puppy for you? At his place?"

Mac joined them just in time to hear Ruth's words. "Lucien's getting a puppy? Mr. Meticulous is actually going to let something that doesn't use toilet paper into his sanctuary? Unbelievable," he added as he accepted the cup of coffee Ruth was holding out to him.

Nicole was placing the serving dishes on the table and stopped cold. "Lucien doesn't like dogs?"

Mac hastened to assure her that he did. "Lucien loves animals. He's just very orderly. He likes things to be very neat and clean. He and Philippe used to keep up an ongoing argument when they shared a room because Philippe is much more casual about his surroundings. I'm just surprised that he offered to do it, that's all."

Nicole was in the middle of explaining about the puppy again when Lucien came in the back door. "Oh, you're here! Are you ready to go?"

"What's your hurry? Something smells really good in here, and I'm kinda hungry," said Lucien.

"That's right, I did make breakfast," Nicole mumbled. She sounded as though food was the last thing on her mind.

"And I have a friend here who's a little hungry, too," Lucien added, taking his right hand from behind his back. On his large palm was Nicole's puppy, looking a little puzzled by this new game.

Nicole's mouth formed an *O,* and she looked dazzled. It was love at first sight as she took the little dog from Lucien and cuddled her. "She's beautiful! Hello, sweetie, how are you? Do you want to be my Yum-Yum?"

Yum-Yum barked once, a tiny little bark that seemed to indicate her acceptance of her new name. Nicole was elated with her new love. She had big brown eyes and a heart-shaped black nose that was just adorable. One ear went up and one went down, which was typical of Westie puppies. In a few weeks, both her ears would stand up straight. Her fur was pure white and slightly wavy, especially on her back. Her tail was wagging frantically, and she seemed determined to devour Nicole lick by lick.

"But I thought we were going to pick her up," Nicole said. "What happened to that plan?"

"I wanted to surprise you," Lucien said. "Are you happy?"

"You know I am," she said, smiling as Yum-Yum burrowed into her neck. She turned to Ruth and Mac, displaying the wiggly little ball of fur. "Isn't she adorable?"

Ruth took her from Nicole, cooing at her and saying what a cutie she was. Mac raised an eyebrow and looked at Lucien, suggesting that he wash his hands and sit down to eat. "This looks like it's going to take a while. Maybe you can explain how you decided to become a bed-and-breakfast for transient pets."

Lucien gave his father a half smile and said he'd do just that.

The simple fact was that Lucien had preempted the visit to Philippe's by going to pick up the dog himself. The fact that

Nicole had praised Philippe the night before still irked him and he was going to eliminate another meeting between them. He also had some words for his brother after he pounded down his door. When the door opened Lucien had pushed past his brother with a scowl.

"I'm going to tell you this one time and that's the end of it. Don't be giving my woman presents, slick. I'm the only one to give her anything, and that includes dogs, diamonds or any other desire of her heart," he said angrily. "What the hell did you think you were doing giving her something without checking with me first?"

"What do you mean, checking with you first? You aren't her daddy or her keeper and you sound like a real big fool right about now. She said she wanted a puppy, I said I had one. Why are you making such a big damned deal out of this?" Philippe sounded angry and genuinely puzzled.

Lucien had sat down on the couch with a heavy sigh. "I have no idea," he admitted. "All I know is that for some reason when you said you were going to give the puppy to her, I saw red. I've never been jealous or possessive in my life and now I'm a two-for-one special," he admitted.

By then Nicole's puppy had raced into the room, followed by her mother. They both stopped at Lucien's feet and stared up at him. The puppy was standing on her hind legs, trying to get his attention, but the mother went to stand by Philippe as if declaring her allegiance. Lucien scooped the little dog up and admired her. "Nicole is going to love you," he said. He made an awkward apology to his brother.

"Look, I have no idea what's wrong with me. I'm going off the deep end and I know it but I don't know why," he mumbled.

Philippe looked at his twin with love and pity in his eyes. "You've gone down for the count, that's what's wrong with you. You're in love with Nicole and you have no idea what that entails so you're reverting to being a caveman. When you were doing all that loud talk about Nicole being your woman and you marrying her didn't it occur to you that you were going to fall for her? Are you that dense or is this an act?"

Lucien let his brother's words sink in for a moment. Philippe was right. He hated admitting when one of his brothers was right and he was wrong, but his twin was dead on the money. He'd never really thought about what loving Nicole would mean. He held out his fingers so that the other dog would come to him and was happy when she did. She sniffed his fingers and licked his palm while he admitted the truth to Philippe.

"I'm just that dense, bro. Really, *really* dense."

He pondered the situation on the way to his parents' home. Yes, he had been doing a lot of big talk about marrying Nicole but he'd been basing his remarks on instinct and nothing else. Nicole moved him in a way that no other woman had. There was something about her that both excited him and soothed him at the same time. He'd known from the very beginning that she was the woman that he wanted to spend the rest of his life with, but it hadn't dawned on him that he'd fallen in love. He should have felt like the biggest fool in the world, but somehow he didn't. The revelation cheered him up for some reason and he couldn't wait to see Nicole now that he'd had this awakening.

When he stepped into the kitchen and saw Nicole, a sense of peace pervaded him and he knew that what Philippe had said was right. He was in love with Nicole. Now all he had to do was make sure she returned those feelings.

Chapter 12

After a long and very full day, Nicole and Lucien ended up at his house with Yum-Yum. Her new crate, where she would sleep and spend time when Lucien was out of the house, was set up, and her food and water were next to it and so were her puppy pads. Nicole cautioned Lucien that there wasn't a lot he could do about housebreaking her until she was a little older. He answered that he knew all about it and it wasn't a problem.

"She's just a baby. I'll take her out first thing in the morning and then again after she eats. And when I get home, I'll do the same thing. If I keep taking her outside, she'll get the idea. She's a smart little girl," he told her.

Nicole was still concerned. "But there's going to be times when she makes mistakes," she said worriedly. "Are you sure you're okay with that? Your house is so immaculate. I hate to think about what Yum-Yum could do in here."

They were sitting on his sofa in his living room, and Nicole's eyes traveled around the room. His home was very nice, although a little austere. The furnishings were classically designed, and everything followed his color scheme of oyster, navy and chocolate-brown. The walls were creamy oyster-white and the furniture was brown with navy accent pillows and draperies of the same color at the tall leaded pane windows. There was an Oriental area rug in the center of the polished hardwood floor that blended all the colors and added a little brightness to the room. The only other colors came from the paintings on the walls, and even they were subdued. There was a flat bowl on the coffee table that held some pewter balls and a neat row of candleholders on the mantel, also in pewter. The decorating scheme was tasteful, but restrained to the point of being boring. Nicole looked around with a bemused expression, taking it all in. Lucien assured her that there was nothing to which Yum-Yum could do permanent damage.

"Don't worry about it, Nicole. She's only going to be little for a short time, so just enjoy her. I can clean up whatever little messes she makes, so don't concern yourself," he said comfortingly. "Look at her, I think she feels at home," he said.

Lucien was sitting with his feet on the floor and his arm around Nicole, who was curled up next to him. Yum-Yum was in Nicole's arms, her head resting against her bosom. She did look perfectly content. Her big bright eyes were slowly closing, and it was obvious that she was getting sleepy. There was no denying that the puppy seemed to feel perfectly secure.

"I think she feels safe. She knows we're going to take care of her," Nicole agreed. "It's just that your father mentioned that you like things to be just so. And I can see from looking at your home, you like things to be very orderly."

"I like you better than I like order," Lucien drawled. He rubbed his cheek against her soft hair and whispered in her ear, "I keep telling you, these things are just things. She can't do any permanent damage to this stuff."

Nicole looked around the room again, leaning forward just a little so she could take in the dining room, too. It was just as refined and tasteful, and just as severe. There were beautiful French doors separating the two rooms, but the almost clinical air of his decor continued. "I'm really surprised to hear to say that, Lucien. Looking at your home, I would have thought the opposite," she admitted.

Lucien raised an eyebrow and asked what she meant.

"Everything looks so perfect," she explained. "If I didn't know you, I'd think this was the home of someone who was rigid, controlling and totally devoid of emotion. I don't see you in these rooms at all," she said honestly. She realized that she'd gone too far and apologized. "I'm sorry. That wasn't a criticism—it was just an observation. I shouldn't have said anything."

Lucien looked around the room and then turned to her with a wry smile. "Actually, since you're an interior designer, it was a criticism. You're very much an expert in the field and are therefore qualified to offer an evaluation of the decor in my home. Besides, I happen to agree with you. This place looks like the waiting room of a psychiatrist."

Yum-Yum issued a little bark, which made both of them laugh. She stretched and climbed over to Lucien. She tried to find a comfortable position in his lap and when that failed, she inched her way up his chest until she got to his shoulder. Then she flopped down with a little sigh and went back to sleep.

"I think she agreed with your description," Nicole said. "Why, may I ask, did you decide to decorate like this?"

Lucien started to shrug his shoulders, but stopped before he disturbed Yum-Yum. "I was basically just looking for things that matched, or seemed to match. I wanted everything neat with a minimum of clutter. I ripped out some magazine pictures and went to some different stores and it was like, 'I'll take that and that and that.' Simple."

Nicole looked thoughtful. "You have some good instincts about the basics, but the decor doesn't show your personality. Anyone could live here. I think a home should reflect the spirit of the person who lives there. When someone comes in the door they should feel the warmth and energy of the owner. I don't feel that here," she said frankly.

Lucien's arm was still around her, and he caressed her shoulder before giving her a little squeeze. "So why don't you hook a brother up? Fix this place, Nicole. Give it whatever it needs."

"I'd love to. It's not really going to take that much, and it will be my way of repaying you for—"

Her words were cut off by Lucien's kiss. It was short, but hot and as passionate as all of his others. She was dreamy-eyed when he stopped. "What was that for?" she murmured.

"To stop you from thanking me again," he said firmly. "And because I like kissing you. Your lips are so luscious they have their own flavor. Tastes like chocolate," he said, kissing her again. "And strawberries and mango," he added before laying another one on her that made her toes curl.

"You make me sound like a Baskin-Robbins with thirty-one flavors," she said with a sexy smile.

"No, baby, you've got one flavor. It just defies description. It's just luscious and juicy like you."

Warning bells were going off in Nicole's head, but they were so faint she wasn't paying them any real attention. Lucien moved to put his other arm around her and found he couldn't without dislodging Yum-Yum so he said it was time for her to go to bed.

"Let's put her in her crate. She's pretty knocked out, so she'll probably just go right back to sleep," he said.

They went into the kitchen where the crate was housed. It was top-of-the-line, big enough for her to feel secure and roomy enough for her to play in. There was a soft pillow for her to sleep on and a couple of toys. Lucien gently placed her in it and closed the door. Before he could turn back to Nicole, Yum-Yum started yipping and whining to let him know she didn't like this place, not at all. Nicole looked distressed, and Lucien told her not to worry. "I know what to do for this. Take off your top."

Nicole crossed her arms and stared at Lucien with narrowed, unfriendly eyes. "Say *what?*"

Lucien smiled and assured her he meant nothing out of the way by his request. "I want to wrap her up in it so she'll smell you and be comforted. You can put on my T-shirt, and I'll get something else to wear." Suiting action to words, he whipped off his shirt and held it out to Nicole. "There's a powder room right there, first door on your right in the hall. We can give her something else that smells like you tomorrow so you can get your shirt back."

Nicole was too stunned by the sight of Lucien's body to respond. She mumbled something she hoped was identifiable as English while she took the shirt and sped toward the powder room. She closed the door behind her and fanned her hand in front of her face to calm down. *Great day in the morning, that man was foine.* Anyone could see how tall he was, but the hard, muscular chest covered in silky black hair under his clothes was an unexpected and delightful surprise. Nicole prided herself on being observant, but why hadn't she noticed just *how* broad his shoulders were before? And why hadn't she imagined the sculpted glory that was hidden under his shirts? She was woman enough to admit to the truth: it was because she wouldn't have known how to resist him. A shudder born of pure sexual desire rippled through her when she imagined what his body would feel like on top of hers with nothing between them but skin and passion.

She hurriedly took off her top, a Phat Farm golf shirt, and slipped Lucien's shirt over her head. His scent surrounded her and seemed to force his essence into her every pore. She could smell the light fragrance of his aftershave and another more essential odor: the scent of his skin that branded him as Lucien. It was the unique combination of pheromones that was evocative of him alone. She was dismayed to see that her body was betraying her feelings: her nipples reflected her interest in the owner of the T-shirt. "All the expensive bras I buy for you two and this is how you treat me? I'm going to stop putting lotion on you, how would you like that?" she mumbled. Her face got hot when she realized that she was standing in the bathroom of the object of her red-hot desire talking to her boobs. *Straighten up, girl. He's just a man with a good body, that's all. Just a man with a good body.*

With steely resolve she returned to the kitchen, shirt in hand, only to find a still-shirtless Lucien holding Yum-Yum. *Crap.* She quickly took the little dog from him and said, "I can get her tucked in. Why don't you go put a shirt on?" She tried hard not to look at him, but it was pointless. He ignored her suggestion and deftly took the shirt from her nerveless fingers and squatted down to make a little nest for Yum-Yum. While he was doing that, Nicole looked her fill at his back, which was just as appealing as his front. She was thinking about what his golden skin would feel like to her hands and wondering what it would taste like. If she were just to take her tongue and run it down the indentation of his spine... She was jarred back to reality by a large male hand waving in front of her face.

"Earth to Nicole, earth to Nicole," Lucien said. "Baby, are you in there? You kinda spaced out on me."

Nicole sent up a quick prayer for strength and tried gamely to smile nonchalantly. "Sorry. I was thinking about how late it's getting. I should probably be going now. I have a long day tomorrow."

Lucien glanced at his watch. "You're right, baby, it's getting late. Let me get a shirt and we can leave."

Nicole heaved a sigh of relief as he took his tempting body out of her sight. She sank down next to Yum-Yum's crate. She watched the puppy nuzzle her shirt and burrow into its folds. Her thoughts were racing as fast as her heart was beating. Lucien hadn't seemed to be making any kind of overt pass at her and he'd managed to make her melt. Heaven only knew what he could do to her if he put his mind to it. How was she supposed to handle all that temptation?

Lucien found her sitting next to the crate like a little girl with her legs crossed and her chin in her hand. He smiled down at her and held out his hand. "She'll be there in the morning, sweetheart. In fact, you can take her with you tomorrow if you like. I have a key for you, so you can come in and out whenever you want. How's that?"

It was one of the few occasions in her adult life that Nicole couldn't think of a single thing to say.

* * *

"Chastain, isn't she the cutest thing you've ever seen in your life? And she's smart, too. Aren't you smart? So pretty and so smart."

The two women were in the workroom that Chastain had set up. On the top floor of Gris-Gris there were two apartments. Chastain was staying in one and the other was vacant for the time being, so she'd set up a long table with all the supplies they needed for their work. She'd also brought in a comfortable chair and a daybed so there was someplace to sit other than the tall stools they would use while working. And happily running from one end of the place to the other was Yum-Yum, exploring everything she could find. Chastain was sitting on her stool, watching the sight with a slightly stunned expression.

"Okay, tell me this again," she said slowly. "You're over at Julian and Maya's and Philippe brings Corey a puppy. Then you say you want one, and he says okay, and Lucien, the original neat freak, says he'll keep her for you until your return to Charleston, and he gives you a key to his house. Is that about right?" Chastain's face plainly showed her confusion.

Yum-Yum had stopped running around and went to Nicole, who was sitting on the daybed. Nicole cooed at her and picked her up. She was rewarded by some kisses on the tip of her nose. Her distraction didn't stop her from hearing the question, however. "Yes, that's about it. You sound surprised," she said.

"I do? Well, I'm not being very expressive, because I'm not surprised, I'm *shocked!* I'm stunned, that's what I am. Lucien, the original Mr. Clean, volunteered to keep a non-house-broken dog for you *and* he gave you a key to his house," she said with wonder. "This is one for the record books. Lucien is *sprung,* honey. This is like the ultimate test of his intentions, and it's quite obvious that he's serious about you, Nicole. What are you going to do about it?"

"Do about *what?* Lucien is just being nice. This isn't a declaration of his intentions or anything like that, he's just being thoughtful. Don't get it twisted, Chastain. This isn't a marriage proposal or anything close to it," Nicole said. "You're getting way ahead of yourself, girl."

Chastain disagreed. "That's only because I know him so well. Lucien has never given a woman his key. He would never allow a woman twenty-four-hour access to his home unless she was the woman he intended to marry. And before you ask, I know this because he told me so himself. We were talking about dating and cohabiting and modern love in general, and he made his position quite plain. The only way he'd get that involved with a woman was if he was planning to settle down with her," Chastain said with an expression that was completely serious.

Nicole made a face that clearly showed her doubt. "The only reason he gave me the key was so I could look after our charge here. If it wasn't for Yum-Yum, he would have never offered me a key. This is just so I can get in there to walk her and feed her and stuff. You are seriously overreacting, Chastain." She set the wriggling puppy on the floor and watched her race over to Chastain to see what she was doing. She stood on her hind legs and sniffed Chastain's bare toes, giving them a little lick.

Chastain laughed at the little dog and bent down to scoop her up. "She really is adorable, Nicole. But this alone is what lets me know that Lucien is serious. He was never one to cater to some woman's hyper little dog or eccentric little cat. That stuff used to turn him off in a heartbeat. He's too neat and too organized to want to have a lively little animal running around, so if he was willing to take on little sugar britches here, it's practically a proposal. You saw his place—does it look like the home of a pet owner?"

"No, it actually looks like a really nice funeral parlor," Nicole said cheerfully. "He admits it, too. That's why he asked me to fix it up," she added.

"*What?* He asked you to change things around in his house and you still think this is some kind of casual thing on his part? He's definitely serious, Nicole. Anytime a man wants a woman to leave her mark in his house, that means he wants her to be a permanent part of his life. For him to want you to redecorate is a sign that he wants you in his life for always."

Nicole was anything but elated by Chastain's attitude. Whether or not she believed her was a moot point; it was plain that Chastain believed every word she was saying.

"Chastain, don't you think you're reading too much into all of this? When you look at it objectively, we have a man who offered to keep a dog. Period. Philippe said he could continue to keep her until I went home, and Lucien said he'd do it. He's just doing me a favor, that's all. And as far as the decorating is concerned, well, if I could get the services of a top interior designer for free, I'd go for it, too. He's being practical, that's all, practical and thoughtful. You need to get over the rest of it," she said firmly as she left the daybed and went to the worktable to inspect her project. It was one of many oil paintings from an arts collective that had been damaged in the storm. She put on white cotton gloves and began removing the frame.

Chastain was letting Yum-Yum lick her chin. "That's enough, sugar britches. I'm putting you down now," she said as she gently placed the puppy on the floor. "Nicole, I'm only going to say this one time. Words like practical and thoughtful aren't in Lucien's emotional vocabulary, or they weren't until he met you. You can believe me now or believe me later, but Lucien is after you in a big way and he's not going to stop until he gets you. Y'all have kissed and gone out. Just remember, I get to be a bridesmaid," she said with a wicked smile.

Nicole was tired of arguing with Chastain and resorted to the time-honored "whatever" to shut her up. It didn't work, though. Chastain had to have the last word.

"If you don't believe me, ask Paris. Paris knows him better than anyone, and she can tell you that he's never acted like this with a woman before. If you think I'm just blowing smoke, ask his sister," she challenged.

Those words did anything but comfort Nicole. On the contrary, they made her distinctly uncomfortable. She had just gotten to the point where she could admit that Lucien was a nice guy and a potential summer fling. Now she was supposed to believe that he was serious about a relationship with her? It was too much for her to think about right now. She would concentrate on the painting in front of her and that was all. She reached in her pocket to answer her cell phone and got even more uncomfortable when she heard the voice on the other end.

"Hello, Lucien. I'm fine, and you?"

Chastain heard her greeting and gave her an annoying smile while mouthing, "I told you so." Nicole clenched her teeth and tried to pay attention to Lucien, but it was hard. Why were things getting so complicated? And why did it have to happen now, just when she was beginning to let down her guard? Life could be so unfair sometimes. But she wasn't going to let it beat her down. After she ended her conversation with Lucien, she pointed her finger at Chastain.

"You're going shopping with me. We're going to have to

do Internet shopping and phone shopping, but you're going to help me get the things I need for Lucien's place. And no, I'm not telling you what he said so forget it."

She laughed at the expression on her friend's face and picked up Yum-Yum. "Mommy's going to teach you how to shop, sweetie. Maybe I'll get you a leopard-print collar with rhinestones. Would you like that?"

Yum-Yum licked her chin and barked enthusiastically. Chastain shook her head. "You've got a baby diva, Nic. She's just like you."

"And you know this!"

Chapter 13

The real complications didn't set in at once. It took another storm to set loose a chain of events from which there might be no return. But before that Nicole was pleasantly surprised by how much fun she was having with Lucien and her lovely Yum-Yum. Everyone was enchanted by Yum-Yum and Popcorn, with the possible exception of Bojangles. The first time he encountered the puppies the look on his face was priceless.

That night they were all in the big sunroom at Ruth and Mac's house. Corey had brought Popcorn over to meet her grandparents, and Nicole and Lucien had brought Yum-Yum so she could bond with her sister. Bojangles came into the room and the puppies went running past him so fast they didn't seem to see him. He saw them, however, and he almost passed out. His look said, "What in the world have you brought into this house?" so plainly that everyone laughed, and he was so offended he left the room in a huff. Nicole was the first one to express concern for him.

"I think we hurt his feelings," she said. "I hope he gets used to the puppies. He's bound to see them around from time to time."

Mac assured her that he'd get used to it. "My bride and I are going to Hawaii next week, so he'll have plenty of time to adjust. Feel free to bring them over every day if you want. He could use some exercise, and I think those little ones will provide it."

Lucien raised an eyebrow. "You're going to Hawaii? How come?"

Mac put his arm around Ruth and kissed her neck. "We're newlyweds, if you recall, and we don't need a reason to get away. We're also grown, and we don't need permission to leave town."

Ruth smiled at her husband's answer, but she explained, "We're going to Hawaii to sell my cottage. I don't use it that much, and I decided to sell it and use the proceeds for hurricane relief. But first we're going to enjoy it together for a few days," she said, giving Mac a beautiful smile.

Nicole was about to tell Ruth how much she admired her generous gesture when Mac fixed Lucien with a stern gaze. "We're counting on you to take care of our guest while we're gone. This is a big house, and it can get lonely for one person. Everyone else has left for new homes now that rebuilding has begun. You keep an eye out for her, hear?"

Lucien gave his father a look that was completely serious and assured him that Nicole's comfort was his only concern. "Don't worry, Judge, I've got this," he said. Then he flashed Nicole a bold yet intimate smile. "I'm like that insurance company, baby. You'll be in good hands with me."

His words were reassuring, but the look in his eyes was anything but. This was just what she didn't need—more temptation. She was trying to listen to something Ruth was saying to her while she was taking a guarded look at Lucien. Suddenly Yum-Yum ran to him and stood on her hind legs, waving her little paws frantically for his attention. He stooped to pick her up, and their mutual adoration was plain. That was when everything became crystal clear to Nicole.

She didn't have to fight her attraction to Lucien—she could just give in. Why was she acting like it was life or death? If he liked her and she liked him, they could have a nice time for the duration of her stay and life would go on when she went back to Charleston. A romantic summer romance. Her sisters had told her she was being narrow-minded and rigid, and this was a perfect way to get back in the game. It was the perfect solution, and she was extremely proud of herself for realizing it.

Lucien noticed her smiling. "You look awfully happy all of a sudden. May I ask why?"

"You'll find out," Nicole promised. "You'll be the first to know, as a matter of fact."

Lucien couldn't have been happier with the way things were progressing. Nicole came over every day and they walked Yum-Yum together before sharing breakfast. They had long talks, which to Lucien signaled the beginning of a real intimacy. He now knew so much about Nicole that he felt like he'd known her for years. They usually had dinner together, too, either alone or with Ruth and Mac, or Chastain. One night he and Nicole had barbecued for Wade and Philippe and they discovered grilled tofu wasn't that bad. It would never be one of their favorites, but they tried it for Philippe's sake. It was the "they" factor that Lucien savored. He and

Nicole were becoming a couple. They were sharing their lives and they were entwining so sweetly and naturally marriage would be the only logical culmination. Things were coming together nicely.

He was out with Yum-Yum one afternoon and they were walking along a street where several small shops were clustered. He looked up and saw two stores he wanted to check out, but he had to take Yum-Yum home first. Most shopkeepers weren't too fond of having small canines in their establishments, even when it was one as cute and nearly well behaved as Yum-Yum. "C'mon, sweetie, let's go home. I saw something in that window I want to give your mama, and I can't take you in there. I'll have to come back this afternoon," he said as she tried to wind her leash around his leg.

"Lucien? I thought that was you. Where have you been, honey?"

He turned to see a curvy woman of medium height with a huge smile on her face. Stifling a groan, he returned the woman's greeting in a decidedly less-animated manner. Her name was Tonya and she'd made no secret of the fact that she wanted Lucien in the worst possible way. "Hello, Tonya. How've you been?"

"I've been okay. I'm doing much better now that I've seen the handsomest man in all of Louisiana. Where have you been hiding out?"

"Me? I've been right here," he answered absently as he disentangled Yum-Yum's leash from his leg. "Tonya, are you in a hurry? Can you do me a favor and watch my little friend for about five minutes? I need to get something in that store, and she's not exactly their ideal customer," he said. He picked her up and showed her to Tonya, who squealed with delight at her cute little face.

"Lucien, that's the cutest dog I've ever seen! Of course I'll hold him for you. What's his name?"

Lucien didn't bother to explain that she'd gotten the sex of the dog wrong. "Yum-Yum. I'm going in that store for about five minutes, and I'll be right back. You be good for Tonya, hear?"

He went into the store, which sold an eclectic mixture of jewelry, artistic accessories and things for the home. Something had caught his eye, and he just knew that Nicole would love it. True to his word, he was only in the store for about five minutes, and when he emerged, he walked into a scene that was unexpected to the point of being surreal.

Nicole was standing about six inches from Tonya, looking like she was about to explode. No one else could have known how angry she was, but Lucien knew her well enough to not mistake that little smile on her face for amiability. She was furious and just barely disguising it. She was speaking in a calm, even tone of voice that meant disaster for the unwary, and Tonya was walking right into her verbal snare.

"I asked you what you're doing with that dog," Nicole said.

"He belongs to my boyfriend," Tonya prattled happily. "His name is Yummy. Isn't he cute?"

Yum-Yum was frantically wiggling, trying to get to Nicole, which seemed to escape Tonya's notice. Nicole put an end to that by plucking the dog out of Tonya's hands.

"I see. Well, you're wrong on all counts, sister. *He* is a she, *her* name is Yum-Yum and she belongs to *me*. And that," she added venomously, "is not your boyfriend. He's mine."

Tonya's eyes grew huge, and she was about to rebut Nicole's words when Lucien put his arm around Nicole. "Tonya, thanks for watching Yum-Yum. Nicole, this is Tonya. Tonya, Nicole. You have a nice day and thanks again," he said as he hustled Nicole in the opposite direction of the bewildered woman.

Lucien was trying not to laugh, but it was too funny. Nicole might be madder than a hornet, but she'd claimed him and that was all that mattered. They reached his car and he opened the door for Nicole, who got in with a haughty sniff. He carefully placed the package on the backseat and got in the driver's side. He turned to Nicole with a big smile.

"You need to take that cheese-eatin' grin off your face, because you can't charm your way out of this one, buddy. You're in so much trouble it's going to take a special dispensation from the Vatican to get you out of this one," she warned him.

Her words didn't bother him a bit. Neither did the fact that Yum-Yum barked at him sharply, as if she, too, were upset with him for leaving her with a strange woman. They might be a little miffed at him, but he didn't care. Nicole had made it plain that she had a more than vested interest in him, and at the moment that was all that mattered.

By the time evening came, Nicole had calmed down. She tried to think of a time when she'd gotten so angry as quickly as she had earlier, but try as she might, she couldn't think of one. It had been a few years since she'd been that mad, and with good cause. *I must be getting mellow,* she thought. *The last time anyone got me this upset, he was sleeping with a younger woman.* She chewed gently on her lower lip while she pondered the idea. It was true; no one had that much power over her emotions since that drip, Leland. Somehow, though, Lucien had slipped under her radar to the point where his actions could really upset her, like letting that nitwit touch her dog. The mere memory of that scene made her grind her teeth.

She and Chastain had been working steadily for hours and they decided it was time for a break. Nicole volunteered to go get lunch because she wanted some fresh air and she also wanted to explore a bit of New Orleans on her own. Chastain had given her directions to a small market with its own bakery and Nicole had driven over there in her rental car. She found the market easily, but she deliberately parked a little ways from it so she could look at all the little shops on the street. She adored the little market, where she purchased a crusty loaf of bread, Boursin cheese, smoked turkey and some Gala apples, which were one of her favorite varieties. She also got milk for her and a bottle of springwater for Chastain. She was heading back to her car when she saw a red-haired woman holding a Westie pup and she smiled until she realized the strange woman had hold of her baby.

Nicole had walked right up to the woman and confronted her. If Lucien hadn't appeared when he did she might have popped her one. Lucien had led her to his car and she insisted that he take her back to her rental car, fuming silently the whole way. Or at least she intended to remain silent. Instead she found herself taking verbal potshots at Lucien.

"What did you think you were doing letting that dimwit have my dog? Are you impaired in some way that no one talks about?" She turned her attention to Yum-Yum who was alternating between licking her chin, trying to get into her shopping bag and barking her joy at seeing Lucien again. "Don't be so glad to see him, sweetie, he left you with an idiot. You shouldn't be so forgiving," she said sternly.

Lucien didn't even have the decency to be ashamed of himself. All he did was answer her calmly and politely.

"It was a bad idea, Nicole. I saw something in a store that I wanted to get, and they had a sign that said no pets allowed. So when I saw Tonya I asked her to watch Yum-Yum for a few minutes. I shouldn't have done it. I apologize."

"Tonya's not very bright, is she? Called her Yummy and thought she was a male," Nicole had retorted.

"Yeah, well, Tonya's not known for her intellect," Lucien had agreed.

"So why didn't you just ask her out on a date instead of involving my poor innocent puppy in your debauchery?"

Lucien had finally defended himself, but mildly. "That's kind of harsh, don't you think? I asked her to hold Yum-Yum so I could buy something for you. And I didn't ask her out because I have no desire to be with her. I thought you knew me better than that, Nicole."

"Obviously I don't. Shall I take Yum-Yum with me or can I trust you to take care of her and not palm her off on another airhead?"

"You can trust me completely, Nic. I was under the impression that you did." Lucien had actually sounded a little hurt, which did nothing to assuage Nicole's anger.

Now, after taking a long, hot bubble bath and painting her toenails, her anger had dissipated and she felt a little foolish over how she'd acted toward Lucien. She'd overreacted and given him more of a tongue-lashing than he deserved, and he'd taken it like a man, too. He'd offered a reasonable explanation and apologized. Had she accepted it graciously, like a sophisticated woman of substance? No, she'd reacted like a true chickenhead, spitting venom all over the place.

The house was eerily quiet, since Mac and Ruth had left early that morning for Hawaii. Nicole had to adjust to being alone in the big house with only Bojangles for company. Her nerves were a little frayed because her bubble bath hadn't worked its normal soothing magic on her. She wasn't feeling the peace that normally permeated her after one of her baths. Even though she'd applied a generous amount of her favorite lotion and body butter from Carol's Daughter, she wasn't enjoying the lingering fragrance and the moist freshness of her body the way she always did. She put on a new nightgown, one she'd purchased before leaving Charleston. It was a flattering shade of peach with spaghetti straps, lacy bra cups and a matching thong. The babydoll length showed off her shapely legs, and she looked sexy and feminine at the same time.

Taking a look in the full-length mirror on the closet door, she smiled at her reflection. Her hair was brushed and lay on her shoulders in a gleaming mass, and she just looked fabulous. Bojangles purred loudly from his perch on the bed, as if to tell her she looked hot.

"Too bad I'm all alone, Bojangles. I look pretty good even if I don't feel it. C'mon, let's go downstairs and get a glass of milk."

It had started raining earlier in the evening and it showed no signs of stopping. Nicole wasn't fond of thunderstorms, because she was afraid of them. When she was little the first crack of lightning would send her running for comfort from whoever had an available lap. Even though she was "grown and overgrown" as her grandmother would put it, she still didn't like storms. She and Bojangles had just reached the kitchen when a loud clap of thunder seemed to rattle the glass panes that made up the ceiling of the room. She covered her mouth to stifle a scream and then screamed in earnest as a huge bolt of lightning flashed overhead. At the same time the back door burst open and there was Lucien, soaking wet.

"What's the matter, baby?"

"What are you doing here?

They were both talking at once until a second crashing boom of thunder made her jump and run into his wet arms.

If he was surprised, he didn't show it. He just laughed gently and said, "Don't squash the baby."

Only then did she notice that Lucien was wearing a Windbreaker with a front pocket in which Yum-Yum was happily ensconced. Her little head popped up and her eyes were sparkling.

Nicole was stunned to see the two of them, but very glad. "So what brought you out in this storm?"

Lucien set Yum-Yum on the floor, and she ran around crazily, trying to chase Bojangles, who hopped onto the counter with a hiss. "I couldn't leave you in this big ol' house in the storm, Nicole. Pop might not have told you, but lately when there's a storm like this—"

Another bolt of lighting flashed so brightly it was like a pyrotechnical extravaganza. It sent Nicole straight into his arms again, and the next sound she heard was a loud buzz and then dead silence as the house fell into darkness.

"Yeah, that's what happens in a storm. Now aren't you glad I came?"

Chapter 14

Nicole was actually trembling. "Hey, baby, it's okay. It's just a little rain," Lucien said soothingly. "Let's go over to the counter and get that flashlight, then I can get the candles and stuff. The lights won't be off that long, I promise you. They come back on really fast."

While he was talking, he was walking her backward to the kitchen counter. At the end closest to the back door there was a battery-operated lantern mounted on a charger. He felt around for it, and when he grasped it, he turned it on, flooding the kitchen with light. "There we go. Now we have light," he said. She finally released her tight grip on him and stepped back. He wished fervently that she hadn't, because his wet jacket had soaked her and the sheer gown was clinging to her body. He had to swallow hard and try to continue talking normally. "Now, why don't you let me get this wet jacket off and I'll get some more light going in here." He pressed the lantern into her hand and said, "Hold this for me, okay?"

He took off the wet Windbreaker and hung it on the knob of the back door. Taking Nicole's hand, he led her to the pantry and showed her an array of cordless lamps and flashlights, along with several boxes of candles. "See? Pop learned how to be prepared for this stuff. There's a stash like this upstairs, too. Let's get some candles and one of these lamps, and we can get comfortable until the lights come back on. How's that?"

"Okay," she murmured.

In a very short time they were in the living room, seated on the floor in front of the fireplace, which Lucien had filled with candles. He had put them in there for two reasons. One was to create a romantic atmosphere, and two was to keep the lit candles from being knocked over. Yum-Yum was determined to get better acquainted with Bojangles, a desire the cat didn't share. They didn't appear to mind the dark of the house at all. They kept zooming through the room, sometimes with Yum-Yum chasing Bojangles and other times with Bojangles chasing Yum-Yum. They galloped in silence for the most part, although the occasional bark was heard from Yum-Yum when Bojangles jumped on a table or chair to escape.

It was still raining, but the thunder and lightning had abated, which was a great relief to Nicole. Lucien had put a blanket on the floor and they shared a bottle of wine along with a bowl of fruit and some cheese and crackers. Nicole had also put on something that was less revealing than her little nightie. It was long, pink and cute, but Lucien didn't particularly appreciate her change of wardrobe, because he liked her in the short gown much better. But he didn't protest. She was still gorgeous, with the candlelight flickering over her face.

He reached over and stroked her cheek, telling her what pretty skin she had. He was lying on his side, propped up on his arm.

"You have the most beautiful skin I've ever seen," he marveled. "It's like baby skin, so soft and warm. Do you do something special to it to make it that way?"

She laughed. "No, I use plain ol' Neutrogena soap and water. I was blessed in the skin department, I guess."

"Did you get it from your mom? She's really gorgeous," Lucien said.

Nicole shook her head. "She's not my birth mom, you know. I was adopted, like Titus."

Lucien kept stroking her face and leaned in for a kiss. "I think I did know that," he said slowly. "I think I forgot because you do look like your mom and your sisters. That's kind of odd, isn't it?"

Nicole laughed again. "Not really. A lot of times adopted children start looking like the rest of the family for some reason. I think Nona, Natalie and I resemble each other because we're all about the same complexion. Poor Titus always kinda stood out like a sore thumb because he has a different complexion, but we loved him so much it never mattered to us. He was just our brother. I was his special baby, and he spoiled me rotten," she said gleefully.

"Girls should be a little spoiled," Lucien said. "It gives them a better opinion of themselves and they won't fall for some ol' okey-doke from the first slimebag who comes along."

"Well, if that's the case, Titus had the right idea. He not only ensured that I had high self-esteem, he taught me to fight. I can render a man unconscious with one hand," she said proudly.

"Good for him. Wade and Julian taught Paris to fight, too. She can take care of herself in any situation. As a matter of fact, she taught me and Philippe a few things," he admitted.

Nicole held a big blackberry over his lips. "Open up. So your big sister taught you two how to scrap? That's cute."

"You're cute," he replied after swallowing the berry. "Tell me more about you, Nicole."

"You tell me about you," she said. "We've talked about me enough. You do a good job of listening, but I want you to talk. What's your favorite movie?"

"The Godfather." And yours is *Eve's Bayou,"* he answered.

"Who's your favorite author?" she asked.

"Walter Mosley. And yours is Pearl Cleage," he said, holding a piece of pineapple to her lips.

She took the pineapple into her mouth and licked the juice from his fingertips. "Mmm, thank you."

"Kiss me, Nicole." He said it softly, but he meant it on a much deeper level. He needed to feel those lips on his again.

She was bending down to give him his wish when a flurry of white arrived on the blanket. Yum-Yum planted herself on Lucien's chest and barked sharply at Nicole.

"Excuse you? I know you're not barking at me, little girl," Nicole said. She leaned in to kiss Lucien again, and Yum-Yum barked even louder. Nicole burst into laughter. "I think she's jealous. What kind of mess is this?"

Lucien rolled over on his back and laughed with her. Yum-Yum thought this was a new game and barked happily.

"Lucien, we should put her to bed. Did you bring her crate?"

He sat up and looked a little embarrassed. "Uhh, she hasn't actually been sleeping in her crate."

"Why not?"

"Aww, Nic, I put her in the crate, and she cries and whines and I can't stand it," he said sheepishly.

Nicole raised her arched brows. "So where has she been sleeping?"

"With me."

"You big pushover! No wonder she's getting all territorial over you—you've got her rotten! You've been letting her *sleep* with you?"

"Yeah, I have. She curls up on my other pillow and goes right to sleep," he admitted. "Looks like we're busted, sweetie," he added, tickling Yum-Yum under her chin.

"Well, it stops tonight," Nicole said emphatically. "You're going to sleep by yourself tonight, sister. Come here, cutie."

When the puppy ran to her, she scooped her up and held her so that they were nose to nose. "You're going to be a big girl tonight. You're going to sleep all by yourself, yes you are."

Lucien smiled at the cute picture they made. "I admire your determination, but Rome wasn't built in a day. How do you plan to accomplish this miracle?"

"That's easy. Take off your shirt," Nicole said.

In about fifteen minutes, things were going well as far as Lucien was concerned. Yum-Yum was sleeping soundly in the bathroom off Nicole's room. The door was open a little. She was in a cozy nest made of Nicole's hooded robe lined with Lucien's shirt, and she looked adorable. The lights had also come back on, so she had a night-light in case she woke up.

The return of electricity also meant that they could turn on the stereo, so there was soft music playing, which made the atmosphere nice and romantic. Nicole had put on a new CD by Ryan Shaw, and the sexy R & B sound enhanced the mood. The rain had turned from a raging storm to a calm, steady shower, and the bedroom windows were open to let in the sweet-smelling breeze. Overhead the ceiling fan turned lazily and the scented candles on the dresser filled the room with an amber rose perfume. Lucien was standing in the doorway watching Nicole, who was sitting on the bed with her legs tucked demurely under her. When she took off her hoodie robe to make the puppy's bed, Lucien was real happy to see that she was still wearing the sexy gown. Right now she looked like the embodiment of all the fantasies he'd been entertaining since he met her.

"This used to be my bedroom," he said.

Her face lit up with interest. "Really? Was this your bed?" She put her hand on the pillow next to her and stroked it slowly.

Lucien said yes. "Philippe and I used to share a room when we were little, but when we moved to this house, we each got our own space."

"So you used to sleep in this same bed?" Her hand continued to travel across the pillow in slow circles.

"Yes, I did." Lucien moved from his position in the doorway to the side of the bed. His eyes locked on Nicole, he lowered his body to the mattress. He sat down and just looked at her. She smiled so her dimples were showing, and he smiled back.

"I hope you're comfortable in my bed," he said softly.

"Very. It's a nice bed. Why didn't you take it with you when you moved into your own place? Too many memories?" Her smile got mischievous, but it was still sexy.

"Memories of *what?*"

Nicole giggled. "Memories of all the girls you sneaked into your bedroom, of course."

Lucien laughed. "I have no memories of anything like that, because I wasn't crazy. I wasn't trying to bring a young lady up here with my looney-toon brothers around. Not my style. I had other ways of handling my business. Why would you ask me something like that anyway?"

"Because I wanted to know the answer. This is part of

getting to know you," Nicole reminded him. "Which side of the bed did you sleep on?"

Before he answered, Lucien kicked his loafers off and stretched out on the bed. He rested against the pile of pillows at the head and said, "I usually slept right in the middle. Would you like a demonstration?"

Nicole looked indignant. "Are you just going to push me out of the bed? That's not very chivalrous, I must say."

With a sudden quick move, he captured her in his arms and held her next to his still-bare chest. "I'm not pushing you anywhere, Nicole. I want you just where you are." He proved his point by kissing her, a hard, passion-filled kiss that slowly turned into a long, languorous exploration of her mouth. He could feel all his senses respond to the sublime sensation of Nicole's warm curves pressed against him. Her hands were on his arms, stroking his big biceps up and down. His hands explored her soft skin, seeking out her firm, enticing breasts. He rubbed his palms over the lace-covered mounds, and Nicole gave a soft moan of pleasure.

He squeezed gently and used his thumbs to circle her nipples, loving the feel of them growing hard and huge in response to him. He had to pull away from the juicy treasure of her mouth because he needed to look at her; he had to see the beautiful body that had been driving him out of his mind. The kiss, however, was too good to end quickly. He prolonged it by continuing to suck her lips, first the top one, then the bottom. It was his turn to moan as Nicole used her hot, sweet tongue to entice him to keep on kissing.

"Nicole, baby, Nicole, stop," he said, his voice hoarse from longing.

"No, I don't want to stop," she said breathlessly. "I like this, Lucien."

"I love it, too, baby, but we have to slow down." He sat up, propping himself up on the pillows so he could see Nicole better. Her dark skin was glistening and her eyes glowed. The thin straps of her gown had slipped off her shoulders and her breasts were almost totally exposed. It was an incredible sight to him, it was breathtaking. She got into a kneeling position next to him and turned off the bedside lamp so that the only light in the room was the flickering candles. She reached for the straps of her gown, but Lucien stopped her.

"Oh, no, *cher*, that's my pleasure. Come here, darlin'." As he spoke, he moved so that he, too, was kneeling and they faced each other. He cupped her face in his hands and kissed her gently on each cheek. He tugged at the straps of her gown until her breasts were free and the gown was down around her hips. Putting his hands around her waist, he guided her down to the softness of the mattress and began making love to each breast in turn, kissing them all over and taking the engorged nipples into his mouth for an even more intimate kiss. While his mouth was on one breast, his hand was on the other, caressing it with his long, strong fingers and circling her nipple with his thumb over and over. Her head was moving back and forth on the pillow, and she moaned his name in the most delicious purr he'd ever heard.

He helped her remove the gown while he stroked her silky skin all over. "Nicole, you're gorgeous. You look incredible, baby. I may keep you naked for the rest of our lives," he said softly. It was true; her rounded curves were so delectable he couldn't believe she was in his arms. He loved the way she was put together, her small waist, ample hips and thighs and her breasts; everything was just the way he liked it, but more so. He slipped his hand inside the lacy thong that she still wore and groaned out loud when he found her hot, tender flesh wet to his touch. He used his index and middle fingers to explore her femininity and his thumb to manipulate the throbbing tenderness at the center, the magic core of her being that sent her into her own private storm of fulfillment. He knew the moment she started climaxing because he could feel her womanhood flexing and contracting on his fingers. He watched her ride out her first orgasm, and when it was over he wanted nothing more than to give her another one.

"Let's take this off, baby," he whispered as he removed her panties. He quickly rid himself of his jeans and briefs, pausing only to retrieve condoms from his pocket. Those he put on the other pillow; he wouldn't need them just yet. He slid down the bed, kissing all the way down her breastbone while he caressed her breasts. His hands slid down her rib cage, down to her hips, with his lips traveling the same path. He stopped to bestow a kiss on her belly button, using his tongue to excite her even more. When he reached his target, he took his time. The delicious smell of her mango body butter mixed with her own personal scent was arousing Lucien more than any other woman had before. Her taste was equally delectable, and he took his time with her, exploring every bit of her juicy sweetness and enjoying every drop. By the time he was finished, she had climaxed two more times, so deeply that she seemed spent. But as he soon discovered, she wasn't exhausted: she was exhilarated.

When he kissed his way back up to her mouth, he was alarmed to see tears in her long lashes. He opened his mouth to ask her what was wrong, but she swallowed his words in her kiss. When she was through with the sweet torture of his mouth, she smiled at him.

"Lucien, that was wonderful. I've never done that before. Ever," she said with a sigh.

"Then I'm truly honored to have been the first man to pay you that tribute. You're, ahh, not a virgin, are you?" He held his breath as he waited for her answer.

"Well, if I was, it's kind of beside the point now, isn't it?" Her teasing tone relieved him, especially when she told him that she wasn't. "I've had very limited experience, but I've had some," she said. "But nothing like this." Her hands were busy stoking his chest, smoothing the thick hair that cushioned it. "This was something totally different, Lucien."

His masculine pride was gratified at hearing those words from her lips. "Thank you, darlin', but when a woman is as luscious as you, she brings out the best in a man. And you haven't experienced that yet. Come here and let me show you what I mean."

A soft, long sigh was her response as she turning willingly and trustingly into his loving arms.

Chapter 15

They lay close together, so close that they were breathing as one. Nicole was so sated she could have easily fallen asleep in his arms and stayed there forever, but she could feel the strength of his powerful erection against her thigh and she knew she had a lot more loving to look forward to that night. She stroked his arms and his powerful shoulders as she kissed his neck. Before he knew what she was doing, she took a look at the big hardened length that was resting against her. Even in the dim candlelight it seemed disproportionately huge. It wasn't going to fit!

"Umm, Lucien? We might have a problem, honey."

He turned so he was on his back. He crossed his arms behind his head and smiled at her. "Like what, darlin'?"

She brushed her hair off her face and pointed at his penis. "Lucien, I'm small and that thing is at least an extra-large," she said frankly. "I don't think it's going to fit."

To her relief, Lucien laughed long and hard. She wasn't trying to insult him, but she didn't see how this was going to happen.

"Touch it, Nicole," he said his voice soft and sexy.

She did so at once, circling it with her hand and finding it hard as a boulder but amazingly velvety to her touch. She moved her hand up and down the shaft, marveling at how something could feel as strong as steel and enticingly warm and tender at the same time. She looked at him with huge eyes. It throbbed in her hand, which made her gasp in surprise.

"Lucien, this is amazing," she said. "I had no idea that they came in this size," she said frankly. Her hand was still caressing him, loving the feel of him. She was also surprised that his private area was neatly manicured just like his mustache and his hair. He was covered with silky chest hair, and his arms and legs bore the same soft coating that felt wonderful against her skin. But not down there. She was about to question him about it when he spoke.

"Listen, luscious, God knew what he was doing when he made us. Just like a baby can come out of your beautiful body, I can fit inside. And it won't hurt, either. You're flexible in there, trust me. You put this condom on for me, and I'll show you what I mean. It'll be easy and gentle going in, and you're going to like the way it feels, inch by inch. Trust me."

Nicole did as he instructed and took a packet, tearing it open with fingers that shook just a little. She opened it carefully and made sure it was turned the right way. She had to straddle him to get it on properly, but she found that she liked this new position. With great concentration on her part, she got it on correctly the first time and looked so pleased with herself that Lucien had to compliment her work.

"That was perfect, Nicole. You've never done that before?"

"No, I never did. My ex-fiancé used to just… Well, let's not talk about him. Now what?" she asked eagerly.

"Now we're going to do something wonderful," he assured her. He put his hands on her hips, holding her firmly. "Lift those big pretty hips, luscious, and put your hands on the headboard. You trust me, right?"

"Absolutely," she said. Then she gasped as she felt the broad crown of his sex begin its entry into her body. Beyond pleasant, actually, it was deeply pleasurable. She'd never felt this sexy, this pleased in bed. Lucien pushed against her slowly and gently at first, then with more force as she responded to his movements. She felt every inch of him as he went deeper and deeper inside her body. She wasn't used to being on top, but she loved the sense of control she had. She also liked the fact that she could feel sensations in more than one place. She was filled with him, but he was so big and broad that if she leaned forward a little she could feel him pressing against her clitoris as well as his strong strokes in her vagina. It was perfect and it was hot.

She looked down at Lucien, and he was looking at her, looking so sexy and loving that she could feel her walls clench him again and again. Her hands moved from the headboard to his shoulders, and she moaned his name aloud. She tightened and held him as she was shaken by another orgasm, this one more powerful than the others had been; this one made her drop helplessly onto his chest, sobbing his name. He turned her over on her back so fast she didn't realize what he was doing until he was on top of her. He showed her the true meaning of the word *stamina* as he began to make love to her yet again, filling her body with his expert strokes. She wrapped her legs around him and bucked with him, clinging to his strength as he pumped into her willing flesh over and over again. Their mouths were joined and their bodies were slick with perspiration as he showed her a wild, reckless passion she didn't know existed.

She couldn't believe it, but she was coming again. "Lucien," she breathed. "Lucien, Lucien, ooh, Lucien." There was nothing in the world besides Lucien and the amazing things he was doing to her body. Suddenly he stopped moving and his arms tightened around her, almost cutting off her breathing. His hips ground into hers, and he groaned her name in a harsh rasp.

"Nicole, damn, Nicole! I love you. I love you, baby. Oh damn, Nicole," he whispered, and his body shook from his effort to wring every drop of sensation from the powerful orgasm that made him tremble in her arms. It was the most sensual, the most intimate thing Nicole had ever experienced in her life, and she knew that she'd never have this with any other man. When the movements finally stopped and they were breathing together, their hearts beating as one, she was totally at peace in his arms.

Nicole fell asleep cuddled next to Lucien, and she woke up the same way. He was still sleeping peacefully, looking so handsome that Nicole's breath caught in her throat. His wavy hair was thoroughly messed up from their strenuous lovemaking, and it made him look younger and oddly vulnerable. His long eyelashes, his thick eyebrows, his sexy mustache and the cleft in his chin all combined to make him beautiful in Nicole's eyes. In anybody's eyes, really. Nicole's hand was propping up her head and her free hand was stroking his chest, the warm golden expanse that had brought her so much joy. They had finally turned back the covers and gotten under the sheet. It was up to their waists, and even though his long, muscular legs were hidden from her view, she was quite enamored of what she was seeing. She was enamored of the whole man; there was no point in pretending otherwise. She was, in Chastain's eloquent phrasing, "sprung." Her hand stopped moving as she considered the enormity of the situation. This was supposed to be a summer fling, nothing else. How had he sneaked into her heart like this? Suddenly Lucien's hand covered hers, pressing it into his chest.

"Don't stop, darlin'. I was enjoying that very much. I love your touch," Lucien said.

"You're awake," Nicole said. "I didn't mean to wake you up."

"You didn't. I've been awake for a while. I just didn't want to move." He finally opened his eyes and looked at Nicole with so much affection she wanted to cry. Instead, she kissed his forehead, his cheek and his neck and put her head on his shoulder with a little sigh. Her hand started stroking his chest again, and it was his turn to make a sound of satisfaction. "Thanks, luscious," he said. "I could get used to this."

"Used to what, Lucien, being massaged? I can give you one if you like. I'm pretty good at it," Nicole replied.

"Thanks, sweetheart, I'll remember that. But that's not what I meant. I meant I could get used to this, to *us,* to waking up with you in the morning."

Nicole's eyes widened, and she didn't know what to say. Further conversation proved unnecessary, though. Lucien took her hand in his and kissed the back of it. "Turn over on your side, Nicole."

She raised one eyebrow, but did as he asked. He turned so that they were spooned together, and it felt wonderful. His warmth spread through her and made her feel protected and loved. How could such a simple thing give so much satisfaction? He was just holding her, and she was just enjoying it, but it was more than that. It was, in a way, as intimate as the way they'd made love. She leaned back a little more and stretched into his body, unaware that she was issuing a soft sound of surrender as she did so. That innocent sound of yearning turned into something else as she realized that Lucien was massaging her breasts.

"You're very sneaky," she scolded him playfully. "Sneaky and insatiable, that's a dangerous combination."

He kissed her neck and whispered in her ear, "I'm the one your mama warned you about, baby."

She was laughing helplessly while he helped her turn over onto her back. Now he was lying on his side, still exploring her body with his hand. There was something about the way his hand felt on her skin that made her feel weightless, as though she would float away without him anchoring her down. He kept stroking her as he kissed her forehead, her eyes and her cheeks. She was beginning to feel an urgency that only he could relieve as she turned her head to fully receive his kiss. Little tremors of delight consumed her as he thrust his tongue into her waiting mouth and the mating dance began again. It had become a familiar source of delight, yet it was always new, like the first time. Kissing Lucien had become one of her favorite activities, right up there with taking her next breath.

She clutched his shoulder urgently to brace herself because his busy hand had sought and found her treasure. While his mouth was seducing her lips, he was loving her with his clever fingers, renewing the wanton abandon she'd experienced earlier. Every time his tongue stroked hers, his fingers did the same until she was being rocked by the rhythm into a frenzy of erotic bliss. She was moaning his name, and her hips were moving faster and faster until she felt like she was floating above the bed. With a smoothly agile movement, Lucien replaced his hand with his mouth, finishing the sensual task he'd started. Nicole cried out in ecstasy as she felt her entire body come apart like a galaxy rent into a billion atoms by a supernova.

When she was able to speak again after several minutes of rapid breathing and murmured endearments, she looked at Lucien with wonder in her eyes. "My, you're nimble," she said.

He gave her an audacious wink. "I've been influenced by my environmentally aware brother. Waste not, want not, you know. I couldn't let all that sweet—"

"Woof." The sleepy little bark alerted them to the fact that Yum-Yum was awake and had come into the bedroom to find them.

"Oops, looks like we have to stop now. We can't be corrupting our baby," she laughed. She leaned over the side of the bed to rub the puppy's ears.

"Hey now, our 'baby' can't be interrupting us. I should have locked that door," Lucien said ruefully.

"Too late. Why don't you let her out and then we'll take a shower and I'll fix breakfast," Nicole offered.

Lucien grumbled but seemed somewhat mollified. "What was that second thing?"

"Taking a shower," Nicole replied. "You and me, hot water, bath gel, rub-a-dub-dub, you get it?"

"Oh, yes, I do." He got up quickly, pulled on his jeans and scooped up Yum-Yum. "C'mon, little girl, you're blocking."

As he left the room, Nicole could hear him explaining to Yum-Yum what blocking was and why she should never, ever do it. She laughed out loud at his silliness. She'd had no idea that his sense of humor was so strong. She'd had no idea that she could experience the art of making love like that. And she truly had no idea what she was going to do about Lucien.

Sometime between the rainstorm and the misty dawn, she had admitted to herself that she was in love with him, and that was not part of the plan.

True to her word, Nicole made Lucien a very nice breakfast. She figured it was the least she could do for him since he'd been such a busy man that morning. He'd taken Yum-Yum out. He'd changed the sheets and made up the bed and put his clothes in the washer. And best of all, he'd shown her a whole new definition of bathing when they showered together. She was standing at the kitchen counter stirring the batter for pancakes when her knees buckled at the memory of the playful, sensuous shower they'd shared. The way he'd looked at her, the honest admiration in his eyes and the sweet affection with which he'd lavished compliments on every part of her figure made tears form in her eyes. This wasn't how things were supposed to go. They were supposed to act on their mutual attraction and just enjoy each other for the next week. She was going back to Charleston in less than ten days; it wasn't like she had a lot of time to devote to this little affair. To her horror, her lower lip trembled from the weight of the emotions that she was experiencing. *What have I done? And how am I going to undo it?*

She quickly wiped her eyes as Yum-Yum came charging into the kitchen, skidding to a stop and smiling up at Nicole for all she was worth. Nicole laughed fondly. Whoever said animals didn't have real emotions didn't know what they were talking about. She already knew the different expressions of which Yum-Yum was capable; she would smile when she was happy, look worried when someone she loved left the room, look indignant when she couldn't get her way and look mischievous when she was running away with a sock or dragging a shoe through the house. Now she was just happy to see Nicole, which never failed to melt her heart. She was so attached to the little dog she couldn't believe it.

"Hi, sweetie! Are you ready for breakfast?"

"Why, yes, I am, luscious. What's on the menu?" Lucien entered the kitchen with his usual smile and kissed her on the cheek. He was wearing the same clothes he'd just taken out of the dryer, a fraternity T-shirt and his jeans. His feet were bare and he looked clean, handsome and sexy. It was hard for Nicole to look at him without bursting into silly tears, but she rallied.

"Pancakes, turkey bacon, sausage, scrambled eggs, fresh fruit and coffee. Well, that's for some of us. Someone is having Puppy Chow, although I'm not mentioning any names," she said.

"How did you know that Puppy Chow is my weakness? Woman, you read my mind," Lucien said with a grin. He put his arms around her and was leaning in for a kiss when Wade came into the room.

"Nicole, are you okay? I was worried about you during the storm," he said.

Before Nicole could answer, Lucien turned on his brother. "If you were so worried, why didn't you *call?* Like on a *phone,* the way most normal people do. How did you get in here, anyway?"

"The phones aren't working yet. They went out last night. And I got in here with my key. We all have one, or did you forget? Nicole, were you okay last night?"

"I was just fine, Wade, thank you for asking," Nicole said.

"Well, you're *fine* this morning, too. You always look good, but I didn't know it was possible for a woman to look so pretty at this hour," he said gallantly.

Nicole was wearing a pair of jeans that cupped her curves

just right and a lavender tank top. She had on purple sandals and her hair was in a ponytail with a white-and-lavender polka-dotted scarf tied around it. She looked adorable, something that Wade reiterated.

"And whatever you're cooking smells good. I hope there's enough for me," he added as he looked down at Yum-Yum, who was trying to get his attention.

"No, there isn't enough for you, unless you want to share Yum-Yum's breakfast," Lucien said acidly. He looked at the puppy and warned her to stay away from Wade. "He's evil, sweetie. Run away fast before he works his evil magic on you. Run!"

"Nicole, pay no attention to him. I think he fell on his head one too many times when he was little. May I please have some breakfast? Pretty please?"

Nicole smiled up at Wade, who looked so much like his brother but was so different. He was as tall as Lucien, but he wasn't lean like Lucien and Philippe. Wade was bigger than his brothers, but he was big with muscles, not fat. He was fair of complexion, but darker than the twins. He had the same wavy hair, but he wore a neatly trimmed goatee with his mustache, and his voice was a little deeper than Lucien's. He was just a big sweet hunk of man, Nicole decided. She made a little sound without realizing it.

Wade looked at her quizzically. "Please? I didn't quite hear you," he apologized.

"I was just thinking that I could sell you, honey. How is it that a big hunk like you is walking around single? I have sorority sisters that would sign over their 401(k), their Beemers, Benzes, waterfront condos and their trust funds to get with you," she said frankly.

Wade's laugh seemed to start in his toes and work its way

up his big body. It was a loud, booming sound that startled Yum-Yum. "You flatter me, Nicole. My secret is the same one I used when I was playing football in college—duck and run, duck and run. That's how you avoid getting tackled."

Despite Lucien glowering at his brother, Nicole invited him to stay. She made Lucien add another place setting at the table and tested the electric griddle to make sure it was ready. She made the pancakes quickly, with a minimum of fuss, and they were soon sitting at the table with Wade saying grace. They held hands, and he said a heartfelt blessing that was just right until he ended by saying, "And bless the lovely hands of the beautiful cook," at which point Lucien's hand tightened on hers and cut off her circulation for a moment. She looked at him with consternation and said "Ouch" under her breath. He mumbled an apology and kissed her hand before taking a bite. After that, all that was heard was praise for Nicole's cooking.

The pancakes were perfectly shaped golden circles that were moist and flavorful and melt-in-your-mouth tender, topped with fresh peaches, sliced thin and mixed with a little brown sugar, cinnamon and nutmeg. The bacon and sausage were still hot since Nicole had kept them warming in the oven. There were individual bowls of strawberries, blackberries and ripe, fragrant Persian melon and piping-hot coffee laced with chicory, which Ruth had taught her to make. The men couldn't stop raving about her culinary skills. Wade asked her where she'd learned to throw down like that in the kitchen.

"My grandmother is an excellent cook, and my mother is, too. My sisters are also very skilled, although you have to drag Natalie into the kitchen screaming and kicking. She hates to cook, but she knows how, that's for sure."

"These pancakes are amazing. How do you get them so perfect? Mine are always kind of triangular," Wade admitted.

"That's because they look like your head," mumbled Lucien.

Nicole had to bite her lips to keep from laughing, but she managed. "Wade, I think the secret is practice. Once you've worked as many church pancake breakfasts and sorority fundraisers and church camps as I have, it becomes second nature. I can even flip them," she said modestly.

"You're going to have to teach me how to do that," Wade said. "That's the sign of a true expert."

Lucien was devouring his food with a distinctly grumpy look on his face. "Why are you here and when are you leaving?"

Wade ignored his tone and said yes when Nicole asked him if he wanted more pancakes. "I told you, I came to check on Nicole. I wanted to make sure she was okay because I know the storm knocked out the power."

Nicole had gone over to the stove to make another batch of pancakes. "Wade, it's so sweet of you to be so concerned. But I was just fine. Lucien was here and we had lots of candles and lanterns," she told him.

"Yeah, I saw all those candles in the fireplace. Why didn't you just turn on the generator?"

Nicole whirled around and stared at Lucien. "There's a generator?"

Wade spoke before Lucien could open his mouth. "Pop's had a generator for a while now. It works pretty efficiently, too." He looked at Lucien quizzically. "Did you forget how to turn it on?"

Nicole flipped the pancakes neatly. "There's an answer I'd like to hear myself," she said in a slow, ominous tone. "Just why *didn't* you turn the generator on?"

She gave him a look that dared him to lie to her. She already had her answer. He'd set up a fake seduction scene to catch her off her guard, and it had worked. She was just another conquest to him after all.

Chapter 16

"Wade, your mouth is as big as your head," Lucien said irritably. "I didn't turn the generator on because I wanted it to look romantic in here. I've been working like a Hebrew slave to get Nicole to like me, and this was an opportunity that just fell in my lap. Look at her! If you had the personality to attract a beautiful woman like Nicole, wouldn't you pull out all the stops? Don't lie and say you wouldn't, because you know you would, slick." He rose from the table and went to Nicole.

"I'm sorry for the deception, luscious, but I wanted to impress you. I wanted you to see me as this romantic guy, because for you, I am that guy. I really am," he said earnestly. "I hope you're not so angry that you won't forgive me," he added.

Before Nicole could answer, there was a quick knock at the back door, followed by a "Hey girl, are you decent?" The wooden door was open to let the morning air flow through the screen door, which was opened by Chastain as she entered the kitchen.

She smiled warmly at everyone, but her first word was "Breakfast! I brought beignets, but this is better. Please say I can stay, because if you don't I'll just stand here and beg," she warned.

Nicole welcomed the distraction. "Of course you can stay! Let me get you a plate." She pulled her hands away from Lucien and took the pancakes off the griddle before they got too brown.

Chastain brushed off her offer to set a place. "Honey, I know this kitchen like the back of my hand. I can get my own plate," she said. She tossed her small purse onto the counter and washed her hands. Glancing out the window, she said, "We have more company. It looks like Philippe is coming up the driveway."

"When did this house turn into a soup kitchen? Do none of you people have homes?" Lucien sounded disgusted.

Chastain laughed at him. "I have a home, but it doesn't have pancakes," she said gleefully.

"Pancakes? I was just thinking about food," Philippe said as he walked into the kitchen with Yum-Yum's mother on her leash.

"Philippe, that's the most adorable dog I've ever seen except for Nicole's baby," Chastain said. She squatted down and made a kissy sound to get the dog to come to her. "What's her name?"

Philippe let go of her leash, and she went to Chastain with her tail wagging. "Her name is Talulah Belle, but I call her LuLu."

Nicole was busy making another batch of pancakes when Lucien left the room and came back with his shoes on and Yum-Yum's leash. "C'mon, baby, I'm taking you for a walk before more critters show up. This place is getting to be like Noah's daggone ark. C'mon, LuLu, you want to come with us?"

Philippe and Wade were talking in the sunroom after

Lucien left, which left Nicole and Chastain alone in the kitchen. Chastain had a plate full of food that she was eating with great appetite while she sat at the work island. "Somebody looks mighty put out this morning. I think he might have had another plan for breakfast, one that didn't involve a house full of company," she said merrily.

Nicole put her hand on her hip and said, "Well, he'll just have to get over it, won't he?"

"Okay, Nicole, quit playin'. Something went on here last night, and I want to know what it was. If you tell me, I'll give you a beignet," she wheedled.

Nicole pretended to hesitate, which made Chastain up the offer to two pastries. "You really are every bit as nosy as my sisters, aren't you? I'll tell you later. When the giraffes have left the ark," she said glumly, nodding toward the sunroom. "Once they're gone, I'll tell you."

"You better," Chastain answered. "Dang, these are good! I want the recipe for these."

Philippe came into the kitchen to get his share. "Why do you want a recipe? You can't cook," he said with a sly grin.

Chastain rolled her eyes at him and kept eating. "I can do lots of things you don't know about, Philippe."

"So when are you going to show me?" he drawled.

She didn't answer him, but a pink blush surged up her cheeks.

Nicole was relieved when the men left. It was Saturday and no one had to work, but all of them had plans. Lucien had a few errands to run, but he didn't leave without cornering Nicole and kissing her goodbye. "I'm going to take Yum-Yum with me, if that's okay. I have to stop by Maya and Julian's house, and I thought Corey might like to see her. I'm going to take LuLu, too. I'll call you later, okay?"

And just like that, as if he hadn't pulled a low stunt on her, he left with the dogs. She watched the devastating Deveraux men walk out the back door with an odd expression on her face, and then she slammed her hand down on the counter. "Men!"

Chastain stopping eating to stare at her. "What brought that on?"

Nicole sat down on the other stool at the counter with a glum look on her face. She gave Chastain an edited version of the previous night's activities and ended her narrative by saying how angry she was with Lucien. Chastain finished eating and wiped her hands on her napkin.

"I don't see what the problem is, Nicole. He admitted what he did, and it's not like it was a capital crime or something. He took what could have been an uncomfortable situation for you and made it sweet and romantic, and he admitted that's what he was doing. Most men wouldn't have bothered. They'd have just tried to jump your bones and been done with it. Or better yet, they would've stayed home instead of coming out in all that rain. Why are you trying to make something out of nothing?" she asked reasonably.

Nicole got up and started cleaning the kitchen, which was already spotless because Lucien had cleared away all the dishes and put everything back to rights. She knew she was being ridiculous, but she felt like she had to, like her anger was the only thing standing between her sanity and a complete meltdown. Chastain had to repeat her question before Nicole could answer.

"Chastain, I know I'm being stupid, but the alternative is much worse. I did something incredibly crazy," she admitted. "I fooled around and fell in love, like that old song says. I'm in love with Lucien, and I can't imagine what's going to happen next."

"What's wrong with you? What do you mean it's the worst thing that could happen? Looks like it's the best thing, if you ask me," Chastain said. "Lucien is crazy about you, you fool. How many times do you have to hear that before you believe it? You're just looking for excuses so you can avoid the reality of the situation. The reality is that you've met a wonderful man who has the misfortune to be good-looking as well as intelligent, charming and well-off. Instead of doing cartwheels like a normal woman, you're going to Nutsville on me. You really need to chill, Nicole."

She got up and rinsed her plate and silverware in the sink before putting them in the dishwasher. She turned around and faced Nicole with her arms crossed and a stern expression. "You're intelligent, beautiful, you have personality and style and you're acting like having a man like Lucien care about you is the worst thing in the world. That's just crazy, girl. I hate to resort to this, but I should tell you there're plenty of women out there who'd love to take your place."

Nicole smiled wanly. "I met one yesterday. Her name was Toya or something. She had the nerve to tell me that Lucien was her man."

"She *what?*"

At Chastain's exclamation, Nicole told her the whole incident. Chastain laughed and said, "Not Toya, Tonya. Her name is Tonya Merriwether, and she's been after Lucien since they were in middle school. But that's what I'm talking about, Nic. There're a whole slew of women who'd love to have a Deveraux, any Deveraux, to call their own. And there are whole bunches who've had their caps set for Lucien since he was just a kid. He can't help it, because he's desirable. Are you going to just let him go because you're insecure? Because of your ex-fiancé?"

"I'm not insecure," Nicole protested, but her protest fell on deaf ears.

"Yes, you are. Either that, or you're just real neurotic and I never noticed before. Lucien is a great guy, and you've admitted that you're in love with him, so what's the problem? I just don't get it, I really don't." Chastain shook her head. "If I had a man like that, you can believe I wouldn't be hemming and hawing and acting like I didn't know what to do. I'd know what to do, trust me."

Nicole saw a chance to change the subject and jumped on it. "So why have you never gotten involved with any of the Deveraux men? You seem to be all too acquainted with their good points. Why hasn't one caught your fancy?"

Chastain looked surprised, but she shrugged it off. "I told you, they're like brothers to me. We grew up together," she reminded Nicole. "Besides, I'm not Deveraux material, if you haven't noticed."

"What on earth are you talking about?" Nicole demanded.

"They like tall women with full figures and long hair, preferably with dark skin," Chastain said dryly. "I don't fit that profile."

Nicole stared at Chastain, who was about five feet seven inches, slender and honey-colored with short dark brown hair with copper highlights. She also had honey-colored eyes that glowed copper when she was excited about something. "But you're beautiful, Chastain! Any man would be happy to get with you and would thank the good Lord for giving him such a wonderful gift," Nicole said indignantly.

Chastain laughed, but the laughter didn't light up her eyes. "Yeah, well. Men are visual creatures. They like what they like and that's what they stick with. Even if they weren't like my brothers, I wouldn't stand a chance. Trust me. And don't think

I don't know what you're up to. You're trying to get me off the subject, and it's not working. True love is a beautiful thing, Nicole, and for you to treat it like it's a disease is beyond me. All I can tell you is that you've been given a gift, a wonderful gift, and if your life is so fantastic that you can do without it, then good for you. But if you're like the rest of us, you'll take that gift and be grateful," she said hotly.

Nicole didn't know whether to laugh or cry. "Chastain, I admit it. When you put it like that, I do sound like a neurotic heifer, don't I?"

"Yeah, you sound like one of those chicks from that sex show on cable. Just relax and enjoy it, woman! And tell me this, just when did you know you were in love with Lucien? Was it before the lovemaking, during the lovemaking or after the lovemaking? Hmm?" The familiar light was back in Chastain's teasing eyes.

Nicole raised an eyebrow and said, "All of the above." Her eyes turned dreamy as she thought about last night. "Every single one of the above," she said and sighed deeply.

"Ooh, girl, you are definitely sprung. C'mon and let's get going so you can get back here to fix him a nice dinner or something."

They were going shopping to get the rest of the items Nicole was looking for to complete the project Lucien had asked her to undertake. She had ordered a lot of things online and was very pleased with them on delivery, but there were some other things she needed to purchase and that was their plan for the day. When Chastain mentioned cooking for Lucien, Nicole shook her head. "He's actually going to cook for me tonight. He says he wants to show off for me," she said coyly.

Chastain rolled her eyes and put her hand on her hip. "See, now you're just rubbing my nose in it," she said with disgust.

"If I already didn't like you, I could really hate you right about now. *Heifer,*" she added.

"Don't hate me 'cause you ain't me," Nicole said saucily. "You need to step up your game. Besides, all that play-brother stuff gets old after a while. My sister Nona married her child-hood sweetheart, and they were truly like brother and sister most of their lives. They were raised together from the time they were arm babies because our mothers were best friends. But when the time was right, everything clicked into place. And since there are two perfectly good single Deveraux men hanging around uninvolved as far as I can see, you may as well help yourself. Why let two much-right men go to waste?"

"Two *whats?*" Chastain looked puzzled.

"Much-right men, honey. You got as much right to them as anybody else, I'm just sayin'," Nicole said with a wicked grin.

Chastain didn't have a snappy comeback to that. "Hmmph" was all she said. "Let's get going before it gets too hot out there."

Nicole had taken a great deal of care with her appearance that evening. After she and Chastain finished their shopping, she'd shampooed her thick hair and blown it dry before curling it. She'd put big rollers in to hold the curl while she bathed. She patted herself dry and used the matching body cream and powder so that she was lightly but thoroughly scented with the lovely fragrance. As a final touch she sprayed the eau de parfum in the air and walked through it so that the layers of fragrance would last all night. She looked at the outfit she had chosen and smiled to herself. Lucien was going to love it.

While she was putting on her underwear, Bojangles appeared from nowhere. He'd been sulking most of the day because he didn't appreciate having his home invaded by those bouncing, yapping white balls of fur, and he yowled his disapproval at Nicole. "There you are. I was wondering what you've been up to all day," she said as she rubbed him behind the ears. "I'm going to give you something nice for dinner because I'll be out late tonight. Very late. I might not even come home. Would that upset you?"

Apparently it didn't bother him, because he yawned at her and curled up on the pillows to watch her dress. She did so carefully, making sure that every hair was in place and her ensemble was just so. She was going to enjoy herself tonight despite any manufactured anxieties that her subconscious was trying to drum up.

Chastain's lectures had the right effect on her; they made her see that she was being ridiculous, and she wasn't going to do it anymore. She wasn't completely convinced that Lucien was as enamored of her as Chastain said, but she wasn't going to worry about it. There was no point in speculating, or dramatizing. It was what it was, whatever it was. She was going to have a good time tonight and store up some memories to take back to Charleston. It might have been a dangerously bad idea to expose herself to more of Lucien's charms, but nothing short of a hurricane could have kept her away.

She drove the short distance to his house, even though he had offered to come pick her up. He was concerned about her safety, he said. She smiled when she thought about how thoughtful he was, especially about little things like that. His brothers were that way, too. She was thinking about why Chastain was so adamantly opposed to dating one of the single brothers when she realized she'd reached his house. He was waiting for her, holding open the front door with one hand while his other hand held Yum-Yum's leash.

"It's easier than letting her run out the door. We've already done that once today, haven't we, sweetie?"

Yum-Yum was dancing around Nicole's feet with delight as though she hadn't seen her in days instead of mere hours. Nicole was going to pick her up, but Lucien stopped her. "What a minute, luscious. I want to get a look at you before you get all caught up with the baby. You look fantastic, Nicole. Damn, baby, you could be in a magazine looking like that," he said fervently. "Come here, I have to kiss you quick before your little friend gets her licks in."

Nicole laughed, but the laughter died as Lucien took her in his arms. The familiar warmth of his hard body and the delicious scent of his aftershave took her back to the passion they'd shared the night before. She tilted her head back and welcomed his lips with her own. It was meant to be a brief salute, but as always, they were overcome by mutual heat. They might have gone on kissing for a long time, but Yum-Yum wrapped her leash around their legs and barked loudly to let them know she was uncomfortable.

"Yums, baby, what did Daddy tell you about blocking? This is what he meant by that," Lucien said as he unhooked her purple leash from her purple collar with little rhinestones on it.

She dashed around the room panting happily, and Nicole laughed at her antics. She looked around the room while Lucien continued to admire her. "It looks a lot different in here now, doesn't it?" Her purchases had come in last Friday and she'd spent the weekend putting her special touches in Lucien's house. It was more of a redecorating project than decorating, but the effect was amazing. This was the first time she'd seen it since she'd finished and she still loved the new look. So did Lucien.

He put his arm around her waist.

Lucien agreed with her. "It looks great in here, Nicole. I can't believe how quickly you made it look like a home instead of a waiting room. You're very talented."

She had to agree that the living and dining rooms looked much warmer and more welcoming. She had added pillows in red and gold to go with the navy blue. The draperies had been changed to gold, and the pictures on the walls were now more colorful and visually exciting. She had removed the row of candleholders on the mantel and replaced them with some Thomas Blackshear figurines that added an element of interest to the area. The pewter balls had been replaced by big colorful balls of capiz shell, and there was a medium-height candleholder on either side of the bowl. The pewter candleholders were now arranged on the buffet in the dining room and they were clustered on either end, mixed with some taller glass holders in red and cobalt blue. A big mirror was on the wall above the buffet, and a Thomas Blackshear wall hanging was on the other wall. A colorful runner went down the middle of the dining room table and the area rug in the living room had been changed to a brighter one in an African-inspired pattern that was much livelier.

There were also thriving green plants everywhere, or so it appeared. Lucien had warned Nicole that his track record with plants wasn't very good, so she had gotten him some very realistic-looking silk plants. There were a few real ones, but Nicole warned him they were test cases. "They're hardy plants that even you should find difficult to kill, but I'm going to keep my eye on you," she said playfully. "If you take good care of these, you can have more."

Lucien was looking around at the changes she had wrought with awe. "It looks a thousand times better than it did, Nicole. I don't know how you managed to find just the right thing for every room, but you did a fantastic job. I really can't thank you enough for your hard work."

"Yes, you can," Nicole assured him. "You can feed me, I'm starving."

They both laughed, and he bowed over her hand. "You won't be in just a minute. Come with me, luscious, and we'll take care of that hunger."

Nicole smiled gamely, but she was glad he couldn't read her thoughts. *If only you knew how hungry I am for you. I don't think that will ever be satisfied.* She put on her best party smile and went into the kitchen with him.

Chapter 17

Lucien looked across the table at Nicole's lovely face and felt the same rushing current of desire that engulfed him whenever she was near him. When he'd opened the door to see her coming up the walk, he'd been stunned. Nicole always looked wonderful to him, but tonight she was just exceptional. She had on a red cotton dress that made him want to forget all about dinner and just peel it off her body. It was a sexy little sundress with a fitted bodice and a swirling skirt. The top had a neckline that was daring and ladylike at the same time; it was strapless, but she wasn't hanging out of it. It seemed to wrap itself around her breasts and make them look enticing, but there wasn't a lot of cleavage showing. She had a matching wrap over her shoulders that she discarded when she came into the house. On her feet were some black sandals with a lot of straps and a flat heel. Her hair was in loose curls and waves and she smelled fantastic, as always.

She looked too good to be eating in the kitchen, and he told her so. "You should be in a five-star restaurant looking like that, Nicole. I set the table here in the breakfast room because I thought we'd just be casual. Now I wish we were in the dining room at least," he apologized.

Nicole disagreed with him. "This is perfect, Lucien. Everything looks wonderful. I'm going to enjoy this much more than eating in the dining room. This is much more intimate. You worked hard on this, I can tell," she said.

"I did my best," he said modestly.

In the breakfast room, which had windows on three walls, he had covered the table with a red-and-white checked tablecloth. In the center of the table was a short round black vase with a dozen red roses with their stems cut so they formed a compact dome of fragrant flowers. There were white votive candles around the flowers and the candlelight made everything look inviting. The table was set for two with white dishes and black charger plates. The linen napkins were also black with red napkin rings. "Lucien, this looks so festive! I can't believe you went to so much trouble for me," she said.

Lucien kissed the back of her hand. "It wasn't any trouble. It was my pleasure. Now let's see if this meal is up to your standards."

He had chosen a few Creole dishes that were easy to make and not too exotic. He sensed that Nicole wouldn't appreciate something like fried oysters or braised rabbit, so he kept his selections to things he knew she'd enjoy. They started with a cup of crab bisque, which Nicole praised highly. "Lucien, this is delicious! I'm definitely going to want the recipe. It reminds of me of she-crab soup, but it's got a really distinct flavor. Mmm, it's wonderful," she said.

The main course was crawfish étouffée served over rice,

followed by a green salad with a simple vinaigrette dressing. Nicole was in heaven. "Ooh, Lucien, if I'd known you could cook like this, I would have been over here begging for scraps every day." She sighed. "This is so good," she added rapturously.

"I'm glad you like it. Would you like some more wine?" he asked.

She shook her head no but held out her glass to him. "I shouldn't, but I will. This wine is lovely. I'm not much of a drinker, but I do appreciate a good wine every now and then."

And I appreciate you, he thought. He was enjoying the evening tremendously. He could have been content just to watch her animated expressions all night, but he knew the evening held much more than lusty looks. He couldn't wait to take her in his arms again and hold her tight. He was drifting off into a fantasy when Nicole's voice shocked him back into reality.

"I really do want these recipes, Lucien. When I go home to Charleston, I'm going to make them for my parents. They'll love this meal as much as I do," she told him.

His buoyant mood came crashing down in the face of the truth, which was that Nicole wasn't truly his yet. She had a home, a job and a life in Charleston. She would go back to that life and leave him unless she had a compelling reason to stay.

He had to give her that reason soon or she'd be gone. The bleakness of that thought didn't have time to settle on him, because Nicole put her hand on top of his on the table. She gave him her pretty smile and leaned in for a kiss, which lightened his angst considerably.

"Lucien, thank you so much for doing this for me. It was absolutely flawless, and I really appreciate you going to all that trouble just for me," she said.

Her lips touched his and set his soul on fire. He reluctantly ended the kiss and then gave her a soft one on the cheek and said, "Nicole, I keep telling you that you don't owe me any special thanks. What I do for you is my pleasure. I enjoy doing things for you. You're very special to me."

He cleared his throat and got up to take away the dishes. Nicole offered to help, and he gave her a look that told her what a ridiculous notion that was. "Would you like some dessert?"

She looked tempted, but she patted her tummy and said she was full. "However, I do reserve the right to call that dessert to the table later," she said with a big smile. "See how my legalese has improved from being around you? You're an educational experience for me."

He finished putting the dishes in the dishwasher and came back to the table to pull her chair out. "You're a revelation for me, too. Let's go listen to some music," he suggested.

He took her hand and they went into the living room, where there was already soft music playing. He put in a different CD and smiled when Nicole turned around with a surprised look.

"You got the Ryan Shaw CD," she said.

"Yes, I did. You didn't think I was paying attention to it, did you? Well, I was. I was paying attention to everything last night."

He walked over to the sofa where Nicole was sitting with Yum-Yum in her lap. He stopped to look at the two of them looking too cute for words. "I've got to get something. I'll be right back." He went into his study and returned with his digital camera. "I have to get some pictures. You look way too good, luscious, I have to get some shots of this."

Nicole let him take as many pictures as he wanted without any protests about not looking good in photographs or her hair not looking right. She and Yum-Yum were naturals in front of the camera, and he got several shots that were just outstanding. Finally he quit taking pictures and sat next to Nicole. "Okay,

I've captured this evening for posterity. The next time you come over, I'll have a framed picture on my nightstand," he said.

Nicole picked Yum-Yum up and cooed at her. "Did you hear that? Your picture is going on display! Are you excited?"

Lucien snorted. "Very funny, Nicole. You know I'm talking about your picture. It's customary for a man to put his girlfriend right next to his bed." He leaned over to give her a kiss, but she pulled back.

"Oh? And what makes you think I'm your girlfriend?"

Lucien ignored her to get what he was after. He slid his hands up her warm bare skin and cupped her face while he applied a gentle suction to her lower lip, coaxing her mouth apart to receive the kiss he'd wanted to give her all night. He could kiss Nicole forever, and that was no joke. Her lips were so sweet and soft, he couldn't get enough of the taste of her. The kiss would have gone on longer if Yum-Yum hadn't chosen to put her nose into it, trying to pry them apart.

Nicole laughed and wiped her chin. "I think this is your girlfriend right here," she said. "She's staked her claim on you."

"If that's the case, she's too late," he drawled. "You already did that yesterday."

Nicole looked bemused, and Lucien was happy to elaborate. "You told Tonya yesterday that I was your boyfriend. You claimed me, Nic. I heard you, so don't try to wiggle out of it now. I'm going to take Yums out for her last little walk. Do you want to come?"

"I think I'd better," Nicole said tartly. "You seem to be hallucinating, and I don't want anything to happen to my baby."

"Nothing's gonna happen to me, luscious. Yum-Yum will make sure of that, so you don't have to worry."

He laughed all the way out the door after Nicole threw a pillow at him.

* * *

Lucien walked Yum-Yum quite a bit longer than he normally did because he wanted to her to be good and tired when he brought her home. His ploy worked, too, because she went right to sleep in her crate with no protests. Now he'd have all of Nicole's attention, which was just what he wanted. While he was walking the puppy, Nicole had gone to her rental car and brought in the items she and Chastain had purchased that day. He discovered this by the presence of a couple of large bags at the foot of the stairs and the absence of Nicole. He could hear her upstairs, and he went to see what was going on.

He stopped in the doorway and watched her arranging some new throw pillows on the bed. She was engrossed in what she was doing and didn't seem to be aware of his presence. "I like that, Nicole. They bring some color in the room."

She jumped at the sound of his voice, and then fussed at him. "Do I have to put a bell around your neck? You need to learn to make some noise before you come sneaking up on a person."

He walked over to the bed and sprawled across it, holding out his hand to her. "I'm sorry. I wasn't trying to scare you. I was trying not to make any noise. Your baby is sound asleep, and I want to keep her that way. Come sit down with me," he invited.

She did so, slipping off her sandals and scooting over so that she was next to him. She was sitting demurely with her legs tucked under, and he was warmed by the sight. He was aroused, as he always was when she was near him, but he felt an unexpected contentment that he liked very much. He took her hand and held it next to his heart. "So what are you going to do with me now that you've claimed me?"

Nicole tried to pull her hand away, but Lucien increased the pressure gently until she gave in. "I don't recall the incident in question," she said primly. "Are you sure you don't have me confused with someone else?"

"Listen, luscious, I was there, and I saw it with my own two eyes. You were all up in her face, and you said, 'Well, you're wrong on all counts, sister. *He* is a she, *her* name is Yum-Yum and she belongs to *me*. And that is not your boyfriend—he's mine.' Don't trip, Nicole. I have an excellent memory. It comes in real handy in my profession. You said it, baby. You spat it out in the heat of the moment, which means it came directly from your heart. I'm yours and you wanted her to know it," he said.

Nicole successfully took back her hand and gave him a soft playful pat on his chest. "You don't have to sound so smug about it. How do you know I really meant it? I could have just been trying to get on that harpy's nerves. It could have just been an emotional reflex."

Lucien reached for her and pulled her down to him until she was cradled in his arms. "*That's* an emotional reflex, baby. Stop fighting and give in so we can be happy," he whispered.

Nicole relaxed against him and kissed his chin. "Is this how you got all your other girlfriends? Did you just snatch 'em up and badger them until they fell into your waiting arms?"

Lucien laughed. "To tell you the truth, I never really had a girlfriend."

Nicole sat up so fast that it caught Lucien off guard. "Oh, please! How did you become Hound Dog with no girlfriends? You're gonna have to come better than that, buddy. How are you going to sit there and tell me you didn't have a girlfriend?"

Lucien closed his eyes and groaned. "Chastain has a big mouth," he mumbled. "And don't say she didn't tell you that, because I know she did." He sat up and leaned against the pillows. He held out his hand to Nicole and she took it, allowing him to guide her into the place next to him. When she was curled up against him with her head on his shoulder, he began to explain his dating history.

"I dated a lot, Nicole. I mean a *lot,* from the time I was, like, fourteen or fifteen. But I never really had one girl that I went with exclusively. I was too busy chasing and being chased to settle down with one person. And the older I got, the more I chased around. When I got to college, it was like a big all-you-can-eat buffet," he said ruefully. "I don't want you to think I treated anyone badly or anything like that. The women I went out with seemed to be just as interested in sex as I was, and that was about it. I'd meet somebody, we'd go out one or twice and then it was on to the next one."

He didn't say anything for a minute or so. "When I say it like that, it sounds really raunchy, doesn't it? I didn't think it was at the time," he said thoughtfully. "Probably because I wasn't thinking at all, at least not about anything worthwhile. I can honestly say I never deliberately deceived a woman, I never mistreated one and I never put them in peril by having unsafe sex. And not one of them ever asked for more," he said in that same distracted tone of voice.

Nicole spoke in an equally quiet tone. "That's because they had what they wanted. You were like a trophy to them," she said. "They wanted to prove something by going to bed with you, and that's all they wanted." She turned her head and kissed him on the neck. She sounded indignant on his behalf, which was the most endearing thing he'd ever heard.

"Okay, some of them might have wanted to use me, but I wasn't exactly trying to be Prince Charming. I was pretty happy with the way things were. I want to be honest with you, Nicole. I wasn't trying to attain a higher level of understanding or commitment. I was just going with the flow. I was having a good time, or so I thought."

"And what changed your mind? What made you decide to turn in the Hound Dog collar?" Nicole turned her head again so he could have better access to her neck, which he was kissing.

"You happened, Nicole. When I met you at Paris and Titus's rehearsal dinner, I thought you were exceptionally beautiful and I wanted to get to know you better. I really enjoyed talking to you and felt so at home with you. But then your date came to the wedding reception... So I waited, because I knew I'd see you again. Your brother is married to my sister, so I knew our paths would cross. And then you came to Pop and Julian's double wedding and I knew."

"You knew what?" she murmured.

"I knew you were mine. But what I don't understand is why you were available. You are so beautiful and talented and so damned sexy. Why are you still single? Tell me it was because you were waiting for me."

"Well, I could say that but it wouldn't be true. I was hiding from you," she said in the same soft voice.

"Hiding from me? Why?"

"It wasn't you specifically," she said. "It was all the men like you, the handsome men who thought they could just plow through women like a field of, of..."

"Wheat?" Lucien said helpfully.

"Whatever. Whatever it is that gets plowed through. You know the kind of man I'm talking about, *Hound Dog*."

"I'm never going to live that down, am I?"

Nicole ignored his plaintive remark and played with his fingers. "I was engaged to a man named Leland Fricke. He was very handsome and he cheated on me. I caught him at it, but he didn't realize it at the time." She told him about the ugly scene she'd witnessed and she was surprised by his reaction.

"Nicole, I'm so sorry that happened to you. You shouldn't

have had to deal with that. You must have been devastated," he said.

"I was, for about ten minutes or so. Then I got mad and did what I had to do. Did I mention that I had my camera with me?" She told him about the pictures, the wedding dresses and the reception and how she'd had the last laugh. Lucien laughed a little, but he was still angry on her behalf.

"Yeah, you handled yourself well, Nicole, but that doesn't excuse what he did. He'd better hope I never meet him," he said darkly.

Nicole was touched to hear his words. "Okay, I admit that the experience made me leery of men. I was distrustful and a little bit mean, actually." She stopped talking because Lucien kissed her. "Mmm." She sighed. "You should be glad it happened, though."

"Why would I be glad about something like that? You're the last person in the world I want to see hurt, Nicole. He should have treated you like a queen. He should have treasured you and loved you completely. How could he ever look at another woman when he had you?"

"Lucien, you should be glad because if he'd treated me right I wouldn't be here right now. I'd be Mrs. Nicki Fricke," she reminded him.

"You're right. You are so right, baby. If I ever see him I'll shake his hand and tell him thank you."

Nicole was playing with the buttons on his raw silk shirt and had undone two of them. Her fingers were tracing his collarbone, and he wasn't listening anymore. He was feeling a hot sensation that was like channeling a bolt of lightning through all his major arteries. Nicole seemed blissfully unaware of the effect she was having on him. She blew on his chest, and the soft burst of warm air was unexpected but delightful. She opened the rest of the buttons and lowered her head to lick one of his nipples and blow again. He had to regain control and quickly.

"If you keep doing that, clothes are going to start coming off," he warned.

"Good. I'm getting wrinkled, and this thing is a bear to iron," Nicole said with a sexy giggle. She slid over to her side of the bed and put her feet on the floor, looking over her shoulder as she did so. She gave him a sultry look and turned to face him. Reaching behind her back, she slowly unzipped her dress and pulled it open. Her eyes closed as she slid the dress down over her hips until she stood before him in her underwear. Lucien's erection was hard as tempered steel as Nicole climbed back onto the bed wearing a red lace bustier and matching thong panties.

"One of us is overdressed," she whispered. "What are we going to do about that?"

Lucien rose and tossed his shirt to the floor. He unzipped his jeans and they followed the shirt to the floor, along with his briefs. He rejoined Nicole on the bed, taking her into his embrace so quickly she let out a noise of surprise that turned into a moan of pleasure.

"Now I'm overdressed," she whispered.

"You won't be in a minute," he promised.

Nicole's entire body reacted to Lucien's touch. She knelt on the bed with him behind her, one arm around her waist as he reached for a condom with his free hand. She held on to the headboard to steady herself while he sheathed his manhood. He put his hands on her hips and gently urged her to bend forward. He moved the thong to one side and stroked her rounded bottom with both hands while he entered her. The impact of their joining was immediate and overwhelming. He filled her so completely she felt an explosion rising at once. She tried to say his name but only a low moan escaped her lips. While he thrust into her with long, measured strokes that were bringing her to ecstasy, he was removing her bustier, something she was unaware of until she felt his warm palms on her breasts, his fingers squeezing her hypersensitive nipples to bring her to an even higher level of pleasure. She felt hot, she felt cold, she felt everything rising up inside with the urgency of a volcano about to erupt. His movements changed tempo, becoming stronger and deeper and faster until they both exploded in a shattering climax that wrung a gasping cry from deep inside her, from a place she'd never been before. Lucien's thrusts slowed until he was gently stroking her in and out. His hands moved up and down the sides of her body, rubbing her velvety skin. He turned her over so they were face-to-face. He brushed her now-damp hair away from her face and kissed her. "How do you feel?" he asked softly.

"I feel like more," she answered and moved her hips seductively. He groaned and breathed her name. She moved again and pulled him into her body, clenching her hot moist walls against his rigid length. He moaned long and hard as his long fingers flexed over her round breasts, squeezing them gently as his thumbs circled her sensitive, erect nipples. His mouth covered one and his hot tongue circled it before he began to apply a long kiss that made Nicole tremble all over. He moved so that every stroke was hitting her just right. She could feel him deep inside her but he was also touching her wet pulsing pearl, over and over and the twin friction caused a sensation that brought her to the brink of release again.

She moaned aloud, saying his name over and over in a passionate cry from her heart. He finally released her breast and locked his arms around her as they rode out a massive climax together. They stayed in the same position for a long time, their hearts beating as one.

"I'm not trying to hurt you, baby. You're just so sweet I can't stop loving you," Lucien said as his breathing returned to normal.

"I feel the same way," she confessed. "You're not hurting me, you're making me happy."

"That's good to know," he said, kissing her forehead, then her lips. He turned over on his back and she turned so she was cuddled next to him.

"Are we going to sleep?" Her disappointment was clear in her voice.

"I'm not tired. I was thinking about continuing this in the shower," he said seductively.

She smiled. "That sounds like a plan."

Afterward, when they had bathed each other and were holding each other under the sheet, Nicole sighed with utter contentment. "What were we talking about?" she asked playfully.

"We were talking about the fact that you've staked your claim on me," he said as their fingers laced together in a tight clasp. "I'm all yours, Nicole. What are you going to do with me?"

She looked at him sleepily and kissed his shoulder. "I think I'll keep you. You smell good, you kiss really well and you can cook. And you're sweet," she added. "You're very loving, and you really care about my puppy." She rubbed her cheek against the smooth warm skin of his shoulder and sighed again. "It's official. You're my boyfriend." She gave a soft, sleepy laugh as he rubbed his cheek on her forehead.

"So how many have you had?" Lucien was beginning to sound sleepy.

"I had lots and lots," she admitted. "My first one was in kindergarten. He used to bring me a marble every day, one of those big glass ones. They were all different colors, and I still have them in my jewelry box. He also used to bring me FireBalls. His name was Benjie, and we got in trouble for talking all the time." She laughed. "I haven't thought about him for years."

"Well, you can stop thinking about him right about now. I'm sorry I brought it up," Lucien grumbled.

"But there's more," she teased. "I had another boyfriend in the second grade. His name was Oliver, and he was so cute! He was my church boyfriend because he went to a private school. He would sit with me every Sunday, and he would bring me a Tootsie Pop every week. We would give each other birthday and Christmas presents, and he kissed me under the mistletoe at the Christmas pageant."

"You were a fast little girl, weren't you?" He groaned as she nipped his fingertip.

"No, but I was chubby and chocolate and cute and the boys liked me. What can I tell you? Don't hate, appreciate," she said with a cascade of giggles as Lucien tried to kiss her quiet.

"I don't want to hear about any more of your conquests, thank you very much. I'll bet you were hell on wheels by the time you got to high school." His arm tightened around her, and he used his thumb to tickle the palm of her hand, which was still clasped in his.

"I absolutely was not," she protested. "I was a sweet little church girl who obeyed her parents. I was just popular. You aren't jealous because I used to have boyfriends way back in the day, are you?" She yawned again, still ladylike, but deeper this time.

"I've never been jealous in my entire life, but I am now. How about that? I don't even like to think about another man looking at you, much less touching you. And it doesn't matter whether it was in kindergarten or last week. Does it bother you at all to know you have my heart in the palm of your hand?" he murmured.

Nicole gently extricated her fingers from his and touched his face. "Not at all. I'll take good care of it, Lucien." She kissed him lightly on the mouth and put her head in the crook of his neck. So softly he could barely hear her, she whispered, "You can trust me, Lucien. I love you," just before falling asleep.

Chapter 18

The next morning found them in the kitchen eating a rather unorthodox breakfast. Since they'd never gotten around to eating the dessert Lucien had prepared for dinner, they were eating it now. He'd made a traditional bread pudding, but instead of the usual raisins he'd used pineapple. It was Nicole's idea to have it for breakfast.

"It has eggs, cream, sugar, butter, bread and fruit. What's the difference between this and French toast? I'll make some coffee if you take Yum-Yum out," she offered.

"How can I turn that down?" Lucien had put the bread pudding in the oven to heat and kissed Nicole before taking the happy puppy outdoors for her morning walk. He was in such a good mood she could have asked him to scale Mount Everest in his underwear and he'd have done it cheerfully. He'd meant what he said to her the night before; she was a revelation for him. He'd never been with anyone who was as much fun or as challenging. She was exciting, sexy, funny, compassionate and intelligent, besides being talented. He couldn't imagine having a dull day with her, ever. They were going to have an amazing life together. True, he hadn't asked her to marry him yet, but that was a mere formality. He had talked to his friend Maurice a few days ago. He designed and made incredible jewelry, and Lucien had presented him with the plan for the ring he wanted for Nicole.

"Come on, Yums, can you keep up with me? Can you run as fast as I do?" He tried jogging a little, which made Yum-Yum look at him like he was crazy. She liked to stroll along, smelling each individual blade of grass when she was walked. She would race around in circles when she was in the backyard, but she wasn't about to try keeping up with his long legs. She barked indignantly and sat down.

Lucien laughed and picked her up. "I'm sorry, sweetie. When you get a little bigger, we can do that, okay? Let's go home and see what your mommy is doing."

Nicole had just set two places at the breakfast table and was pouring milk into her glass. The rich aroma of coffee filled the room and everything seemed blissfully domestic. It was surprising to him how contented he felt at the moment. This was something he never thought he wanted, something he'd never sought, but here it was, right in front of him. It was like he'd found a winning lottery ticket in his pocket that he didn't remember buying. He unhooked Yum-Yum's leash and put her on the floor so she could run to Nicole.

"This was supposed to be a walk, not a carry," she said with a smile. "You're such a pushover."

Lucien was about to answer her when her cell phone chimed. She picked it up off the counter and glanced at the caller ID. Her face lit up in a big smile as she answered it.

"Good morning! How are you?" She motioned for Lucien to wash his hands and sit down, and he went to the sink to do so, although he was wondering who she was greeting with such affection.

"You are? Really? Oh, that'll be nice. I can't wait to see you! Do you want me to pick you up?"

Lucien sat down while Nicole brought the bread pudding over and placed it on the table. She put a serving spoon into Lucien's hand and took her seat, still chatting and smiling. "Okay, I'll look for you tomorrow afternoon. I can't wait! Love you," she said and ended the call.

"So who was that? Sounds like you're expecting a visitor," Lucien said gruffly.

Nicole ignored his tone and held her hand out to say grace. They both said amen when it was done, and she smiled as Lucien placed a portion of the warm pudding on her plate. "This smells delicious," she said. Taking a bite, she closed her eyes in rapture and said, "Mmm, it tastes delicious, too. It's moist and delicate and not too sweet. It's just perfect," she said. "What were you asking me?"

Lucien tried hard not to sound as rough as he had previously; he tried to discipline his tone of voice. "I was asking who you were talking to on the phone. I take it you're expecting company?"

"No, *we're* expecting company," she corrected him. "That was Paris. She's coming in tomorrow with Titus. She wants to shoot a segment on the aftermath of the storm for her show, and he wasn't about to let her make the trip by herself. So they'll be here for my birthday," she said happily.

Lucien felt a hot flush brush his face. He'd actually felt a little jealous because Nicole was talking to someone on the phone. He'd truly gone off the deep end, no doubt. He was going to have to watch himself in the future, because Nicole, if he knew her at all, wasn't going to put up with much of that kind of behavior. And he was happy to know that his only sister was coming to town. "I'm glad they're coming. I don't get to see much of my sister these days."

"I feel the same way about Titus. We talk on the phone and e-mail each other, but I still miss my big brother," Nicole said.

"So what do you want to do for your birthday? Do you want to have a party?"

Nicole shook her head. "Oh, nothing like that. Just a nice home-cooked dinner with family and friends. That's more than sufficient. Your folks will be home tomorrow, too, so that's a good reason to celebrate. Nothing fancy, just a few people," she said.

Lucien laughed. "That's the challenge of having a big family, luscious. We outnumber everybody. A family dinner turns into a party whether you want it to or not. Speaking of parties, I bought you something the other day, and I haven't given it to you yet. It's not your birthday present, though—it's just something I saw, and I thought you'd like it. It's still in the car, as a matter of fact. I'm going to go get it now."

In a few minutes Nicole had opened the box he'd presented to her and was staring at the contents with an odd look on her face. "You bought me a monkey? Why?"

Lucien felt distinctly uneasy. The monkey in question was a small antique lamp. The base was like a palm tree with a small capuchin monkey on its trunk. The monkey was dressed in a short red jacket and was holding a banana. The top of the palm tree housed the bulb. It was made of bronze, which gave it a nice weight, and the colors were nicely preserved. It was in excellent condition and was considered a highly collectible piece. When he'd seen it in the shop window, something told him that Nicole would love it. Now, as he looked at the expression on her face, he thought the inner voice that told him to get it was a traitorous liar. She hated it.

Luckily, his cell phone went off and he welcomed the chance to answer it so he wouldn't have to explain his choice of gifts. It was his father, and Lucien was never gladder to hear his voice. "Yo, Pop, what's up? I hear you two are coming back tomorrow," he said with forced joviality. He got up and walked into the dining room, talking the whole time. The conversation with Mac was brief; he was just calling to say what time their flight landed.

"So how's everything going there? Have you been taking good care of Nicole? It wasn't our intention to abandon our guest, but this trip had been planned and we had to see it through. How's she doing?" Mac asked.

"She's magnificent. She's the best thing that's ever come into my wasted life," Lucien said honestly.

"I'm glad to hear that, son. She's a lovely woman, and she'll make you a wonderful wife. Try not to scare her off," he added before ending the call.

Lucien groaned. The monkey may not have frightened her off, but it wasn't exactly reeling her in, either. He was going to have to get her the most perfect birthday present in the known world to make up for the ill-advised lamp. He went back into the kitchen to find Philippe eating the rest of the bread pudding with gusto and LuLu playing with Yum-Yum at Nicole's feet. For once he was glad that he and his brothers didn't stand on ceremony. Unannounced visits were par for the course with them, and this one couldn't have come at a better time.

Nicole announced that she needed to go home and change clothes. "I need to go to the grocery store, too. I think Chastain is going to go with me. We'd said something about that yesterday. Do you need anything?"

"No, luscious, I don't. But thanks for asking, that was very thoughtful of you. Will you call me later?"

"Of course I will," she said sweetly. "I'm going to leave Yum-Yum here because she's having too much fun with her real mommy. Okay, I'm going to clean this up and go."

"No, you're not. I've got this, Nic. You go have a good day with Chastain, and I'll see you later. Be safe," he added. "Wait a minute, let me put this in the car for you," he said as he hastily boxed up the lamp. He didn't want to revisit her reaction to the gift in front of Philippe.

When he came back into the kitchen after walking her to her rental car, he looked at Philippe with a plea in his eyes. "I need help, man. Nicole's birthday is in a couple of days, and I've got to get her something really nice. I'm taking suggestions. You got any ideas?"

Philippe reacted the way any concerned brother would when his sibling needed help. He laughed in his face.

After letting Philippe dog him mercilessly about being love struck, he enlisted his twin's help in finding the perfect birthday present for Nicole. They got into his Mini Cooper to find a store that would supply whatever it was he was looking for, and Philippe continued to pick at him. He thought Lucien was going overboard in trying to please Nicole, but Lucien disagreed.

"Look, I know next to nothing about this whole process. Nicole is the first woman outside of our family that I've bought something really meaningful for, and obviously I don't know what I'm doing. You didn't see the look on her face when she saw that lamp. She wasn't loving it," he said glumly.

Philippe shook his head. LuLu was sitting in his lap, and

he scratched her ears as he offered a rebuttal. "You're wrong. When I came in the kitchen, she was looking at it, and she showed it to me like she was really proud of it. Why would she do that if she hated it?"

Lucien scratched his head. "She was probably being polite or something. Who knows. I just got the distinct impression that she didn't like it, which is why I have to redeem myself with this birthday gift."

"So what are you going to get her?"

"Some of her favorite perfume, for one thing. I know she likes Juicy Couture, so that's a no-brainer. And a framed picture of Yum-Yum that I took the other day for another. There's no way she wouldn't like that. And I'm getting her roses, because those are her favorite flowers. But I want to get her something else, something unexpected and special. Something she'll really love," he said thoughtfully.

"Before you drive yourself totally crazy, can we stop at Gris-Gris for a minute?"

"What for?" Lucien glanced at his brother.

"Chastain is going to keep LuLu for a few days." No further explanation was forthcoming, so Lucien had to ask Philippe why he'd asked her to dog-sit. His twin could be close-mouthed to the point of being really annoying. But he finally answered, and the reason was rather surprising.

"Basically because LuLu is a good little watchdog, and I don't like Chastain staying above Gris-Gris by herself. I asked her to come stay with me, but she won't do it."

"Ha! I always knew you were sweet on her," Lucien said, gloating. "Why do you always act like you don't get along? Why don't you start acting like mature adults instead of bickering children?"

"Why do you run off at the mouth, especially when you

don't know what you're talking about?" Philippe sounded bored rather than annoyed.

Lucien was parallel parking at the moment and didn't bother to answer. But he was making a big mental note. Someday, when he least expected it, Philippe was going to get the royal treatment about Chastain. Lucien was many things, but unobservant wasn't one of them.

Mac and Ruth's homecoming was a lot of fun. Chastain and Nicole had made a big lasagna dinner with an antipasto platter, green salad, garlic bread and tiramisu for dessert. There was even a separate pan of vegetarian lasagna just for Philippe. Mac and Ruth looked well-rested and madly in love, and they weren't the only ones. Paris and Titus were so much in love that it radiated from them like a beacon of light. Lucien was touched and heartened by the sight of the two couples. In a very short time he and Nicole would be another set of happy newly-weds. All he had to do was pick up the ring from Maurice, present it to Nicole and they'd set a date for the wedding. Nothing could be simpler—or more complicated. He hoped his surprise party would pave the way for his proposal.

Even though Nicole had indicated that she wasn't inter-ested in having a party, he was going to give her one. Her birthday was the day after the family dinner, and he wasn't about to let it go uncelebrated. It wasn't going to be elabo-rate, just the family and Chastain. Of course, as he had told Nicole, "family" meant a crowd because there were so many of them, but it would be okay. He was going to barbecue because he and his brothers had made it into an art form and he could count on them to help out. Baking wasn't high on his list of accomplishments, so he bought a beautiful cake and had her name put on it. He'd bought a few dozen roses and arranged them in the dining room, sunroom, the living room and the bedroom. He'd even gone so far as to purchase linen napkins in pink and green to establish a color scheme. He knew better than to get matching paper goods like paper plates and cups because he'd endured enough lectures from Philippe about the wastefulness of such. They would use regular plates and glasses and be happy.

The idea was that everyone would be at the house except Nicole, Ruth and Mac and Paris and Titus. Paris was going to tell Nicole that she wanted to see the new decor at Lucien's, and the three of them would drive over to his place, followed at a discreet distance by Mac and Ruth. They would bring Nicole to the backyard, where everyone was waiting to say "Surprise!" and the party would begin. He was pretty pleased with himself, and he thought Nicole would be, too. Sure, she'd said she didn't want a party, but she did say she would like a nice dinner with friends and family and essentially that's what this gathering was.

He glanced at his watch and said, "Okay, they should be here in about two minutes." He heard voices coming up the driveway and changed his previous statement. "They're here," he said, turning around to see Nicole coming into the yard, followed by Paris and Titus.

"SURPRISE!"

Her mouth fell open and her eyes were wide, but then she laughed out loud and got into the spirit of the party. "Ooh, you sneaked this one up on me, didn't you!" she said to Lucien. He took her hand and kissed her, greatly encouraged by the fact that she kissed him back and kept a tight grip on his hand. Everyone was there: Maya, Julian and Corey, Chastain, Philippe, Wade, Paris and Titus and Mac and Ruth. The little dogs were all in attendance, looking festive with big bows on their collars, and a noisy chorus of the birthday song went up. Nicole actually looked very happy, even though she gave Lucien a playful poke with her elbow.

"I told you I didn't want a big party," she said. "I'm so glad you didn't listen to me! You're so sweet," she added as she stood on tiptoe to kiss him.

Lucien was gratified by the kiss and her happiness. As long as she had the same reaction to the gifts he'd gotten her, everything would be great. He made her sit down at the big table on the patio so he could serve her dinner. He came back with a plate just in time to hear Paris talking about the dogs.

"Nicole, I've never seen anything as cute in my life. Well, except for Kasey, that is. I wish we'd brought him with us. He'd be having a ball right now." Kasey was the half Pomeranian, half cockapoo that Titus had given her for her birthday. "I can't believe Lucien gave you a puppy," she mused.

Lucien handed plates of food to his beloved and his sister. "Correction, Coco. Philippe gave her the puppy. I, however, am keeping her. And she loves me best," he said smugly.

"That's because she's a little tramp. She just loves men, period. Look at her right now, if you don't believe me," Nicole laughed.

Yum-Yum was sitting in Titus's lap, looking up at him like he was the most wonderful thing she'd ever seen. He was rubbing her head and talking to her, and she was lapping it up like her favorite treat. Everyone laughed except Paris, who was looking at Nicole and Lucien with a stunned expression. She leaned over to Nicole and spoke in a low voice that only Nicole could hear. "You've been holding out on me, sister-in-law. We're going to have some serious girl talk tonight."

After the sumptuous feast of ribs, chicken, veggie burgers and hot dogs with corn on the cob, baked beans, coleslaw and sliced tomatoes, it was time for the cake and presents. Lucien could tell that Nicole was pleased with all the gifts, although she kept protesting that the party was more than enough. She got bath products from Chastain, gift certificates for Carol's Daughter from Mac and Ruth, a beautiful pink cotton night-gown and robe from Paris and Titus, and more gift cards from Wade and Philippe. Maya and Julian gave her CDs, includ-ing the newest one by Norah Jones. Corey presented her with a double picture frame. On one side was a picture of Popcorn, Yum-Yum and Lulu, and the other side was a picture of Corey and Popcorn. Corey told her it was so she wouldn't forget her.

"Auntie Nicki, you can keep this with you and then you won't forget me," she said earnestly.

Lucien saw Nicole's eyes fill with tears at the remark, and he tried to distract her by giving her the gifts he'd selected for her. She loved the picture of Yum-Yum and the Juicy Couture perfume and lotion. The last package he handed her was the one he'd been searching for, the one he thought she'd really adore. He watched her closely as she opened the box and took out the object that he'd selected so carefully. It was a figurine of a plump, sexy sister wearing a white dress and hat, walking a small white dog on a leash.

There were oohs and ahhs from everyone, and Corey said, "Auntie Nicki, look! It's you walking Yum-Yum!"

Nicole smiled and said, "Yes it is, sweetie. It's very beau-tiful, isn't it?" Lucien was relieved until he sat down next to Nicole. She didn't say anything at first, but when Corey and the others dispersed she turned to Lucien with an odd little smile on her face.

"Is this what you think my thighs look like?"

She hates it, Lucien thought. *I should have just let it go with the perfume. She hates it.* He'd seen the statue and thought it was adorable, but apparently he was wrong. True, the woman had exaggerated thighs, but the whole effect was to make everything else about her seem really feminine and dainty. Besides, she was obviously sexy and confident; he thought Nicole would find it charming. All he could think about was how wrong he'd been. He was truly happy when Paris and Chastain distracted Nicole and Titus gave him a nod from across the table. "Come take a walk with me, Luc. I think your little friend here wants some exercise," he said, indicating Yum-Yum, who was actually asleep at the moment.

"That's a good idea." *Any port in a storm.*

Chapter 19

The two men walked down the long driveway and down the sidewalk. Titus watched Yum-Yum frisking along in the grass for a moment before saying what was on his mind. "You're in love with my baby sister." It was a statement rather than a question.

"Yes, I am," Lucien answered. "I plan to marry her, so if you have a problem with that, you'd better let me know about it now."

"No problem here, Luc. I just have a word of advice. Don't let Nicole play you. She's crazy about you, but if she can give you a hard time, she will."

This wasn't what Lucien was expecting to hear, and he asked Titus to elaborate. "Look, man, Nic is a handful, always has been. You think she didn't like that statue you gave her, right? I saw the look on your face when she made that crack about her thighs. She was shocked by the statue, no doubt, but that's because she collects them. She loves those things. She has about ten of them in different outfits and poses. She has one in her bathroom, and she talks to it! For all I know, she talks to all of them. I know my sister, and she's just thrown that you managed to get her something that she really loves. She's not used to having a man be that tuned in to her. You really get to her, and she's not sure she can handle it. Just take my advice and don't let her bulldoze you," he advised.

Lucien stopped to untangle Yum-Yum, who was investigating a shrub. "Dang. Here I thought I'd done something stupid. I gave her an antique lamp, and I thought she hated it, too."

"The monkey lamp? She's crazy about that thing. She was showing it off to us today. You probably don't know this, but Nicki loves monkeys. She's wanted a monkey since she was three, but we weren't crazy. There was no way in hell we were gonna get her a live monkey." Titus shook his head. "She got into enough mischief on her own. She didn't need a monkey to help her create havoc. But she got a lot of toy monkeys. She collects Curious George stuff, and she loves movies with monkeys in them. As long as there's a monkey in it, she'll watch it, and that includes *King Kong*. Like I said, Nicole isn't used to having someone really know her and sense her every desire. You scare her a little, which is a good thing. Otherwise she might run over you."

Lucien defended her at once. "Nicole wouldn't do anything like that. She's too loving and honest. She'd never just mess with my head," he protested.

Titus patted him on the shoulder. "I'm glad you see the best in her. She's a wonderful person, and she can be sweet as pie. That's when she's Nicole, Nic, or Nicki. But she has a little alter ego I used to call 'Cole-baby. 'Cole-baby is the dark side, the side that really does like to mess with someone's head, the side that beat the crap out of my ex-fiancée because she thought the woman needed a beat down, the one who'll give you a nice-nasty smile and then eviscerate you verbally. 'Cole-baby is the one you have to watch."

Lucien was laughing now. "Yeah, now that you mention it, I've gotten a couple of glimpses of 'Cole-baby. But I have to tell you, I love all of Nicole. She keeps me on my toes, she makes me think, she's unpredictable and lively, and I like that," he said.

"That's good to hear, because Nicole got herself engaged to some chump who actually thought he could get over on her. She was mad as hell, but it also made her very distrustful of men." He went on to tell Lucien the whole story of the infamous Leland Fricke, who thought he could have some illicit sex on the side and Nicole not find out about it. "After that loser, Nicole didn't swear off men, but she may as well have because the men she started dating were, well, kind of *subdued* is the most polite way I can put it," Titus said.

"Nerds?" Lucien asked.

"Nerd*like*. They exhibited behaviors normally associated with those known as nerds, and that's all I'm saying." He laughed as Yum-Yum suddenly plopped down on the sidewalk and refused to move. He picked her up and said, "You're not used to having two big flat-footed men run you all over the place, are you?"

Lucien was still taking in what Titus had told him. Titus grinned at him. "I'm just real glad to see Nicole with a man who can handle her. She needed someone in her life who doesn't jump when she says jump and who can meet her on her own level. This tells me that Leland Fricke doesn't have any hold over her anymore. So let's get back to the party and have a good time."

They turned around and began to head back toward the

house. His brother-in-law was a very wise man, and he was making a lot of sense about a lot of things.

Paris had meant what she said about girl talk. As soon as the party was over, she had turned to Nicole with a merry but determined twinkle in her eye. "You can have one hour to make kissy-face with your man, but after that you need to come to my room, because we've got a lot of catching up to do. Be there or I'll come find you," she warned.

"Yeah, and I'm comin' with her," Chastain cackled.

Paris was so serious it struck Nicole as being funny, and she giggled every time she thought about her mandate. Lucien wanted to know what she was laughing about. They were in his living room, listening to one of her new CDs while they cuddled on the sofa.

"What's so funny, luscious?"

"Your sister called me on the carpet. She says I have one hour for kissing, and then I have to report to her to spill my guts about our relationship, or else." Nicole laughed again.

Lucien joined his laughter to hers as he nuzzled her neck. "Yeah, I'm sure she has a few pithy things to get off her chest. She shouldn't be surprised that we're together. I told her you were the woman I wanted," he murmured.

Nicole raised her eyebrows, and she stared at him. "You did? When did you tell her that?"

Lucien kissed her slowly before answering. "At the wedding. The morning after the wedding," he corrected himself. "I told her you were the one."

"Which one? One what?" Nicole asked, clearly stunned.

"I told her you were the woman I planned to marry," he said. "I told you when I saw you at the wedding, I knew you were the one. Weren't you listening?"

Nicole's mind raced back to the night Lucien had cooked dinner for her. They had talked about a lot of things, and she vaguely recalled him saying he knew something, but she was also remembering some very hot and steamy love-making, and everything was blurred. "Yes, I was listening, but I'm pretty sure you didn't say anything about marrying me. I'm pretty sure I would have remembered *that*," she said.

Lucien didn't seem to be paying attention. He was kissing her neck again and telling her how good she smelled. "Did you enjoy your party?"

"Yes, I did, Lucien. It was a great party and I had a won-derful time. I love you for doing that for me. I also loved my presents. You're very thoughtful, aren't you?" She kissed his fingers and then repeated the gesture on the palm of his hand.

"When it comes to you, yes, I am. I want you to be happy, Nicole. I want to make you happy." He buried his nose in her fragrantly silky hair and rubbed his face against its softness. "So you liked everything I gave you? Even the statue?"

"I liked that the best," she admitted. "I love those girls. They're made by this Italian artist, and they're called Chubby Models. They come in different nationalities, and I have several of them. And Corey was right—it looks just like me and Yum-Yum. How did you know I collected them? I don't even think Paris knows that."

Lucien tipped her face up to his. "I didn't know. I saw the statue, and it just called out to me. I thought you would like it, and you did," he said before kissing her again.

"You know me too well," she murmured. "Like that darling lamp, for example. What made you get me a monkey lamp? I love monkeys. My daddy still calls me Monk-Monk because I was so crazy about monkeys when I was little. I always wanted a monkey," she said reflectively. "I might marry you if you got me a monkey," she teased.

"Don't play," Lucien warned her. "I have a frat brother who runs a zoo. I can get a monkey. I can have a monkey here tomorrow, a dirty, unsanitary, banana-eating, screaming ape swinging from the chandelier and torturing Yum-Yum." He paused for a moment and said, "Never mind. That's a deal-breaker. You're going to have to take me as I am, without a simian. Can you handle that?"

"I guess that remains to be seen," she said saucily. "In the meantime, my hour is just about up. If I'm not at your parents' house soon, Paris is going to send out a dragnet to bring me in."

"Then we need to be making better use of our time," he growled and took her in his arms for one last sizzling kiss.

"That's enough of that. I'm taking you home now before I keep you here all night," he said roughly.

They drove home listening to Mark Murphy and holding hands. He parked in his parents' driveway and turned off the ignition. Turning to Nicole, he gave her a look that was both deeply passionate and totally serious. "Are you going to marry me?"

Nicole looked equally serious. "Are you going to ask me?"

"Yes, I am. I love you and I can't even imagine living without you."

"Are you sure? Absolutely one hundred percent sure? Because you know what I do when I'm scorned," she warned him.

He laughed softly and kissed her. "I know all about you and I'm willing to take the chance. You are the best thing that's ever happened to me and I plan to make you happy every day of our lives."

"That's a tall order," she whispered.

"I'm a tall man, sugar. Nice how that worked out, isn't it?"

They kissed again and Lucien had to make himself stop. "Listen, juicy, let's get you in the house before I do something really wrong."

"Nothing we do could be wrong," she protested.

"In my father's driveway? Don't test me, Nicole. I'm not that strong," he said as he got out of the car.

Now Nicole was surrounded, with no hope of escape. She was in Paris's bedroom, sitting cross-legged on the bed. Paris was sitting there, too, in the same position. Chastain was also there, in a pretty chair with floral upholstery. Ruth was leaving the room, although Nicole was begging her to stay. "Don't leave me. They might hurt me," she pleaded laughingly.

Ruth gave her a loving smile. "You'll be just fine, sweetie. You know the rules. If you hold out on Paris, you have to pay the price for your silence. Besides, I'm still a newlywed," she teased. "You'll know what I mean real soon," she added as she slipped out the door.

Paris gave Nicole a very intense look accompanied by a pointing finger. "I can't believe you didn't tell me! You and Lucien are all in love, and I have to find it out when I see it with my own eyes. That's just not right, Nic. You know I have to know all the dish before everyone else, especially when it concerns a loved one. And you've been keeping this giant secret from me for weeks! How can you be so selfish? I'm getting ready to have your niece or nephew, and you treat me like a stranger," she sniffed, trying her best to look aggrieved even though she was laughing.

Nicole was laughing, too, even harder than Paris. "What was I supposed to do, call you up and say 'Hey, girl, I'm in love with your brother and we're boinking like crazy?' I don't think so! Besides, it kinda sneaked up on me," she admitted. "It wasn't like I came here with lust on my mind. No one is more surprised than I am, believe me. And I understand that you were given a little heads-up about his intentions that you didn't bother to mention to me. He says the two of you had a little chat about me at the double wedding. You could have given me some warning, now, couldn't you?"

Paris's face flushed, and she entreated Chastain to protect her. "She's picking on me, help!"

"You're on your own, toots. You didn't clue me in, either, and I'm practically part of the family. If you knew Lucien had designs on her, you were obligated to tell. That's the rule," she said cheerfully.

Paris conceded that point. "Okay, I admit that I had information which I didn't pass on, but I couldn't do that without messing everything up. You have to admit that if I'd told you what Lucien told me at the wedding, it would have put your back up and things would have gone terribly wrong. It's a good thing I kept my nose out of it," she said candidly.

Nicole tilted her head to one side. "What exactly did he say to you?"

Paris gave her a bright smile and proceeded to tell Nicole what she had discussed with Lucien in Atlanta. "He was upset with me because he said I wasn't taking his emotions seriously. That's when I knew he really meant what he was saying, Nicole. As unlikely as it seemed from his track record with women, there was something about you that truly touched his heart. He knew you were the woman meant for him," she told her. "Was he wrong?"

Nicole's face softened into a dreamy smile. "Absolutely not. We belong together," she said softly.

Paris clapped her hands and let out a happy squeal. "Oh

my God! Does this mean another wedding is coming in the near future?"

Chastain jumped from her chair. "I already called bridesmaid, so don't get crazy. I knew this was coming, I just knew it!"

"Calm down. We haven't formalized anything," Nicole cautioned.

Paris was rocking back and forth with excitement. "But that's all it is, a formality. You two will be next, and if I know my brother, it won't be but a minute before he proposes. Then we start planning your wedding in Charleston and your move to New Orleans," she said.

A cold chill raced down Nicole's spine. For some reason, she hadn't internalized what the future was going to hold. She hadn't given a single thought to what marrying Lucien might mean in terms of her career and the life she had in South Carolina. Suddenly things seemed a lot more complicated that she'd anticipated, and for the first time, she questioned what she was getting into.

Chapter 20

Nicole looked at Lucien, who was driving along happily as though he hadn't a care in the world. They'd been on the road for a few hours, and he didn't even mind that they'd had to stop three times because Yum-Yum got a little carsick from riding so much. When she would whine and look uncomfortable, he would obligingly pull off the road and take her out of the car so she could walk around and get her bearings on soft grass. Each time, the process revived the puppy's flagging spirits and she was her usual spunky self when the car started up again. It was an amazing show of patience and caring, as far as Nicole was concerned, and she told him so.

"You know, you didn't have to do this," she reminded him. "I could have flown home, or I could have driven by myself. Or Daddy could have come and picked me up," she added. "I truly appreciate your doing this for me, but you really didn't have to."

"Nicole, don't be ridiculous," Lucien said patiently. "How

could I not take you back to Charleston? What kind of jerk wouldn't take his lady home to her family? Did you really think I'd let you make a twelve-hour drive by yourself? And did you think I'd let Yums be stuffed into a cargo hold on a plane? She would have been miserable. Besides, I'm going to hate being away from you, and this prolongs our time together. It makes perfect sense to me. It's the only possible solution, in fact. And don't forget, I want to start getting to know your family," he added.

Nicole kept appraising his profile as they sped along the highway. Lucien was quite possibly the sweetest man she'd ever met, certainly the most thoughtful, outside of her brother and her father. She was so happy that she'd given herself an opportunity to get to know him and find out once and for all what a kind, compassionate and loving man he really was. When she thought about how she had once dismissed him as a selfish pretty boy, she had to suppress a shudder. She could have let fear and doubt rule her and she might have missed out on the love of a lifetime.

"I love you," she said softly.

Lucien took his eyes from the road long enough to give her a rakish grin. "I know you do. And I love you, too. Nice how that works out, isn't it?"

"I mean it, Lucien. I really love you," she said with wonder in her voice. "I've never felt like this before."

He reached over and took her hand. "I feel the same way about you, Nicole. I had no concept of what loving someone was like. I saw all my cousins in Atlanta going down for the count, and they're all as happy as pigs in mud, but I didn't think it was in the cards for me. And then I met you," he said, squeezing her hand. "I took one look at you and something inside of me went 'Dang, so this is what it's all about.' When

I talked to you, when I kissed you, that's when I found out what I'd been missing all these years. It was like the first time that my head and my heart and my body all connected. It was the first time I understood what love was and what it could mean to be in love."

Nicole was humbled by what she was hearing. "So what does it mean, Lucien?"

Lucien laughed. "It means I make a twelve-hour trip to Charleston to visit with your family. I'm pretty sure they want to get to know me a little better before I become a permanent part of their lives," he drawled.

A week ago those words might have put Nicole in a panic. She'd actually suffered a mild panic attack when thinking about the fact that if she and Lucien took their relationship to the next level, there would be a lot of changes in her life.

She would be moving to New Orleans permanently, because she couldn't see herself in one of those modern commuter marriages. She wanted to wake up with her husband and go to bed with him every night. She wanted to be able to share all the daily mundane things that any married couple shared and she wanted to share them with Lucien. She had talked to Nona and Natalie about it, and they were totally supportive, once they got over the shock.

They knew that she was seeing Lucien, of course. They had weekly telephone conversations, so they were up to speed on what was going on in Nicole's life. But the realization that their younger sister was actually contemplating matrimony was an exciting revelation. Nona had acted as though Nicole leaving Charleston was to be expected. "Of course you'll be moving. It'll be challenging, but what in the world is worth having that isn't?" she'd said. Natalie had a different idea.

She was the most independent of the three sisters, and she

didn't see why Lucien couldn't move to Charleston. "He can practice law anywhere, can't he? Why do you have to do the moving?" She and Nona went back and forth about it while Nicole listened and laughed. But in the end, she made her own decision. She would become a resident of the Crescent City when she became a bride. When that was going to happen was anybody's guess, because Lucien was being maddeningly stubborn about the details, which was a source of annoyance for her. Annoyance, not anxiety; it was a done deal and they both knew it, but he said he wasn't going to propose until he talked to her father. She couldn't believe he was being so stubborn, but he wasn't budging on that point.

"Look, I never thought about me taking the big step into matrimony, but since I've been lucky enough to find the one woman in the world who completes me, I'm going to do it right." He looked serious for a moment. "I think I'm becoming a traditionalist," he said piously.

"I think you're becoming deranged," Nicole said derisively. "Maybe your blood sugar is getting low. Should we stop to get something to eat?"

"Aww, *baby,*" Lucien crooned like the Big Bopper and then launched into "Chantilly Lace."

Nicole burst out laughing. "That's just wrong, Lucien! Is this what I'm going to have to put up with for the rest of my life?"

Lucien stopped singing and gave her a brilliant smile. "If I have my way, you will. That's a promise."

Sarah and Clifton Argonne were two of the nicest people Lucien had ever met. Of course, this wasn't his first time meeting the couple; he had encountered them several times during Paris and Titus's prewedding and wedding festivities. They were a strikingly handsome couple as well as being gracious hosts. When he and Nicole had arrived in Charleston, Sarah had a meal ready for them. They introduced Yum-Yum, who was always glad to make a new friend, and washed up quickly before sitting down to a lovely feast of oven-fried chicken, yellow squash sautéed with Vidalia onions and red peppers, mashed potatoes, green salad and the best homemade rolls Lucien had ever eaten. After taking a long swallow of lemonade, he complimented Sarah on the excellent meal.

"Mrs. Argonne, everything was delicious. Thanks so much for going to all the trouble of preparing it," he said.

"Oh, please call me Sarah," she replied. "And it was no trouble at all. It was the least I could do since you brought my baby home safe and sound."

"That was no trouble," Lucien said, casting a loving eye on Nicole. "I wouldn't have had it any other way."

A loud laugh from Clifton made everyone look at him. "Yum-Yum is patting my knee under the table. It must be time for her to eat," he said.

Nicole cautioned her father not to feed her. "She's just realized that there's a big difference between Puppy Chow and people food. Guess which one she likes best? And," she said mischievously, "guess who started her on the road to perdition?"

Lucien tried to defend himself. "I just gave her a little piece of chicken once. And maybe a little bite of steak. She likes shrimp, too. But most of the time she gets Puppy Chow."

"And she's getting some right now. I'm going to feed her, and then I need to go home and get in the bathtub. I feel so grimy!" Nicole said. "Mama, I'll get the kitchen cleaned up before I go," she added. She didn't wait for an answer as she rose from the table, calling Yum-Yum. "Come on, sweetie. I'm going to give you a little dinner and then you're going to see where mommy lives, okay?"

Sarah called after her as she went into the kitchen. "Don't even think about cleaning up! Your daddy and I can handle it." She looked at Lucien and sighed. "Nicole is the most generous, most conscientious person in the world. She will work herself into a frazzle to help someone else out. You're going to have to watch her to make sure she doesn't spread herself too thin," she cautioned. "Excuse me, won't you?" She rose to leave the table, and both men stood up to acknowledge her.

Now it was just Lucien and Clifton alone in the dining room. The two men looked at each other while a pleasant silence grew. Lucien broke the quiet first. "Mr. Argonne, I'm in love with your daughter. I want to talk to you about that, about how I want to become a permanent part of her life. I want to marry her, sir, and I want to get your blessing, yours and Sarah's." When he finally wound down, he found that Clifton was smiling at him.

"First of all, call me Clifton. And I have to tell you, I'm a little surprised by this. Nicole is a grown woman, and she makes her own decisions. She's the one you need to convince, son, not me and her mother. I appreciate the fact that you're man enough to come and talk to me, but I don't have the final say-so. Have you talked to Nicki about your feelings?"

Lucien assured him that he had. "I told her that I wanted to talk to you before we made it official, but there's no question that we're going to be together, sir. I've never felt like this about anyone else. I've known for some time that Nicole was the woman I wanted to spend the rest of my life with," he said with utter sincerity.

Clifton smiled warmly. "Look, Lucien, we don't have to cover all this right now. Why don't you take Nicole home, and when you come back we'll talk."

Lucien looked blank. "Umm, when I come back? I'm staying here?"

The older man gave him a brief nod that spoke volumes. "We've got the guest room all ready for you," he said smoothly. "Look at it this way, son. You need some rest, and if I know my daughters they'll be at Nicki's door ready to interrogate her until the wee hours of the morning. This way we have our talk, and you get some sleep," he said wisely.

When Lucien and Nicole got to her condo, he could see exactly what Clifton was talking about. Nona and Natalie were already in the kitchen waiting for them. "Welcome home," Natalie drawled. "Before you ask, I used my key to let us in. Hello, Lucien, it's good to see you again."

"Hello, Natalie," Lucien replied. "It's good to see you, too. Nona, how are you?"

"Just fine," she answered. "Do you need some help getting Nic's things out of the car?"

Lucien acted like there was nothing unusual in being greeted by his beloved's sisters in this unorthodox manner. "Nope, I can handle it. Why don't you hold Yums for me, and I'll get started," he said, handing the wriggling puppy over to Natalie.

"Ooh, she's cute! I'm not even a dog lover, but she's adorable," Natalie cooed. Lucien smiled and went out to the car to start unloading. Nicole came with him.

"I had no idea they were coming over," she apologized.

"I did. Clifton warned me to expect an invasion. Don't worry about it. It's cool. I'll get your things inside and head back to your parents' for a quick shower, a long nap and the rest of my discussion with your dad."

"And I'm sorry you have to stay over there, too," she said, and she sounded as though she really meant it. "I really don't like the idea of being away from you, even for a night," she confessed.

Lucien stopped what he was doing to wrap his arms around

her for a long, lingering kiss. "Will that hold you for a while?" he teased her.

"Whoo-hoo! Y'all go on witcha nasty selves," Natalie crowed. "I see why Daddy had to put you on lockdown. Do y'all do this all the time?"

Lucien laughed while Nicole handed Natalie a bag. "We do it as often as humanly possible. If you had someone to do it with, you might manage to stay out of my business. Here, make yourself useful."

In short order, everything was in Nicole's condo. Lucien got a tour of her home while Nona and Natalie took a tour of him. He wasn't surprised to see the feminine yet modern look of Nicole's home. He could see Nicole's personality in every aspect of the place. Yum-Yum apparently liked it, too, because she was running around investigating everything with enthusiasm. Every so often she'd run back to Lucien or Nicole, as if to make sure they were still there. Nona and Natalie were talking about Lucien as though he couldn't hear them.

"You know, he's actually better-looking than I remembered. Taller, too," Nona said.

"He's very patient," Natalie observed. "And he's really kind, too. A lot of men would have just said 'Call me when you get there, Boo' and wouldn't have bothered to bring her home. He definitely gets points for that," Natalie replied.

"Don't forget he kept her little dog, too. That was above and beyond the call," Nona reminded her. "Nic, he's definitely a keeper. We're going to take your baby out so you can say good-night properly, and then we have a very short questionnaire for you. It shouldn't take more than an hour or two to complete. Be right back," she said sweetly.

After her sisters left the living room with Yum-Yum, Nicole turned to Lucien with a look of determination on her face.

"Lock the door! Let's lock them out and go to the bedroom," she said in a stage whisper. Tugging at his hand, she urged, "Let's go! Let's go!"

Lucien laughed at her silliness and enfolded her in his arms. "Your father is expecting me back at his house. If you think I'm going to try to duck out on him, you're crazy. He'll be over here with a shotgun, and I'm not trying to get killed before I propose."

"Well, do it right now and you won't have to worry about it," Nicole said.

Lucien tipped her head up and kissed her gently. "I love you, Nicole, more than I thought it was possible to love anyone. You're the person who opened my heart up to love. I don't know what I did to deserve someone as wonderful as you are, but it's going to be my pleasure to spend the rest of my life showing you how much you mean to me every day. Will you please do me the honor of being my wife?"

Nicole's eyes filled with tears, and she had to bite her lower lip to stop it from trembling. "I love you, Lucien. Nothing would make me happier than to spend the rest of my life with you. I thought I knew what love was, but I was wrong. Now I know for sure because I know your love. I can't wait to marry you," she said with a tear-filled sigh.

"Then how about we put this on your finger?" Lucien reached into the front pocket of his jeans and pulled out a small velvet box. He put it on Nicole's palm and opened it so she could see the ring nestled inside.

"Oh, it's beautiful! Put it on me, please."

He did so at once, telling her about the ring he'd had made just for her. "The big stone is a green amethyst and the smaller ones are diamonds. I had it made for you, so I hope it's to your liking. If it isn't, we'll just find one that is," he told her.

Nicole's hand was trembling, and she was crying freely. The main stone was a six-carat oval of a highly faceted gem in the palest shade of green that shimmered like a drop of dew. It was surrounded by brilliantly sparkling diamonds. "Don't be ridiculous. This is the most beautiful ring I've ever seen in my life. I love it, and I love you for giving it to me."

They were kissing passionately to seal their pledge when her sisters came back in with Yum-Yum. Lucien sighed deeply. "Look, luscious, I'm going to go. I really need to get some rest, so I'll call you later. I love you."

"I love you, too."

Lucien went out to the car and laughed as he heard the high-pitched squeals from Nona and Natalie that meant they'd discovered Nicole's ring. He smiled with deep satisfaction, because this time he had no doubts about whether she liked it. She loved it and it made her very happy, which made him happy. They were going to have a wonderful life together.

Chapter 21

The next morning, Lucien and Nicole were on their way to meet her grandmother, the lovely and formidable Mama Sweet. Nicole knew that he'd charm her right away, because Mama Sweet was an unrepentant flirt who adored men. "She and Yum-Yum have a lot in common. They both love men, especially handsome ones, and there's no shame in their game. But I have to warn you, she doesn't bite her tongue. What comes up, comes out, so be prepared. She may ask you anything, so be ready," Nicole warned him.

Lucien gave her a satisfied smile. "Listen, she can't be as bold as your sisters, and I survived that," he said with a laugh.

"Where do you think they got that boldness from? You're getting ready to meet the queen of everything, honey, so just get your game face on."

"After the breakfast I just had, I can handle anything, baby.

If we didn't have to go have an audience with the queen, we'd still be at it," he said cockily.

He was referring to the fact that he had come to Nicole's earlier to have breakfast with her and the meal had gone to the wayside in favor of some passionate lovemaking. Nicole certainly didn't regret it, but her grandmother had a gift for knowing just what people were up to and she doubted that her afterglow would escape Mama Sweet's notice. She was hoping against hope that Yum-Yum would prove to be a diversion. Mama Sweet had a Pomeranian named Pumpkin, and it was Nicole's fervent desire that the two dogs would keep her attention away from the strong aura of passion that surrounded her and Lucien. She had to force herself to listen to what he was saying.

"Your sisters are amazing, Nic. They're beautiful, smart, funny, everything a man could want. Are they dating, engaged, involved or what?"

"Nona is a widow," Nicole told him. "She really hasn't had anyone in her life since Franklin died. She just can't seem to get interested in anyone. And Natalie specializes in breaking hearts, because men fall at her feet and she just steps over them. She's too independent, I guess, because she's never met a man who could keep her interest. Oh, we're here. That little pink house with the white shutters. Just park in the driveway," she instructed him. She cupped Yum-Yum's little face in both hands. "You'd better behave or else. Don't let that little furball coerce you into some unseemly behavior."

Mama Sweet was dressed fashionably in a cotton-knit jogging set with a pair of New Balance walking shoes on. The violet color of the outfit set off her brown skin and snow-white hair, and she looked energetic and ready for action, which she was. She was a busy lady, always involved in something, whether it was a church activity, some charity or a social event with her senior group. She was on her way to a tennis match, so they wouldn't be there long, but Nicole knew she had to make a formal introduction of her fiancé or face her grandmother's wrath at a later date. Mama Sweet was very impressed with Lucien, as Nicole knew she would be. After Yum-Yum and Pumpkin greeted each other, they went to the fenced backyard to play and Mama Sweet turned to Lucien with a smile on her face.

"Well, let's sit down and have some tea," she invited. "I made some sweet rolls, too, and there's some fruit. I figured you two would be hungry," she said archly.

Nicole could feel her face burning. It was just as she feared; her grandmother had taken one look at them and knew exactly what they'd been up to. She couldn't look at Lucien as she followed the older woman into the kitchen. It was big and sunny and old-fashioned, and it was normally the most comforting place in the world. Right now it felt like a torture chamber to Nicole. Mama Sweet turned her twinkling eyes on Lucien and Nicole braced herself for what was coming.

"You're a big handsome fellow, aren't you? I hope you have a good income. Nicole's not used to going without, and she has a very good career here in Charleston. I trust that you can provide for her properly."

Nicole's head dropped, and she groaned, but Lucien had no problem reassuring Mama Sweet. "I'm in corporate law, and I have a very successful practice with my brothers. I also have a very good investment portfolio and some real estate, as well as a few businesses that I share with my brothers. You don't have to worry about Nicole's future, ma'am."

She nodded approvingly before launching her next salvo.

"How many children do you plan to have? You two will certainly have some pretty ones. How do you feel about children?"

Nicole stifled another groan, but Lucien handled it smoothly. "We haven't discussed an actual number, but I love children and I'll be happy to have as many as Nicole wants. She's going to make a wonderful mother, and I'm very excited about being a father."

"But not before the wedding, I trust. I hope you two plan on getting married very soon, because otherwise we could be knee-deep in babies around here. I suggest you do it as soon as possible to circumvent any accidents," Mama Sweet said firmly.

This time Nicole moaned out loud and covered her mouth with both hands to keep from screaming. Her grandmother glanced at her histrionics and caught a glimpse of her engagement ring. "That's a beautiful ring, sweetheart. What is it?"

Nicole held out her hand at once to show it off and told her all about the stone. "He had it made just for me, Mama Sweet."

"It's very unique and special, just like you are, dear. But you two need to tie the knot quickly because those babies are going to come fast and furious and you don't want to get caught out of wedlock. Have something to eat, dear, you look a little peaked," she said calmly.

"Lucien, my granddaughter is very precious to us, I hope you realize that. We're entrusting her happiness to you, and I hope that you understand what a sacred charge that is," she said, giving him a steady and appraising look.

"Ma'am, I understand completely, and you'll never have to worry about Nicole from this day forward. I plan to devote my life to making sure she's as happy as she is right now. I love her, and my main concern is her happiness."

Mama Sweet beamed. "That's just wonderful, dear. Nicole, you would have saved yourself a lot of trouble if you'd picked this one instead of that bony loser you had before. This is your man right here, honey."

Nicole opened her mouth to protest that she didn't know Lucien was in the world when she was engaged to the lousy Leland, but what was the point. She just smiled at Lucien and said, "You're absolutely right, Mama Sweet. He's the right man for me. The only one," she added as they leaned to each other for a quick kiss.

"You two just do what I say and get married soon. It's obvious that your willpower is a little on the low side."

Lucien laughed loud and long, which should have infuriated Nicole, but she had to laugh, too. "I have to warn you, honey, my whole family is like this. Are you sure, absolutely sure, that you want to do this?"

"I was never more positive of anything in my life. And she's right, you know. We need to do it soon."

"Now this is a young man with some sense, Nicole. You did good, baby. You did real good," she praised.

Nicole found that things were falling into place with incredible speed. Before Lucien went back to New Orleans, they started planning in earnest for her move from Charleston. The first step, the one she was dreading, was informing her employers. Nicole really loved working at The Lennox Group, and she didn't want to leave, but she had no choice, or so she thought. When she went in to see Andrea and David Lennox, they were elated about her news and not terribly concerned about her leaving the firm, which hurt her feelings a little.

"Congratulations, Nicole. We're so happy for you!" Andrea gave her a tight hug and David did the same.

"Look at you—you're positively glowing," David told her. "Have you set a date for the wedding?"

"We'll know soon. We want it festive, fun and fast," Nicole replied. "But there's so much to do with planning a move to Louisiana. I'm trying to get everything organized on this end as well as trying to figure out what my new career is going to be like. There's not a lot of call for interior design in New Orleans right now," she said. "They have much more pressing needs, so I'm going to be unemployed for a while, something I'm not too happy about."

Andrea's eyes widened, and she looked at David, then Nicole. "But why do you have to be unemployed? You aren't leaving us, are you?"

"Well, since I'm moving to New Orleans, I figured it was a done deal," Nicole said frankly.

David spoke up then. "It doesn't have to be, Nicole. You can continue to work with us doing just what you're doing. You can keep your clients and continue to service them. With all the things you can do online and electronically, there's no reason for you not to," he said. "Additionally, we've been thinking about opening offices in other cities. New Orleans is on our list, as well as Atlanta. You're right, of course, interior design is probably the last thing on anyone's mind in New Orleans right now, but there are a lot of projects we can get involved with that will benefit the city and give us a presence there at the same time. It'll involve a lot of work on your part. I'm not trying to soft-pedal that. But it's a way that you can relocate and still be involved with the firm, which is what we want more than anything. What do you say?"

Nicole's eyes sparkled, and she gave him her best dimpled smile. "I say yes, of course. Thank you for the opportunity," she began, only to have Andrea and David cut her off.

"Nicole, you're the best designer we have, and there's no

way we want to lose you," Andrea assured her. "I just wish we could meet this fiancé of yours. He must be very special."

"You can meet him right now. He's in my office waiting for me," Nicole informed them.

The meeting was a great success and ended with them all having lunch together. Nicole was full of happiness. Her family had embraced her future husband, her job was secure and the future was bright. She looked down at her ring, the symbol of Lucien's love for her, and a dreamy smile transfixed her face. When Andrea teased her about it, she didn't even blink; she just extended her hand to show off the sparkling gem.

"So is this going to be a long engagement?" Andrea asked.

"Not at all," Nicole replied.

Lucien grinned. "We don't want to wait. All we want to do is start our new life together as soon as possible."

Nicole gave him an especially sweet smile and agreed. "It's going to be hectic, but it will be worth it. You want to buy a condo?" she added brightly.

Everyone laughed except David, who said he knew someone who was looking. "I'll have him get in touch with you tomorrow," he said.

Now Nicole was truly elated. Nothing was going to stop them now; they were on their way to wedded bliss. She squeezed Lucien's hand under the table, and he squeezed back. Everything was just perfect.

A few weeks later, Nicole was still in her ebullient mood. The condo had sold for her asking price, and her sisters were helping her get her furnishings handled. Anything she hadn't worn or used in six months was going to charity. She had sold some of her furniture to the young man who'd bought her condo, and except for the pieces she was taking with her, she'd sold the rest with the help of Andrea, who had a friend with a resale shop. It was a busy but productive time for Nicole, and she was enjoying it all. The wedding plans were still hazy, but that was because Nicole didn't want a big wedding. On the contrary, she wanted the smallest ceremony possible. After the huge debacle of her aborted wedding to Leland, Nicole wanted nothing to do with a big formal ceremony.

She was trying, with a limited degree of success, to get Lucien to agree. He was in favor of a huge celebration, reasoning that even the simplest ceremony was going to turn into a big one just because of all of their family members. She could see his point, but she just wasn't feeling up to the whole process of picking out a gown, the arduous task of finding bridesmaid dresses, sending out invitations, picking a menu for the reception and the multitude of tasks that went along with a traditional wedding. She shuddered just thinking about it all. She was in her bedroom savoring a rare moment of solitude. The room bore only a rudimentary resemblance to the warm, inviting space it had been before the great move began. Now there were boxes stacked in all the corners, the pictures were off the walls and the closet door was open to reveal a very spartan-looking interior. The only thing that was unchanged was her bed. Even her beloved vanity table was gone; her father had crated it up and shipped it off very morning. When her phone rang, it was a pleasant distraction from all the clutter of moving.

She smiled when she heard Chastain's voice on the other end. "Hey, girl! What have you been up to?" She was surprised to hear a very subdued voice coming from her friend.

"Nothing much, same ol' same ol', I guess. Look, Nic, when are you coming back to N'awlins?" Chastain didn't sound like her normal bubbly self at all. She sounded rather stressed, in fact.

"I was planning on coming in two weeks, why?"

Chastain got right to the point. "I think you need to haul yourself back here ASAP because there are some strange rumblings going on here. I hate to do this to you, but I don't want you walking into this without forewarning."

Nicole raised an eyebrow and stared at the phone for a few seconds. "What kind of situation would that be?"

A heavy sigh was her answer. "Look, I know this heifer and I know she's lyin' through her teeth, but one of Lucien's old flames is back in town with a baby on her hip. Everybody is saying that the baby is Lucien's, and she's not denying it. It's a cute little thing, light-skinned with curly black hair, so that's supposed to make him a dead ringer for Lucien. Hell, you could pick N'awlins up and shake it and it would start rainin' little critters who look like that. I don't believe that little tramp for a minute," she said indignantly.

Nicole sat straight up on the bed. "What little tramp?" she asked in a low, ominous voice.

"Her name is LaDonna Foster, and she and Lucien were a hot item for about thirty seconds or so a couple of years ago. But I happen to know that she was involved with someone else after they dated. And he was somebody she wasn't supposed to be with," Chastain said with grim amusement.

"What do you mean?" Nicole demanded.

"I mean he was somebody else's husband. What do you think I mean? All I'm saying is that this little witch is trying to make it seem like Lucien is the father of her child, and if I know her, she's not going to leave it at gossip. She's gonna try something, you mark my words."

"And you can mark mine. I'll be there Friday, and she won't be trying anything when I get through with her."

Chapter 22

Lucien was in a bad mood, the same bad mood he'd been in for over a week. It had started as soon as LaDonna Foster breezed into town, and it showed no signs of flagging. He'd known something was up when he started getting phone calls from women he hadn't seen in months and in some cases years. All of the messages were about the same in that they all bore thinly veiled references to his rumored love child. He was thoroughly sick of the innuendoes and the snickering amusement that was directed toward him. The crowning insult was the day he ran into LaDonna herself with her son in tow. She had fluttered around and beamed like a thousand-watt bulb as she introduced him to "Little Luke," as she referred to the boy. It was all he could do not to cuss her for old and new. He still cringed when he remembered the incident.

He had been having lunch with Philippe when LaDonna had floated into the small diner like it was Brennan's. She had dragged the little boy, who looked about eighteen months old, by the hand, and he looked less than thrilled with the situation. He looked like he was about to cry, but LaDonna wasn't paying him any attention.

"Hel-*lo,* Lucien! It's been such a long time," she had trilled in a falsely breathy voice. "How have you been?"

Before he could answer, she had pulled the little boy in front of her and announced that she had someone she wanted him to meet. "This is Little Luke, Lucien. What do you think of him?"

Lucien hadn't blinked an eye. "Cute kid, LaDonna. Who does he belong to?"

Without hesitation, she'd given a truly phony giggle and said, "He's mine, of course."

Philippe had cut in then, saying, "He looks just like you. Cute little boy. Good to see you, LaDonna."

It was an obvious dismissal, and she knew it, because she'd left almost at once. Philippe had given him a long, serious look. "She's trying to start something, Luc. She's been hauling that poor kid all over town showing him off and saying he looks just like his daddy. Of course she says it right after she's mentioned your name two or three times, so the implication is clear—she's trying to get people to think he's yours. You and I know he's not, but that doesn't mean that she won't try to stir up some crap," he'd said.

Lucien had truly appreciated the fact that his brother knew him well enough to dismiss the woman's tactics. "I just don't get why she's doing it at all. She might be flaky, but she's not crazy. She has to know that if it comes down to it I'll demand a paternity test and she'll end up looking like one of those dingbats who go on TV to find out who their baby daddy is. What the hell is she up to?"

"That's a good question, Luc. But where there's a question, there's an answer. How are you going to get it?"

Lucien had smiled grimly. "Don't worry about it. I got that all covered. All I'm worried about is what Nicole is going to say. She's liable to go tick-tick-boom if she hears about this. She has a temper, and she's not afraid to use it," he said.

Philippe had laughed but agreed with him. "Yeah, she doesn't seem like the shy, retiring type. LaDonna better watch her back, because if she's not careful, Nic will take her head off and hand it to her."

His brother's words were echoing in his head as he drove home from the office. He was irritated by all the gossip but relieved that his family at least knew without being told that Lucien couldn't possibly have fathered LaDonna's child. Mac Deveraux had done too good a job at instilling in his sons the need to have protected sex for any of them to have done something so careless. Besides that, the timing was off; the child was eighteen months old, which meant he was conceived twenty-seven months before. Lucien had been in Portland, Oregon, at the time, working on a long and drawn-out case. LaDonna had been in Washington, D.C., where she had moved sometime after her brief affair with Lucien. And he had gotten to the bottom of the situation at last, having had a long conversation with LaDonna that still annoyed him because it was the most ridiculous one he could ever remember having with a woman.

He turned into his driveway and almost collided with a strange car that was parked there. He saw at once that it was a rental because there was a sticker with the Enterprise logo on it.

Nicole.

Without a doubt, she was there to confront him because she'd heard about the rumors that were flying around the city like the Katrina debris that was still being cleaned up. *Crap.* He'd deliberately not said anything to her about the situation because he didn't want her to become upset about something that was a total nonissue. Granted, he'd had quite a reputation as a ladies' man in the past, but that was the past, not the present. From the moment he'd realized that she was the woman he wanted, he had cut off all associations with other women because he was through with being Hound Dog. He was ready for a new phase of his life to begin with Nicole, and if she was going to jump crazy the first time some gossip started churning about, they didn't have much of a future. He sat in the car for a few minutes, pinching the bridge of his nose, trying to relieve the pressure that was building in his head.

When he finally got out of the car and went into the house, he had a pretty good idea of what to expect, but he didn't find it. He figured Nicole would be standing in the kitchen with her arms crossed and a mean look on her face, but she wasn't. She was in the kitchen, but she didn't look angry. On the contrary, she looked quite happy to see him.

"Hello, sugar. It's about time you got home. Do I get a kiss, or are you just going to stand there?"

She was preparing a meal, and she actually looked like her normal sweet self. She walked toward him, wiping her hands on a dish towel, a big smile on her face. He bent his head to kiss her and was glad he did. Her lips were as delicious and accommodating as they ever were, and they kissed for a long time.

"Wow. You seem happy to see me," he murmured inanely.

Nicole's throaty laugh rippled out. "Of course I am! Why wouldn't I be?"

Lucien didn't answer her at once. He was holding her tightly, enjoying the feel of her soft curves pressed against his body. "Damn, I missed you," he said hoarsely.

"I missed you, too," she said softly and hugged him back with equal intensity.

Finally he broke their embrace and put his hands on her shoulders. He kissed her on the forehead before asking her a question. "Why are you here, Nicole?"

"I didn't think I needed a reason to come see my fiancé," she replied.

"You don't, but you do," he said cryptically. "You never need a reason to come to me, but I think you have one this time. I think that someone, let's say for the sake of argument it was Chastain, gave you some information that you felt you needed to act on and that's why you came here unexpectedly. Is that about right?"

She didn't look the least embarrassed as she considered his words. "Okay, for the sake of argument, let's say that you're right. What do you think she told me?"

Lucien felt his blood pressure rising. He just wasn't in the mood to play games with Nicole. He stepped back from her and began pacing like he did when he was in the courtroom. "Let's not mess around, Nic. Chastain called you up and told you the same junk that's been spreading like wildfire around here. She told you that a woman I used to date came to town with a kid that she's been trying to pass off as mine, didn't she?"

Nicole nodded. He ground his teeth and kept talking. "That child isn't mine, Nicole. She's been dragging the poor kid all over town, playing games with everybody's head, and she knows the kid isn't mine."

"I know," Nicole said.

"She had some warped idea that by accusing me on the sly, she could get me mad enough to demand a DNA test so it would be obvious that someone else fathered the child. The real father is a married man, someone who won't own up to what he did for obvious reasons," he said hotly.

"I know," Nicole said.

Lucien didn't actually hear her because he was too riled up. "I'd had enough of the gossip and the innuendoes and the jokes, and I went to her and asked her what the hell she was playing at, and she told me she was trying to make him mad enough to claim his child. He and I went to school together, and we were never what you call close friends. We didn't like each other, really—we were academic rivals, and he also tried to get with a lot of women I had gotten to first." He stopped talking for a minute and shook his head. "It was all petty college stuff. I was first in our law class, and I was editor of the law review, and he couldn't stand me. So LaDonna decided that if she made it appear that I was the baby's father, he'd get off his ass and do the right thing. I wanted to wring her stupid, shallow, selfish neck, I really did."

"I'm sure you did," she said softly.

"I didn't tell you about it because I didn't know how you would react. I know you've had some issues with trust thanks to that weasel you were engaged to, and I know you didn't have the best impression of me when we met. I didn't want to get you all upset until I knew what was behind all the talk, and unfortunately, motormouth Chastain got to you first and told you God knows what and now you think I'm scum," he said, raking his hand through his hair.

"No, I don't," she protested, but he didn't hear her.

He finally stopped pacing and turned to face her. "Nicole, I've asked you to trust me, to believe in me when I say that you're the most important person in my life. I would never disrespect you or dishonor you in any way, and if you can't believe that, we don't have anything," he said, his voice full of passion.

"I know that, Lucien. Haven't you heard a word I've been saying?"

Her voice finally penetrated the cloud of emotion surrounding him. "No, I guess not," he admitted. "What were you saying?"

To his surprise, Nicole was smiling. "I said I believe you. I know you couldn't possibly have fathered that woman's child, and I figured it was something she was doing for her own twisted reasons. I came here to support you, Lucien, not to accuse you. I do trust you, because I know you and I know that you're an honorable man who doesn't take chances when he makes love."

"Has sex," he corrected her. "The only woman I've ever made love to is you."

"I'm glad to hear it. And I'm glad to hear that you confronted that hoochie. I never heard of anything so stupid in my life. It was crazy for her to try a stunt like that with a lawyer who could sue the pants off her for defamation of character, but she didn't do her homework or she'd have known that your brother-in-law is the best investigator in the country, and he could have her checked out in a heartbeat," Nicole said with satisfaction.

Lucien raised an eyebrow. "You had her checked out, didn't you? You called Titus and put him on the case, had him digging into her past and whatnot, didn't you? That's why you're so calm about this," he said warily.

Nicole shook her head. "No, I didn't. I admit I thought about it," she said, raising a supplicating hand. "I thought about picking up the phone and asking him to dig up as much dirt as possible on the skank, but then I thought, why? You've proven yourself to be a man of principle, and you've shown your commitment to me over and over again, and if I couldn't trust that, what was the point in being engaged? People are always going to talk whether they have something relevant to say or not. I say screw 'em. All I need to know, I see in your eyes every time you look at me. I knew in my heart what the truth of the situation was, and I came here just to be with you and let you know that nothing else matters. Are you hungry? I made jambalaya," she said with a smile.

He suddenly realized that he was famished, but it wasn't for food. He took off his suit coat and tossed it into the breakfast room while he walked toward Nicole. She laughed at him, but the laughter died when she saw the passion in his eyes, and she took a step backward. "What are you doing?"

He didn't answer at first. He was busy taking out his cuff links and tossing them onto the counter. Then he whipped off his already-loosened tie and started on the buttons of his shirt. "If I had a little music, you'd know what I was doing. I'm starving, luscious, and in about two minutes you're going to know what I'm hungry for," he growled playfully.

Nicole kept backing up until she reached the stove. She quickly turned off the burners and gave Lucien a provocative smile. "I'll bet I can beat you upstairs," she said with a sultry coo.

She dashed off, only to have him catch her at the foot of the stairs. "Don't ever underestimate a starving man, luscious."

The aftermath of lovemaking was always wonderful. Nicole liked nothing better than being in Lucien's arms. They were entwined under the sheet and she was stroking his chest while he drew his hand up and down her back. "I still can't believe you left Yum-Yum in Charleston," Lucien said. "She's supposed to be with us."

Nicole brushed his protests off. "Natalie wanted to keep her, and I flew, so if she had come she would have been miserable. You said so yourself. Besides, she'd be all over you, and I wanted to be alone with you. You can spoil her rotten again real soon," she said, laughing. She kissed him and then reminded him of the obvious. "Lucien, we have to set a date for the wedding," she murmured.

"Yeah, we do. But we also need to decide what kind of wedding we're going to have. I vote for a great big wedding with all the trimmings. Lots of food, lots of music and lots of people," he said drowsily. "I want to celebrate, Nicole. This is going to be the most wonderful thing I'll ever do in my life besides hold our babies for the first time and I want to make it memorable. What's so wrong with that?"

Nicole put her head on his shoulder and tried to bury her nose in the crook of his neck. She mumbled something incomprehensible and Lucien had to ask her to repeat it. She nipped his neck playfully and propped herself up on her elbow so she could look at him. "I'm sorry I'm being such a wench," she apologized. "It's just that my parents spent all this money on the other wedding and I spent so much money and there was all this fuss and bother and for what? I told you about the train wreck that resulted from the first time I tried to get married. I just can't go through that again," she said. "I'm not trying to be selfish and want everything my way, but I don't think I can handle it."

Lucien sat up and pushed the pillows up to made a backrest. He pulled Nicole close to his heart and locked his arms around her. "Listen, luscious, I know that experience was a bad one, but I have to say I never heard of anyone handling it with as much style and grace as you did. You're a remarkable woman, Nicole. You took lemons and turned them into gold, as far as I'm concerned. But that doesn't have anything to do with this," he said as he kissed the top of her head.

"This is your real wedding, your only wedding. I'm the only man who's ever loved you the way you should be loved, and this ceremony is going to celebrate that. We're both intelligent people. We should be able to figure out a way to do this without going crazy. Besides, I promised Corey she could be in my wedding, and I can't disappoint her," he reminded her.

Nicole smiled and kissed his chest. "So how are we going to pull this off? I'm certainly open to suggestion." She laughed softly as his hand explored her willing body.

"Leave everything to me. I promise you it'll be the best day of our lives, and it won't drive you crazy or bankrupt us. It's going to be beautiful, Nicole, just wait and see."

"As long as you and I are man and wife at the end of it, I'm fine. I can't wait to be married to you, Lucien. We're going to have a wonderful life together," she told him.

After a long kiss, Lucien agreed with her. "It's going to be better than anything. I love you, Nicole."

Nicole gave him a sexy smile. "Well, are you going to show me how much or are we going to talk all night?"

Lucien turned her over on her back so fast she gasped. "We're gonna do both, baby. We can do anything as long as you love me."

"Then it's a done deal, because I'm going to love you forever," she vowed.

Epilogue

The sun was shining brilliantly and a soft breeze was caressing the company assembled on the beach at St. Simons Island, Georgia. A white gazebo had been erected on the sand, and underneath its flower-decked arch stood Nicole and Lucien as they prepared to take their vows. The wedding party was huge because it consisted of all the people who loved them and wished them well. Everyone was dressed casually and comfortably because they had all chosen their own outfits.

"Wear anything you want, as long as it's white," Nicole had told them. Nona and Natalie had teased her mercilessly about wearing white to her wedding.

"You're a real hypocrite, Nic. You know that white is for virgin brides, and I know you're not trying to tell us you and Lucien haven't been getting busy," she laughed.

Nicole refused to be rattled. "I'm pure in spirit, heifer. And I look fabulous in my dress, so don't hate." It was true;

she had found a beautiful gown that was off the shoulder with cap sleeves. It was made of raw silk with Alençon lace along the neckline and the hem. It had a close-fitting bodice with a dropped waistline that showed off her curves, and the flared skirt was tea-length. The best part was the price. It was a steal because it had been made for a woman who eloped at the last minute and Nicole got it for less than two hundred dollars. She was barefoot, and so was Lucien. She didn't wear a veil; she just wanted flowers in her hair. And Yum-Yum was also there, along with Paris's dog, Kasey, and young cousin Trey's dog, Patrick, and Mama Sweet's Pumpkin. She saw no reason for them to miss out on the fun, and they all had bows with flowers on their collars.

That was what set the tone for their wedding, a relaxed, happy affair with no rules except to have fun. Corey got her wish to be a flower girl, and Chastain was a bridesmaid, along with Nona, Natalie, Andrea, Jodie and Jamie, Titus's birth sisters, Maya, Paris and Ruth. Philippe was the best man, and Wade, Julian, Mac and Titus were the groomsmen, along with his cousins Clay, Martin, Malcolm, Marcus and Trey. They made an extraordinarily handsome assemblage as the couple faced each other at the altar.

There were lots of handkerchiefs available because there were a lot of happy tears. Sarah was blotting away moisture, as was Mama Sweet, and even Clifton looked a little misty. Nicole and Lucien had thought to keep it to immediate family, but it was next to impossible. They had chosen the St. Simons location because it was between Charleston and New Orleans and it would be somewhat easier for everyone to travel to the spot. The Atlanta Deverauxes had a vacation home on St. Simons and over the years had bought two more properties, so that instead of a home, it was like a compound that was used often by all of the family members. On this particular weekend, it was like a private resort.

The wedding ceremony was simple, eloquent and moving. The music was incomparable, since Ceylon, Martin's wife, was a world-class jazz singer, and she serenaded them with "I'm Glad There is You." And as a surprise for the couple, Lucien's brothers also sang to them. They sang "I Am Your Man," a classic R & B standard that had been given new life by Ryan Shaw. Nicole had no idea that she would cry like a baby, but she did. Lucien even teared up and promised his brothers and cousins that he would pound them into paste if they ever mentioned it again. They promised nothing, however, and were happy to bring it up several times during the reception. It was such a great party, however, that Lucien couldn't have cared less.

The wedding took place in the morning so they could party all day long, and that's just what they did. Lucien's uncle had brought his jazz band for the music and Trey was the DJ, something he was surprisingly good at for one so young. It was hard to remember that he was still in middle school because he acted like someone much older. And his musical taste was impeccable; in the intervals between the band sets he had the place rocking. Everyone was dancing when they weren't eating, and they ate a lot because the food was superb.

The only thing that was catered was the cake. Everything else had been made by the families. The men barbecued, and there was a shrimp and crab boil. Enormous bowls of fruit salad, green salad, potato salad, coleslaw and succulent side dishes of grilled vegetables, green beans, succotash and baked beans abounded. There was a special bar for the children that dispensed frozen fruit drinks and snow cones, and the dogs even had their own buffet.

Everyone was enjoying themselves tremendously. Mama Sweet was looking around the crowd of fun-loving guests, trying to pick out suitable mates for her unmarried grand-daughters, Nona and Natalie. She was sitting next to Vera, Marcus's wife, who was wiping her son's face with a warm washcloth. "Chase, be still, sweetie. You can go after Corey in just a minute, okay?"

"Corey my girlfriend," he relied in true Deveraux fashion.

Vera laughed gently. "No, baby, she's your cousin. You don't need any more girlfriends." It was true—he chased all the little girls in nursery school and church school like a veteran player.

"You know, with this many handsome men in one place, I'm sure Nona and Natalie can find themselves nice husbands," Mama Sweet said appraisingly. "That handsome thing talking to your husband, is he married?"

Vera glanced up and said no. "Dante Bohannon is very single, Mama Sweet. You want to meet him?"

"Yes, I do, dear. I certainly do," she said sweetly and innocently. Paris came over just in time to hear her words.

She sat down, rubbing her tummy and smiling at her grandmother-in-law. "I know that tone. You're matchmaking, aren't you?"

"Not yet, sweetie. But I will be. I'm tired of waiting around for those two."

Nicole and Lucien had more fun than anyone, dancing up a storm when they weren't kissing madly. They were sitting under a huge tree in a hammock, observing the party in relative seclusion. "Lucien, do you realize how many mothers-to-be there are around here? Paris, Angelique, Benita, and if I'm not mistaken Maya has a real glow about her. And Benita's sister-in-law Alicia is with child, too." She kissed him again and smiled. "If we're not careful, we could be pregnant really soon," she warned him.

"Then let's not be careful. I want a lot of babies, Nicole, and I want to have them while we're young, because they can wear you down. Do you see all the gray in Clay's head? And Marcus is just as bad, and so are Martin and Malcolm. They look like old men."

Nicole was about to reply when she saw something that made her mouth drop open. "Lucien, check them out!" She was pointing at a couple who were lost in each other's arms and oblivious to the fact that they were being observed. "Philippe and Chastain? How long has that been going on?"

Lucien just laughed. "Who cares? Right now it's all about us, baby. Let's go back to the party and enjoy ourselves. We've got a honeymoon to go on and babies to make," he said before kissing her once more like she was the only woman he'd ever love, which she was.

Should she believe the facts?

Essence bestselling author

DONNA HILL

SEDUCTION AND LIES

Book 2 of the TLC miniseries

Hawking body products for Tender Loving Care is just a
cover. The real deal? They're undercover operatives for a
covert organization. Newest member Danielle Holloway's first
assignment is to infiltrate an identity-theft ring. But when the
clues lead to her charismatic beau, Nick Mateo, Danielle has
more problems than she thought.

TLC—There's more to these ladies than Tender Loving Care!

Coming the first week of December wherever books are sold.

They had nothing in common—
except red-hot desire!

National bestselling author

Marcia King-Gamble

TEMPTING
M O G U L
the

Life coach Kennedy Fitzgerald's assignment
grooming unconventional, sexy Salim Washington
to take over as TV studio head has become a little
too pleasurable. For both of them. But shady
motivations and drama threaten to stall this
merger before the ink's even dry!

Coming the first week of December
wherever books are sold.

KIMANI
ROMANCE

www.kimanipress.com

KPMKG0931208

One moment can change your life....

Seduced BY Moonlight

NATIONAL BESTSELLING AUTHOR

Janice Sims

When Harrison Payne sees an intriguing stranger
basking in the night air at his Colorado resort,
he's determined to get to know her much better.
Discovering that Cherisse Washington is the
mother of a promising young skier he's agreed
to sponsor is a stroke of luck; learning Cherisse's
ex is determined to get her back is an unwanted
setback. But all's fair in love and war....

*Coming the first wefi of December
wherever books are sold.*

Love, honor and cherish...

•

i promise

NATIONAL BESTSELLING AUTHOR
ADRIANNE
byrd

Beautiful, brilliant Christian McKinley could set the
world afire. Instead, she dreams of returning to her
family's Texas ranch. But Malcolm Williams has other
plans for her, publicly proposing to Christian at the
social event of the year. So how can she tactfully turn
down a proposal from this gorgeous, well-connected,
obscenely rich suitor? By inadvertently falling in love
with his twin brother, Jordan!

"Byrd proves once again that she's a wonderful
storyteller."—*Romantic Times BOOKreviews*
on *The Beautiful Ones*

Coming the first wefi of December wherever books are sold.

ARABESQUE®
www.kimanipress.com   KPAB1151208

NATIONAL BESTSELLING AUTHOR

ROCHELLE ALERS

invites you to meet the Whitfields of New York....

Tessa, Faith and Simone Whitfield know all about coordinating
other people's weddings, and not so much about arranging
their own love lives. But in the space of one unforgettable year,
all three will meet intriguing men who just might bring them their
very own happily ever after....

Long Time Coming

June 2008

The Sweetest Temptation

July 2008

Taken by Storm

August 2008

ARABESQUE®

www.kimanipress.com